WHERE BATTLE RAGES

Weaponized Math and Other Stories

Colonel Jonathan P. Brazee
USMC (Ret)

Semper Fi Press

Printed in the USA

ISBN-13: 978-1-945743-39-9 (Semper Fi Press)

This is a work of fiction. All of the characters, names, incidents, organizations, and dialogue in this novel are either the products of the author's imagination or are used fictitiously.

Acknowledgements:
I want to thank all those who took the time to pre-read most of these stories, catching my mistakes in both content and typing. In particular, I want to thank Kelly O'Donnell, James Caplan, and Micky Cocker. Any remaining typos and inaccuracies are solely my fault. And I'd like to thank Dave Creek, Deborah Davitt, and James Palmer for their help in creating this collection. And most of all, I'd like to thank my big brother, Howard Brazee, for getting me started in my life-long love for science fiction.

Original Cover Art by Matthew Kadish

Dedicated to my big brother, Howard Brazee, for instilling his love of books in me at an early age.

TABLE OF CONTENTS

INTRODUCTION

I have always been a reader, hiding under my covers at night with a flashlight, gobbling up everything I could. I quickly graduated from the Hardy Boys and the like to more adult fare, reading the English translation of *The Ingenious Gentleman Don Quixote of La Mancha* when I was eight, then anything else on which I could get my hands. I was smitten with Burroughs, but the Tarzan stories, not the Mars.

Then my brother gave me a copy of *Andre Norton's Star Man's Son 2250 A.D.,* and I was hooked. I didn't know it was possible to invent totally new worlds, new universes. I'd found my passion. From Heinlein to Asimov, I devoured the classics. Farmer blew me away. He delved into topics that the other Golden Age writers avoided. Same with Andy Offutt. I was blown away at the potential of science fiction.

In 1975, my brother dragged me to a science fiction convention in Des Moines, where I met Gordon Dickson (who became one of my favorite writers), and for $6, I had lunch with a real live member of the Science Fiction Writers of America (later rebranded to the Science Fiction and Fantasy Writers of America). I wish I remembered her name now. At the time, she'd published three short stories, none of which I'd read. Still, she was a *professional* writer.

I went off to the Naval Academy, ready to pursue my career as an officer in the Navy. As Heinlein was an Academy grad, and as my brother was a big fan, I had the temerity to write Heinlein to ask him if he could pen a short note giving my brother a little grief, them mailing it to him in the stamped envelope I provided. To my surprise, three weeks later I received a note from my brother asking me why Robert Heinlein had written to him to chastise him for not writing me.

While at the Academy, I took a creative writing elective. I was so proud of my first assignment, a banal story of two young people in the position to have sex for the first time, but backing out at the last minute. I mean, it was so *adult*, right? My professor didn't think so, giving me a B. But I learned from that class, and my final project, a short story titled "Secession," ended up being published in Labyrinth Magazine, to my tremendous surprise (the story has been republished in this collection).

Also, at the Academy, I had the chance to meet James Webb, a Marine Navy Cross winner and writer of novels, to include the tremendous *Fields of Fire* (he later became the Secretary of the Navy, a senator, and for a brief time, a presidential candidate). I spent several hours in his cramped office discussing writing.

Then I was commissioned, not into the Navy, but into the Marines, and embarked on my career. I abandoned my fledgling efforts at fiction—I mean, who would read anything I'd written, right? I still published, but in non-fiction: nuclear proliferation, cross-cultural management, military science, the tuna industry, leadership, and race relations (I won a national Black History Month Writing award, and the $500 that went with it was the most I'd ever been paid for something I'd written).

Then came Iraq, where I was the military liaison to USAID. I was busy, but I did have free time, and I couldn't go out running as that pretty much made you a moving target. So, I decided to write my first novel. They say to write what you know, so I wrote a short military fiction about the Marine embassy in New Delhi during a takeover titled *The Few*.

I never sent the novel to a publisher because I knew no one would be interested in anything I wrote. But I wanted some copies, so I went to a vanity publisher and paid $470 for twenty copies that I gave out to my mother, brother, and friends. Part of the deal was that they would put the novel on sale on Amazon for $19.99. And over the next several years, I actually made $98 in royalties. I was bemused, but technically, now I was a professional writer.

Jump forward several years, and I was at the United lounge at LAX when I spotted a man with a Kindle. I'd never seen one before, so I was intrigued. When I told him I had a book on the Kindle, he looked and told me I didn't.

I called the vanity publisher when I got home, and I was told that I only had a paperback as I hadn't paid them the extra $70 to have an eBook. By this time I'd heard of self-publishing, so I simply uploaded my word doc. To my surprise, I sold almost 400 copies over the next two weeks. That grew to another 700 copies the next month. And people started reaching out to me, asking for a sequel. I'd killed off half of the characters in the first book, but I managed to come up with two more novels, *The Proud* and *The Marines*.

And I was off to the races. Those three books have been downloaded over 100,000 times since then, and I now have over 75 titles in print. I'm a hybrid writer now, meaning I've taken traditional contracts as well as self-published. And I've had a modicum of success, quitting my day job in January of 2017 to become a full-time writer. My novelette, "Weaponized Math," (included in this collection) was a 2017 Nebula Award finalist, my novella, *Fire An,t* was a 2018 Nebula Award finalist, and my novel, *Integration*, was a 2018 Dragon Award Finalist for Best Military Science Fiction or Fantasy Novel. Then, in 2019, I became a USA Today Bestselling writer.

And that lunch I had back in 1975 with a real, honest-to-goodness SFWA member? In 2015 I became the second member to join SFWA based solely on self-published works.

I've been extremely lucky in my writing career, and I have to pinch myself sometimes. I am extremely grateful that there are people out there who enjoy reading what I write. It boggles the mind.

And now, as my list of shorter works grows, I'm finally able to put together a collection. I hope you enjoy the stories. As a writer, I could ask for nothing else.

Jonathan Brazee
North Las Vegas, NV
2020

"Where the battle rages, there the loyalty of the soldier is proved." -- Martin Luther.

Jonathan P. Brazee

WEAPONIZED MATH

One of my readers favorite characters is Gracie Medicine Crow, a descendent of the real Joseph Medicine Crow, the last Crow War Chief, and a personal hero of mine. Gracie is a sniper in the United Federation Marines and had her own novel, Sniper, as part of the three-book Women of the United Federation Marines series.

I thought I was done with Gracie after the novel, but I had so many requests for more stories about her, that I wrote two more novelettes, "High Value Target" and "BOLO Mission." These enjoyed unexpected success, and when Craig Martelle asked me for a short story for his upcoming The Expanding Universe 3, I returned to Gracie and wrote "Weaponized Math."

To my great surprise, "Weaponized Math" became a 2017 Nebula Award finalist, and it continues to sell well as a stand-alone novelette.

****

Staff Sergeant Gracie Medicine Crow, United Federation Marine Corps, accepted the cup from Rabbit as she scanned the almost-deserted village below. She blew on the coffee, then took a sip, and nodded in appreciation. She thought she recognized the brew as Cushington Blue, and she wondered where her new spotter had scored it. Lance Corporal Christopher Irving—"Rabbit"—had only been assigned to her for a week now, so she hadn't formed an opinion as to his skillset yet. He'd gotten good grades at Triple S, the United Federation Marine Corps Scout-Sniper School, but school performance didn't always reflect performance in the field.

Still, if he can shoot as good as he can scrounge up a good cup of Joe, then he might have potential.

"Take the west side," she told him in dismissal. "Let me know if anyone takes an unusual interest in the library."

"Roger that, Staff Sergeant," Rabbit said as he scurried— as well as a two-meter tall, 120 kg Marine could "scurry" —to the other side of the roof.

Gracie could sense his eagerness. Like all snipers, he'd proven himself in combat as a grunt before being accepted into Triple S, so technically, he wasn't a newbie. Despite that, he still had that new-sniper smell to him, straight out of the package. More than that, he was still only a PIG, a "Professionally Instructed Gunman." This was their first live mission together and, for once, Gracie was fine with the fact that it should be a cold mission. As part of a routine security element, she would have the opportunity to observe him in a field setting while the stakes were relatively low. Scout-sniper teams had to depend on and trust each other, and that usually meant months of training before going in hot. However, after Saracen had been killed three weeks ago, Sergeant Halcik Sung, her previous spotter, had been pulled from her to fill Saracen's slot. Forty-one confirmed kills made Gracie the most accomplished sniper in the platoon, so she'd had to take the newbie.

She took another sip of coffee. Five floors below her, Sergeant Rafiq exited one of the shops surrounding the small square. He and his squad had been conducting a sweep before the rest of his platoon escorted the major to the meeting with the local commissioners. He looked up and caught her eye, then nodded. Gracie acknowledged him with a half-salute.

She really hadn't expected Second Squad to find anything. Tension Gorge—why "Gorge," Gracie still hadn't figured out since the area around the village was as flat as a rugby pitch— was not in a high-risk area. The last incident, an IE attack, had taken place thirteen days prior and eight klicks away. But with a field grade officer coming from division, all precautions had to be taken, and the village had to be swept. So, instead of pursuing the FLNT commandos in the Mist Mountains, she and Rabbit were here acting as glorified security guards.

They hadn't even set up a proper hide with overhead cover and concealment. They were meant to be seen. Gracie felt exposed to the world, which made her nerves crawl. Every instinct told her to get into a hide from where she could deal death unseen, but orders were orders. Not many fighters, even FLNT commandos, would choose to take on a Marine sniper. She was there as a "Warning: Attack Dogs on Premises" sign.

The slightest bit of movement caught her eye. Gracie raised her Windmoeller and scoped the spot. About a klick away, at the western edge of the village, a woman shifted her weight behind a window, looking out. She stood there for a moment before stepping back out of sight. Gracie pulled the map of the village onto her helmet display, noting the two-story house, and then running a line-of-sight to the library. She didn't think the women could see the library entrance, but she might have a sightline on several of the library's upper-story windows. She ranged the building, getting 984 meters, then entered it as a C-level target in her data book, joining the 44 other potential target positions she'd identified since arriving early in the morning with Second Squad.

She ran through the target positions again to see if she could remember the range for each one, starting with the A's. She got 39 of the 45 correct.

Come on, Crow. Get them down! she chided herself before going over the list yet one more time.

It would only take a moment to pull up the range on a specific target, but even a split second could make the difference between taking out an aggressor or allowing the enemy to engage the Marines. Some of her fellow Marines thought her anal-retentive insistence on memorizing details was over-kill, but none of them had notched 41 kills, either. Gracie believed in leaving nothing to chance.

This time, she got 42 out of 45 correct. Better, but not good enough. She'd wait twenty minutes, then try again. It wasn't as if range was the only parameter that went into making a good shot. Her angle to the ground, the temperature, wind speed and direction, humidity, the planet's rotation, gravity—those and more would affect her round's trajectory. The constants were already entered into her scope's firing computer, but the variables had to be measured or determined at the time of the shot. The more variables she could enter into her scope's AI, the better her chances of success, and the faster she could do that, the quicker she could fire. If already knowing the range could slice off even a microsecond, it would be worth it.

At Triple S, a wall plaque proclaimed: *Snipers aren't deadly because they carry the biggest rifles; they're deadly because they've learned how to weaponize math.* This hit the nail on the head. Some people, even fellow snipers, claimed that sniping was an art, but Gracie knew it was purely physics, purely math, and ever since she'd become a sniper, she'd dedicated herself to making her math skills the best possible.

"Staff Sergeant Medicine Crow, your package has been delayed. He's still at Hornsby. Call it 80 minutes late," Lieutenant Diedre Kaster-Lyons passed over the platoon net.

"Roger that," Gracie passed back. "Any idea as to why?"

"That's a negative. We just got the word. I'll keep you posted."

Gracie took a deep breath, letting it out slowly. She wasn't surprised. Nothing ever seemed to go according to plan on this planet. Part of it was normal Marine Corps operating procedures, but more seemed to be because of the local government's maneuvering factions. Everyone agreed that the Frente de Liberación de Nuevo Trujillo was the enemy to all that was good and just on the planet, but in practice, none of the various political factions seemed willing to cooperate lest they cede some sort of advantage to another. She should be used to it by now, but the thought of sitting up on the roof for an additional hour-plus made her want to scream. By the time she got back to camp, she'd have spent at least 14 hours doing absolutely nothing.

"Did you hear that?" she passed to Rabbit on the P2P.

"Roger that. Uh . . . is it always like this? I mean, the changes?"

She suppressed a chuckle. As a junior grunt, he wouldn't have been kept in the loop as much as he was now as a scout-sniper. This wasn't even the first change: the meeting had originally been planned for yesterday. This was now the second delay for today.

"Hurry up and wait, Lance Corporal Irving. You know how it is in the Suck."

"Yeah, I guess so. It's just so . . . well, you know."

Yes, I do know, Rabbit. Boy, do I know.

Gracie could bitch with the best of them—although usually not aloud—but she still wouldn't change her profession for anything. She was meant to be a Marine. A member of the Apsaalooké Nation from Montana on Earth, she came from a long line of warriors, and her lifestyle was embedded in her DNA. She might chafe at the delay, but this was her life.

Without conscious thought, she reached under her collar and rubbed the "hog's tooth" hanging from her neck between her fingers, a recovered round from her first victim's magazine, but more importantly, the symbol of being a HOG, or a "Hunter of Gunmen."

She continued to scan the area below, working quick firing solutions in her mind for various locations, almost on autopilot. Sitting in a hide for days on end waiting for that one shot, there wasn't much else to do, and she'd done this tens of thousands of times over the ten-plus years she'd been a designated scout-sniper. Tens of thousands of calculations and more than a year of combined time in hides, all for 41 kills. Civilians used to the Hollybolly war flicks might think it a lot of effort per kill, but some snipers never even registered a single kill. Never became HOGs. Gracie's total was now the fourth largest among active duty snipers.

"Dingo-Three, Charlie-Two-One, we've got a cargo hover approaching your position from azimuth Two-Zero-Five, range two-point-three klicks. Looks like it's got agricultural products in the bed. There are a few anomalies in the scan, but within accepted parameters. Just keep an eye on them," an unnamed voice passed over the command net.

"Roger that," Gracie and Sergeant Rafiq said in unison.

"You got that?" Gracie asked Rabbit over the P2P, turning her head to look at him.

Two-Zero-Five was to the south west of their position, and her spotter should have a straight line-of-site to what they had designated as Route Bluebird, the road leading into Tension Gorge from that direction.

Rabbit swiveled his body to glass to the south-west before ignoring the P2P to shout "Got it!"

They might not have been in a concealed hide, but Gracie winced. In the open or not, snipers didn't shout like that, giving away their positions. It was a bad habit to start, and she'd have to remind him of that.

"Looks like a typical hauler, one of those gas jobs."

Which was to be expected. Nuevo Trujillo relied heavily on methane for ground transportation, methane extracted from agricultural waste. She ran a scan through the available feeds before picking up a micro-drone that had the hovertruck in its sights. The truck, three-quarters loaded with cargo pods, was making its way north down the road, which was the secondary north-south thoroughfare in the sector. Salinas, another small farming town, was twelve klicks south along Bluebird from Tension Gorge.

Gracie wasn't overly concerned about the truck since Tension Gorge was not a restricted town. While it had been largely abandoned during the fighting of two months ago, some people still lived there, and there were still crops to be harvested and transported to the processing plants. Still, Second Squad would have to stop and search the truck when it reached the village.

"Keep your eye on the truck while it gets here and Second checks it out," she passed to Rabbit.

She was tempted to move to his side of the roof and do it herself, but he needed to get his feet wet. To her side in its case was her Kyocera, her hypervelocity sniper rifle, and with any other spotter, she might have told him to take it. Rabbit, however, had not snapped in with it, and without being able to key in the cheek weld and eye position, he wouldn't be very accurate. No, better he keep his standard-issue M99. It had more than enough range to cover Second Squad, and he had it zeroed in for his shooting position.

She turned back to her area of responsibility. The Navy and Marine Corps' scanners hadn't found anything suspicious about the truck, but using something so obvious as a decoy was not unheard of. With short quick movements, she covered the mental grid she'd constructed, using both her prime focus as well as her peripheral vision to spot anything out of the ordinary.

One of Second Squad's four-man fire teams was moving to where they could intercept the truck. Gracie shifted her focus to the two local security standing outside the library door. They'd arrived with the first three commissioners. Casually sucking on stim sticks, flare-barreled Munchen 44's held at the ready, the impressively lethal-looking men didn't watch the fire team as it left. If something was up of which they were a part, they were hiding it well. Gracie didn't suspect the two guards of anything, but she had a firing solution for them already locked in, and her Windmoeller's WPT-331 rounds had the penetrative power to defeat the Cryolene body armor they wore. Better safe than sorry.

She was more concerned with the young boy she'd nicknamed "Space Dog" due to the brightly-colored image on his t-shirt. Perhaps ten or eleven years old, he sat on the stoop of a home a block off the square. He wasn't armed, the best she could tell, but he'd been sitting there for half-an hour, seemingly interested in the goings on. That might be merely normal adolescent curiosity, but he could be acting as a lookout, feeding information to the bad guys. Gracie had zoomed in on him several times with her scope, but she hadn't seen any signs of him communicating with anyone.

"The truck's almost here," Rabbit shouted across the roof.

"Use your comms, Irving. You trying to paint a bullseye on us?" she passed.

"Oh, yeah. Sorry, Staff Sergeant," he said, this time over the P2P.

"OK, then. Just keep an eye on them."

She pulled up Rabbit's feed, then reduced it and sent it to the top left of her helmet display where she could monitor it but still have a full view of her own area of responsibility. She quickly ticked through her known potential target list. Silver Hair was still in his garden, Red Shirt was walking along Calle Jones after going to the lone store still open, and Limp Man was no longer in sight. She shifted to the right where Route Robin led into the town and from where the major would arrive. A local policeman still stood at the edge of town, ready to hop on his scoot and escort the major and the rest of First Platoon to the library. He looked bored out of his head, something Gracie completely understood.

Closer in, she checked Space Dog, then Gollum 1 and 2, the two security guards at the library. Shifting her view farther to the right, she—

What's with Potbelly? she wondered.

The older man, his protruding gut hanging over his belt, had risen from his seat on a porch where he'd supposedly been reading a novel for the last hour. The reader was now on the small table beside his chair, its screen dark, and the man was looking with poorly disguised interest to his left. Gracie followed his gaze's direction, but nothing jumped out at her. That wasn't a comfort—something was tweaking her instincts.

"I don't have anything for certain, but something might be up," she passed on the local command circuit, which was keyed into Rabbit and all the Marines from Second Squad. "Keep alert."

"What d'ya got, Staff Sergeant?" Sergeant Rafiq asked.

"Nothing for certain, but Potbe . . . the man at Building 23," she passed, using the number Lieutenant Diedre Kaster-Lyons, dual-hatted as the battalion intel officer and the scout-sniper platoon commander, had designated the house, "seems a little too interested in something."

"The fat guy? Eric?" the sergeant asked. "I spoke with him. He seemed OK, happy to see us. Tired of the fighting and all."

Maybe, but something's up, she thought as she continued to watch him. *I can feel it.*

Potbelly—Eric whatever—was now looking in every direction except to the left, which might mean something, but then he sat back down, picked up his reader, and started to read again. Gracie wondered if her nerves were playing with her, making her see things that didn't exist, but something still nagged at the back of her mind. She zoomed in on the man, and that something hit her. The reader. The display was off. Potbelly was "reading" a darkened screen.

"Stop the truck!" she passed. "Something's wrong!"

From Rabbit's feed, she could see the truck, now a mere three hundred meters from the village's edge. Corporal Ben-Zvi, the fire team leader of the team preparing to search the truck, didn't wait for orders from his squad leader. He stepped out onto the middle of Route Bluebird, weapon raised while his amplified voice called out, "You, in the truck. Halt!"

The truck sped up.

Gracie bolted across the roof before conscious thought registered what was happening, yelling for Rabbit to take her place on the roof's east side. Ben-Zvi's fire team had spread out and taken the truck under fire, but it was a big, hulking thing, and their M-99s weren't having much effect on target. There was a whoosh as a Marine launched a Hatchet, but the missile hit high on the truck's right side with an impressive but ineffectual blast, missing the engine block and anything vital.

Firing at a moving vehicle, through a windshield, and from a high angle, was one of the most difficult shots a sniper could make. Gracie had spent countless hours in simulators and on ranges from Tarawa to Alexander, but still, this was no sure thing, and she both hadn't pre-calculated a firing solution and had no time to calculate one now. She'd have to go with her gut.

Firing from a height meant the round's drop would be less, but firing through the windshield meant that the round would most likely deflect downwards when it hit. The WPT-331 rounds she'd loaded to take care of the security officers armor had more punching power than the standard WPT-310 Lapua sniper round, so the deflection would be less—*but how much less?*

Gracie hit the roof's edge, flipping off her helmet as she brought up her rifle and laid it across the top of the low retaining wall. Her scope was zeroed at 300 meters. She had already ranged the edge of the first house where Route Bluebird entered the village at 445 meters. The truck was still 150 meters or so away from that, and the wind had been blowing north to south at a slight eight-to-ten KPH. She didn't have time to enter any of that; it was pure Kentucky windage time. Unable to see through the windshield's glare, she put her crosshairs slightly high and to the right of where she thought the driver would be. Just as she started to squeeze the trigger, she saw the slightest of cracks from the driver's side door.

He's not suiciding! He's going to try and get out!

The car that Gracie had taken out on Jericho had been driven by a suicide bomber. This driver was either not as dedicated or was considered still vital. If the latter, then this was just the initial act in a larger assault.

With a last-second shift to the right, figuring the driver would be scrunched over to be able to bail out, she squeezed off a round, and then shifted lower and to the left before firing off a second. The flower blossomed on the windshield as the 285-grain jacketed round punched through it, and the truck started to veer before the second round hit.

"Axel-Three, this is Dingo-Three. We are under attack. Cancel the mission," she passed on the command net before adding, "But send the rest of Charlie-One. We're going to need them."

"Roger, Dingo-Three. Understand you are under attack. Axel-Three-Five is being recalled. Will get back to you on Charlie-One."

The major had to be pulled back, but Gracie thought they'd need the rest of First Platoon here in the village. She scanned for more fighters as the hovertruck left the road and slowed to a stop in a field of knee-high, green, leafy crops.

On Jericho, the suicide VBIED had exploded when the driver she'd killed released the suicide switch. This truck didn't. Gracie looked over her scope at it, wondering if she'd jumped the gun by declaring a full-out attack.

The truck erupted into a fireball that roiled into the air.

Of course. It was on a timer so the driver could escape with his skin intact.

Gracie was half-listening to Corporal Ben-Zvi giving a quick sitrep on the net when the sound of firing from the center of the town reached her. She bolted back to her original firing point where Rabbit stood, peering over the building's edge.

"Get down. You can see just as well if you're prone, and you won't be exposed," she told him, jerking him down by the collar.

"I'm hit, Sergeant," someone passed on the net.

Without her helmet, Gracie didn't have her display to see who it was, but she swung her scope to the two security guards. One was crouching, weapon ready as he scanned for a target, and the other was running forward. Gracie put her crosshairs on him, ready to take him out if needed, but he reached the wounded Marine and dragged her back to the base of the library.

Guess they're not part of this.

Someone was, though, and Gracie's job was to take him out.

"I've got someone. Looks like he's got a Halstead," Rabbit said.

"Where? Give me a location."

"Uh . . . Building 38, second floor."

"Building 38, 185 meters," she mumbled, then "Take him out."

Such a close distance was child's play to a Marine with an M-99, much less a trained sniper. She left the target to Rabbit as she searched for more. She heard the whisper-snap of darts as Rabbit fired, then an excited "I got him!"

"Well, HOG, go find your number-two kill," she said, wanting him to focus on the task at hand.

"A HOG, really? But that was with my ninety-nine."

He was right. A kill like that wouldn't be tallied as a sniper kill, so she'd jumped the gun on anointing him a HOG. Now wasn't the time to get into technicalities, though.

"Later, Irving. We don't have time to discuss it now."

"Roger that," he said. Gracie heard him quietly add, "Shit, a HOG."

A string of automatic fire opened up, but with the sound reverberating between buildings, Gracie couldn't pinpoint its origin. Putting that weapon out of her mind for the moment, she shifted back to Potbelly. The man was gone, his reader abandoned on the floor of the porch. She kept scanning the direction where he'd been looking. Tension Gorge was not a very densely populated village, but there were still enough buildings to intermittently mask her view. She was dead sure, though, that there was somebody there.

A flash of movement proved her right. Two people, pulling an ancient but effective looking crew-served gun that she didn't recognize but looked like an anti-tank weapon of some sort, passed between two buildings, moving out-of-sight before she could aim and fire. She swung her barrel to cover the other side of the house that now masked them and waited. Automatic fire still echoed in bursts throughout the village, but she slowed her breathing, letting her sight picture become her world. A few moments later, a head peered around the corner. At 210 meters to the home's front door, she could easily drop him, but she wanted the gun in the open.

Come on out! The coast is clear, she implored him.

He turned back, said something, then disappeared for a moment, reappearing holding the crew-served gun's controls, leading it forward. He pointed towards the square as he said something to his companion, who followed him into view.

Gracie and Rabbit were not exactly in stealth mode, and their position had to have been noted, but the two FLNT fighters didn't even look her way.

Your loss.

When they were five meters out from the house's protection, Gracie squeezed the trigger, going for center mass. The man dropped as if poleaxed, and Gracie cycled her action, swinging to take the second man into her sights. With cat-like reflexes, the second soldier bolted back into cover. Gracie snapped off a shot, but she was sure she'd missed.

"Staff Sergeant, do you got eyes on whoever is on our asses?" Sergeant Rafiq asked between heavy breaths.

"Where's it coming from?"

"Through the fucking wall, from the north. It's chewing the shit out of the place, and we've got no cover."

"Lance Corporal Irving, we need to find that automatic weapon. Move to the edge over there and see if you can spot it." She keyed back to the command net and asked, "Rafiq, what's the status on your platoon? I'm not hearing anything. When's their ETA?"

A round pinged just below Gracie, taking a chunk of cerocrete off the wall.

So much for them ignoring us.

"As soon as the major's lifted out of there, they'll break free. We've got a Minidrag on the way, though. ETA is six minutes."

Gracie had half-expected the delay in the platoon. They couldn't just leave the major out there on the road, cooling his heels. The Minidrag was a nice piece of news, though. The Marines had two "Dragon" drones. The "Mini" was the smaller, but depending on its combat load, it could still pack a decent wallop. It would have been providing overwatch for the column bringing in the major, and she was frankly surprised that the S3 had cut it loose to support Second Squad and her sniper team.

As Gracie watched, chunks of the closer wall of the store in which Rafiq and two of his fire teams had taken cover blew out into the square. The enemy gun was shooting all the way through the building.

"Fuck! Can you get them off our ass, Crow?" Rafiq passed. "If we weren't hugging the deck, that would have cut us in two. I don't think we can wait for the Minidrag."

"I think I have the position, Staff Sergeant," Rabbit shouted, forgetting her earlier admonition. "I saw a flash."

"Wait one," she passed to Sergeant Rafiq on the P2P. "Let me see what I can do."

"Hurry up, Staff Sergeant. I've got one down, and I don't have anything to engage.

Gracie slid back behind the retaining wall, then crouched and scooted to where Rabbit hunkered behind his section of the low wall.

"Give me your helmet," she ordered.

She should have put hers back on—then she could have simply downloaded his feed—but it was still 20 meters behind her, so she threw on his. She reversed his feed 60 seconds and started it up again. Her image appeared first from what looked like just after she dropped the FPL fighter.

Don't look at me, Rabbit. Look out at the bad guys.

She heard her voice telling him to move over to try and spot the shooters, then the herky-jeky footage as he ran to the roof's far corner. He was scanning, back and forth when there was a flash at the corner of his vision immediately before the burst of automatic fire could be heard. Gracie made a mental note of the building from where the flash originated: Building 14, the Ag Co-op, which was a two-story office building made from the same cerocrete as the bank on which she now perched.

She gave Rabbit back his helmet, then did a quick turkey-hop to orient herself before dropping back out of sight. From her adjusted position, the window on the building would be about 465 meters, still an easy shot. Gracie's longest kill to date with the Windmoeller was 2005 meters, so this would be child's play—if she could acquire a target.

She entered the data into her Miller, then eased up and brought the window into her sights. A sharp report from behind their position startled her for an instant, but the *cracka-cracka-cracka* was from a Marine M110, the standard automatic slug-thrower for a fire team. Corporal Ben-Zvi's team had engaged, and she hoped they'd taken out the soldier she'd missed. She acquired her sight picture again, and the muzzle of a barrel immediately edged out before firing off another string of 15 or 20 shots. This was their baby, but the gunner hadn't exposed himself. She was pretty sure that whoever he or she was, they knew exactly where she and Rabbit were and didn't want to become targets.

"Can you get them?" Rabbit asked as she slid back down to sit on the deck, back against the low wall.

"You didn't happen to bring a Hatchet, did you?"

"No, Staff Sergeant. You didn't tell me to."

She hadn't expected him to have brought one of the little personal anti-armor rockets, but it hadn't hurt to ask. Semismart, the rocket could take out most armor or blast its way through any civilian construction.

She shrugged, then half-turned her torso to reach up and touch the wall's rounded top. It was about 10 centimeters thick. Only three buildings in the entire village were made of cerocrete, and she had to figure that they had probably been constructed in a similar fashion. Cerocrete was more expensive than the pressed vegaboard that was used for most of the village's buildings, and not surprisingly, it was more robust. The walls of the building in which Rafiq was taking cover might as well have been paper for all the protection they were providing, but cerocrete was different.

How different? she wondered, dropping her magazine and checking the rounds inside.

There was one of her remaining WPT-331 jacketed rounds in the chamber and two in the magazine. The WPT-310 Lapua was a much better round for long distances, but the 331 had more punch. She didn't know if it could punch through 10 centimeters of cerocrete, however. Once again, the math of sniping had raised its head, but this time, she didn't have the numbers to plug into the equation.

Only one way to find out.

More firing was erupting from around the village. With Sergeant Rafiq pinned down, only Ben-Zvi's fire team and maybe the two civilian security officers were returning the fire. That had to change. Marines took the fight to the enemy. They didn't let the enemy bring it to them.

"Sergeant Rafiq, if I cover you from that automatic crew-served, can you make it to the library? It's made of stone, so it'll give you better cover."

"If you can send some rounds to the east, too, I think we can. We're taking small arms from there, and we've got to carry Parker."

"Can you let the two security guys know you're coming? I don't want them to take you out."

"Roger that. They pulled Omato out of the line of fire. She's pretty fucked up, but she's on her comms now."

Another heavy burst from the crew-served gun tore through the building, and Sergeant Rafiq passed, "With you or without you, we've got to go now!"

"Irving, on my go, I want you to put rounds downrange to the east. No one shot, one kill. I need volume."

He nodded, his hand squeezing and relaxing on his pistol grip while Gracie checked her scope one more time.

"On three," she passed on the command net so every Marine could hear her. "One . . . two . . . three!"

Gracie swung her barrel over the top of the wall, set her crosshairs on the wall about 15 centimeters to the left of the window's edge, and squeezed the trigger. She shifted lower and slightly to the right and fired again as Rabbit started sending hundreds of hypervelocity darts across the square and in amongst the buildings.

"Go, go!" Sergeant Rafiq shouted over the net.

The muzzle of the enemy gun disappeared, and Gracie put her last 331 into the wall. She wasn't sure if the rounds had penetrated completely through it, but she'd certainly gotten the shooter's attention. With a WPT-310 now chambered, she swung back to the square and looked for a target. A flash of movement caught her at the edge of the scope, and she brought the crosshairs to bear, but realized that it was the boy, Space

Dog, running away from the square, not toward it. A door opened ahead of him, and a panicked-looking woman came out, wildly beckoning him to her.

She didn't bother to see if the boy made it. Rounds started to impact around her, and she looked over the top of her scope, trying to spot a real target. She immediately picked up an FLNT soldier running full tilt towards the square, firing up at her as he went. With a smooth move, Gracie acquired the man through her scope, adjusted high, then fired. The round hit him just below the throat, and Gracie knew he was dead before he hit the ground.

There was a thud next to her, and Rabbit grunted before spinning around and falling to the deck.

"You OK?" she asked.

He gave her a weak thumbs-up, then rubbed his upper chest, saying, "My bones stopped the round, but shit, that felt like someone hit me with a club."

The "bone" inserts that acted as body armor would stop most small arms rounds, but while darts might barely be felt, larger caliber slugs could still beat a Marine up pretty good.

"Where was the shooter?"

"Over there," he said, pointing past Gracie. "I was turning to you when I got hit."

"Show me."

He picked himself up, and with a grimace, popped his head up and pointed. Gracie followed the direction, then both dropped as another round zipped past where Rabbit's head had been an instant before.

He can't be, she told herself as she tried to analyze what she'd seen.

There was only one structure higher than their building in that direction: the water tower. While water towers seemed to be the platform of choice for snipers in Hollybolly flicks, they pretty much sucked for the job. A sniper on one was completely exposed with no route of egress. Not only a suicide position, but a stupid one because a sniper perched there would be taken out immediately.

But this guy's already proven himself to be pretty dumb. Why try to take out Rabbit instead of me?

Gracie knew that she didn't look much like a Marine at times. At 1.4 meters and 38 kg (and that after a Harvest Festival banquet), she could look like a little girl playing dress-up in daddy's gear, especially when she had on her full battle rattle. But any soldier should have realized that since she was carrying the Windmoeller while Rabbit had his standard-issue M99, she was the threat, not him.

Being a sniper, despite all the advances since the Evolution, was still pretty much a man's game. Gracie had run across misogyny more than once, but this was ridiculous, and she was going to enjoy taking advantage of it. If that cretin didn't think she was the threat, she was going to prove him wrong—and enjoy doing so.

"You ready to play the prey, Lance Corporal Rabbit?"

He looked up at her in confusion. Gracie wasn't one much for nicknames, and she'd always kept military discipline in her professional relationships.

"He doesn't seem to recognize that I'm the sniper here. You're twice my size, so you must be the threat. So, if you're up to it, can you pop up for a moment and run a few steps while I disabuse him of his notion?"

A smile crept over his face. He nodded, saying, "My chest still hurts, Staff Sergeant, so yeah, I think I owe him this."

She held up her hand while she entered the range and the height differential. More math—lethal math. At 884 meters, this would be a longer shot, but the calculations were done the same way.

"No matter how good he is, it'll take two seconds minimum for a round to reach you, so no hero stuff. I want you back down in two."

She muted her earbud to the sounds of Sergeant Rafiq directing his squad and took three deep breaths to calm her pulse, then nodded. When Rabbit bolted up, she rose, rested her barrel on the top of the retaining wall, and only had to nudge her scope slightly up and to the right to have the enemy sniper in her crosshairs. She'd just acquired him when she saw him fire.

"Down!" she shouted at Rabbit as she started squeezing her trigger—just as the man lifted his head to look over his scope as if trying to see if he'd hit her spotter. Gracie raised her point of aim to take advantage of the larger target and fired. She could see the trace as the round pierced the air, so she immediately knew she was on target. Long-range sniping might be math, but it was almost art to see the round arc up, then curve back down and slightly to the right to impact his throat. Blood splattered the white paint of the water tower behind him as his weapon fell forward to tumble to the ground.

"Did you get the bastard?" Rabbit asked.

"What do you think? Of, course, I did."

Firing below them was intensifying. She keyed her earbud back on. Second Squad was getting in it deep. Although now that they were inside the library, they were dishing it out as well as taking it in.

"Back to work, Irving."

She started scanning with her scope, trying to find targets and take the pressure off of Second Squad, but while she caught a few shadows, she was having a difficult time. The Marine Corps Miller was an outstanding scope, its targeting AI second-to-none, but snipers usually engaged at over 1000 meters at a minimum. Even with the scope at its widest display, she just wasn't getting the field of vision she needed to spot the enemy as they maneuvered below her. Rabbit had fired four times since she'd taken out the sniper, and she'd yet to engage.

"I need the Kyc," she muttered.

Gracie was more attached to the slug-throwing Windmoeller, but as they were 45,000 credits each, she only had one Miller Scope. She had attached a normal combat scope to her hypervelocity Kyocera, something quite a bit less sophisticated, but with a much wider and higher-contrast field of view. Normally, she wouldn't have even brought the Kyc on the mission, relying instead on her Windmoeller for sniping and her Rino .358 for personal defense. Since she'd had an eager Rabbit there willing to hump it, however, she had figured it wouldn't hurt to bring it—and now that might prove to have been fortuitous.

Keeping low, she scurried alongside the wall to where Rabbit had left the weapon. She powered it up and checked its readouts. Power was at 98%, and while the Kyc didn't carry the 1000-round dart mags of the M99, she still had 150 slightly larger 3mm darts ready to throw and another two mags ready to use. She brought it to her shoulder and looked through the combat scope. As if a gift from the gods of war, she immediately picked up two soldiers hugging the wall of a building that was giving them cover from Marine fire.

Not all Marine fire, guys.

The combat scope must have brought her back to her time as a regular grunt, because instead of squeezing her trigger in the best Triple S fashion, she snapped off five shots in quick succession. With the Kyc's negligible recoil and semi-automatic action, she could fire three darts per second, which beat the Windmoeller's 1.8 seconds per round. The first two darts punched through the head of the lead soldier, both probably continuing to hit the second soldier in the chest. He didn't drop but lunged backward as the next three darts chased him. He fell, only his legs visible as they churned to push him back out of her line-of-sight, so Gracie fired two more darts, at least one hitting him in the left leg.

The FLNT soldiers had layered plate armor on their torsos, but their legs were unprotected, and the man left a smear of blood on the ground as his legs disappeared.

"Dingo-Three and Charlie-One-Two, we have two armored vehicles, Kuang Fen 10's, approaching your position from three-four-niner, two klicks out. We are diverting the Minidrag to intercept, and Charlie-One is on the way. ETA for the platoon is forty-five mikes, so hold on."

Gracie glanced over at Rabbit, who met her eyes. Kuang Fen, an Alliance-registered company, was a new supplier of relatively cheap military equipment. While nothing they had was as good as Federation, Brotherhood, or even Confederation equipment, they were a match for what Gentry, the major supplier to local governments and mercenary units, could put out. More importantly, a KF-10 was more than capable of taking out a lone Marine squad and sniper team. Intel apparently hadn't caught on to the little fact that there were KF tanks in the sector.

"Hope the Minidrag can take them out," Rabbit passed on the P2P.

"That's out of our hands for now, so keep firing."

Over the next five minutes, Gracie dropped three more FLNT fighters, one as he crouched to fire a shoulder-launched missile at the library. She picked up the Windmoeller again to put a round through the missile as it lay in the dirt so no one else could pick it up and use it. As she searched for more targets, her mind was on the Marine drone as it closed in on the KF-10s.

The fight, more than a klick-and-a-half away and within their sight from the roof, was over in seconds. The lead KF-10 erupted in a ball of flame, and moments later, the Minidrag was knocked from the sky. That left one tank still in the fight, and it looked huge as it pushed forward.

"Now what?" Rabbit asked, firing off another burst of 20 darts.

"Keep shooting."

There was whoosh, then a boom as a missile crashed into the side of the library, blowing a hole through the stone. Gracie tried to spot the gunner to no avail. She could almost feel the enemy close in though. The hammer would fall when the KF-10 arrived.

"You still with us?" she asked Sergeant Rafiq on the P2P.

There was a pause before he answered, "We're down to three effectives. That last one, shit, I'm down hard, bleeding like a stuck pig. I'm not going anywhere. I just gave Ben-Zvi the order to retreat to the west, and I'd suggest you do so, too. We'll try to give you some cover, and when that fucking FLNT tank gets here. . . well, we'll see what happens."

A death sentence, Gracie knew. The FLNT didn't see the value of prisoners.

She tied Rabbit in to the net, then said, "I don't think so, Sergeant. We can keep them off you."

She looked over at Rabbit who nodded his agreement.

"You can take out a KF-10? Don't think so," Rafiq said, then groaned in pain.

"Lieutenant Hjebek and the rest of your platoon are almost here."

"Look, Staff Sergeant, I . . . *we* appreciate the sentiment, but this time, the dice rolled against us. All of us here, we talked about it, and we agree. Get out of here. Semper fi," he said before breaking into a fit of coughing and cutting the net.

"Keep at it, Irving," Gracie said, snapping off another round. It didn't hit the running soldier, but it made him dive for cover.

The enemy tank was getting closer, and Gracie pulled up a threat assessment. The KF-10 would be vulnerable to any Marine anti-armor, but the two teams, or whoever was left of them, had used theirs in anti-personnel mode to push back the assault. A few antennae and the periscope were vulnerable, but not to her when armed with only a Kyocera.

But what about the Windmoeller? she wondered.

She didn't have any more WPT-331 rounds, but a WPT-310 would still be better than her 3mm darts. She changed weapons, then shot a range to the tank. It was about to enter the northern edge of town, 1,245 meters away from her. She took a few moments to enter the environmentals. Gracie was an excellent marksman, but hitting a 4cm-wide periscope lens on a moving tank at that range was going to be a task.

"You can't take out a tank with that," Rabbit said when he realized what she was doing.

"No, but maybe I can blind it," she said as she took her three calming breaths.

The tank was still advancing, and Gracie had to estimate what that would do to her sight picture. She made her decision, then fired. A moment later, she saw the round ping off the periscope turret, four or five centimeters low.

She immediately adjusted, but the driver juked the tank to its right just as she fired again, so she never saw the impact of her round. With the side aspect she had now, the shot would be almost impossible, but she held the target in the hopes that it would turn back to her.

There was an explosion behind her. Gracie spun around as three figures burst through the door to the roof that had been blasted right out of the frame, hitting Rabbit hard on the head.

Gracie swung her Kyocera around and fired an un-aimed shot that took one soldier in the thigh and dropped him, causing the man behind him to stumble. She fired again, hitting the second soldier on the top of his head. The third soldier, however, fired a three-round burst at her. One hit her in the left arm and caused her to drop her Windmoeller, her entire arm aflame with pain, while another hit her square on her left knee.

With a smile of . . . satisfaction? . . . scorn? he lowered his rifle and pulled out an enormous boarding gun. Probably over 100 years old, it fired a short-range rocket that had the power to blow right through her body armor. He was slowly raising it to bear down on her when a string of darts hit him in the side where his plate armor deflected them. He spun and fired, the rocket crossing the ten meters to where Rabbit lay on the ground, the muzzle of his M99 wavering as he tried to keep it on target.

Rabbit never had a chance. The rocket blew apart his upper torso. The man stopped, looking at Rabbit's body for a moment before turning back to Gracie. That small delay was enough to give her a chance to pull her Rino from her thigh holster, and his eyes widened in shock as she fired, double-tapping the trigger. The first .358 hollow-point hit him in the forehead, the round expanding and lodging ten centimeters deep into his brain.

Gracie felt a pang of loss, but she couldn't stop to mourn Rabbit. She stumbled to her feet, arm numb, and picked up the Kyocera again. The final assault was about to kick off below, and she intended on taking out as many of the enemy as possible. Heedless of how exposed she was, she leaned over the top of the wall, firing round after round. She thought she dropped at least four of them, but she wasn't sure. The whole time she was firing, the sound of the KF-10 reverberated between the buildings as it made its way to the square.

She heard Sergeant Rafiq ask the lieutenant how far out the platoon was, but she didn't bother to listen to the reply. She knew there was no way the reinforcements could reach them in time.

"I'm still here with you, Dylan," she told him. "Hang in there."

"Shit, Staff Sergeant, you're as stubborn as they said. But you sure as hell ain't no Ice Princess like they say, though. You've got balls, sister."

"And so do you."

And the KF-10 rolled into the square, big and mean, blue-diesel engine pumping out smoke. She knew her Kyocera was useless against it, but she fired off 100 rounds, more as a statement than anything else, as the tank gunner raised the 80mm gun to take her under fire.

She knew she should do something, but there wasn't much left in her box of tricks. The big gun was going to take off the entire top of the building, and her leg was already swollen and immobile. Math worked for snipers, but also for tanks—80mm trumped 3mm.

Gracie kept firing, though. The gun was halfway up when there was a loud whoosh from beneath her, and a smoky plume raced across the square to hit the tank right below the commander's cupola.

The gun stopped tracking. No massive explosions, no turret flying through the air. The tank just stopped cold.

"Scratch one tank," Corporal Ben-Zvi passed on the command net.

"Fuck, Abe, I told you to take your team and get out of here," Sergeant Rafiq passed.

"Ah, I've always been a fuck-up, Sergeant. You know that."

The *cracka-cracka-cracka* of an M110 sounded below her, its rounds shooting across the square to disappear out of sight.

"I'm still effective up here," Gracie passed. "And thanks for taking out the tank, but this isn't over. We've still got a job to do."

But it *was* over. With the KF-10 gone, the will of the FLNT fighters seemed to slip away—that or the fact that they knew a Marine platoon was minutes out. Gracie fired one more shot at a retreating figure, but that was it before Lieutenant Hjebek led the rest of the platoon into the village.

The fight was over.

"Corporal Ben-Zvi, can you do me a favor?" she passed on the P2P as the new Marines swept the area.

"Sure thing, Staff Sergeant."

"Go find one of the dead FLNT fighters before they get policed up, one who looks like he was taken out with an M99. Get a round from him and bring it to me."

"Uh . . . Staff Sergeant, you know we can't take trophies."

"I know the regs, but just do it, OK? It's important."

"Shit, if you say so, of course. We owe you."

"And I owe you. Thanks."

She moved back to the wall, her Kyocera at the ready. Her arm and leg were aching, but at least she could move them now. She could go down to get one of the docs to check her out, but she was a sniper, and two squads of Marines were clearing the village. Her job was to cover them.

****

After the Heroes Ceremony a day later, the members of Third Battalion, Seventh Marines' Scout Sniper Platoon held their own ceremony. Gracie had attached to a piece of parachute cord the night before to the round Ben-Zvi had scrounged, and when Doc Rhymer turned off the stasis chamber for a moment, she slipped it inside with Rabbit's body. The corpsman turned the chamber back on, then left the snipers alone.

According to rules developed over centuries, Rabbit had not technically become a true Hunter of Gunmen because he hadn't used a sniper's weapon to make a kill at distance. Just as Gracie wouldn't get a kill credit for dropping Rabbit's slayer with a handgun, Rabbit's kills with his M99 were considered merely part and parcel of being a Marine. Gracie had asked that he be put in for a medal, and the battalion commander had agreed, but that didn't make him a HOG.

Gracie was a dedicated Marine, and as a habit, she didn't lie. She'd never made a false official statement—until the night before. She hadn't been sure of what kind of Marine Rabbit was, but he'd proven the temper of his steel. Without him, she doubted anyone would have made it out alive. So, she lied. She said she'd given her Kyocera to him, and from the enemy bodies recovered, five had died from the tipped 3mm darts. Gracie didn't need the kills on her record, but he did.

Gracie was sure that Gunny Adams, the Scout-Sniper platoon sergeant, hadn't believed a word of it. He knew how possessively she treated her weapons. But after staring into her eyes for a full 30 seconds, he had nodded and accepted her report.

While the other stasis chambers were being loaded for return, either for resurrection or burial, each of the snipers in the platoon made their way past Rabbit's chamber. Each Marine quietly said their goodbye. As his sniper, Gracie was last. She wasn't much for long talks, so she kept it simple.

"Fair winds and following seas, HOG."

She gave the chamber a little slap, then turned to join the others.

"Do you need a day or two?" Gunny asked her.

She gave the chamber one last look as the loading crew came to take Rabbit, then said, "Nope, I'm ready. What's my next mission?"

Gracie's full-length novel, Sniper, can be found on Amazon on other outlets.

BOLO MISSION

This is another Gracie Medicine Crow novelette, written at the request of readers who wanted more of her tale.

****

"So, here's our jarhead," the tall, slender man said, his long legs stretched from where he leaned back in his chair to the bottom bunk.

Gracie didn't bother to respond directly but asked, "Where's my rack?"

"Right here, madam," the man said, his voice dripping sarcasm as he raised his feet a few centimeters before dropping them back.

Gracie rolled her eyes, but threw her seabag on the rack, just missing his feet. She'd known this wasn't going to be an easy mission. Top Riopel had warned her about the SEALs. They were the Federation's premier derring-do unit, and they knew it. And as a rule, they also didn't like having to deal with Marines.

Gracie had never worked with SEALs before, and she wasn't sure she wanted to now. But orders were orders, so she was going to do her best. She only hoped they would be as diligent in following orders as well. SEALs had a reputation for going off script whenever it struck their fancy.

Staff Sergeant Gracie Medicine Crow did not go off-script. As a Marine sniper, and probably the best sniper in the

Federation, she was more methodical in her planning. No detail was too small. In her line of work, the slightest detail could mean the difference between a successful kill mission and being the victim of her opponent's kill mission.

She stood over her rack for a moment, looking pointedly at the SEAL's feet. With an exhalation of air that didn't quite form a word, the SEAL took them off her rack. She sat down, her head leaning forward to clear the bottom of the rack just above hers.

"Staff Sergeant Gracie Medicine Crow. I'm your sniper," she said, looking at the five men in the cramped compartment.

"We don't do ranks in the teams," the SEAL whose feet had been parked on Gracie's rack. "I'm Dockery. They call me "Dock."

"I'm Franz," the man lying in the top rack across from Gracie said, leaning over to look down at her. "Welcome to the team."

"Kevin," a short, broad-shouldered man said, getting up out of the bottom rack to hold out a hand.

The man had the look of a gym rat, and Gracie expected a bone-crushing grip, but his handshake was gentle.

"That there's Wister, our fearless leader," Dock said, pointing to the bunk just above Gracie's.

She craned her head around to look. One of the most non-descript men she'd ever seen was racked out on his back, his mouth open, his breath almost, but not quite, a snore.

This is a SEAL team commander? Gracie wondered. *He looks like an Ancient Lit major at some liberal arts school, not a warrior.*

"And I'm Ali," the fifth man said, his skin the darkest ebony Gracie had ever seen on a person.

His shirt was off, and every muscle stood out in stark relief as if sculpted by a Renaissance master. He reached up to one of the pipes that ran through the overhead and proceeded to commence a set of pull-ups. From the lingering scent of sweat in the air, this wasn't his first set. In a normal Navy ship, the air systems whisked away even the slightest of smells. The scow they were on wasn't the most up-to-date, however, and Gracie was beginning to realize that the transit might not be the most comfortable one around, especially being cramped together with the five SEALs.

"So, uh, Doc. I take it you're the corpsman for the team?" she asked.

"No, Franz is the doc. I'm the explosives guy. I make things go boom. Like I told you, my name's Dockery, so, therefore, Dock."

Gracie knew that the SEALs were all multitasked, and their training and skills surpassed that of a normal Marine grunt, but calling this guy Dock seemed stupid when he wasn't a corpsman. It showed a lack of, well, military discipline. And if anything, Gracie was a creature of discipline.

"Any word yet to where we're going?" she asked.

"Nope. Not a word. But since you're gracing us with your presence, I'd have to think we've got ourselves an HVT out there somewhere. Not that we need you. Assassination's well within our wheelhouse," Dock said, before nonchalantly biting a piece of his pinkie fingernail off and spitting it to the deck.

Gracie started to correct the man, but she stopped. He obviously didn't want her with the team, and his condescending attitude reeked of arrogance. She knew something he didn't, and she wasn't in a sharing mood.

For the last two days, Gracie had been snapping in with a Lieper Bullmaster. The Bullmaster was a Confed weapon, a massive 13.4mm kinetic monster that threw out an 880-grain, armor-piercing shell. Despite its size, or maybe because of it, the weapon's range was less than that of a Federation Barrett.

No, this weapon was not used for soft targets. Gracie doubted this was an HVT kill mission.

Ali dropped from his makeshift pull-up bar. Gracie hadn't been counting, but he'd probably done 50 reps, and he was barely breathing hard. There was a noticeable reek of sweat as he finished.

Gracie didn't even know the name of the ship, only that it had all the appearances of a small tramp steamer. No one spotting it, or even scanning it, would see the small compartment deep in the ship's bowels that housed the SEAL team.

Gracie had run out of small talk, and none of the team seemed to want to carry on a conversation. She settled back into her rack. This didn't look like it was going to be a pleasant mission, so she just had to buckle down and endure it. She didn't know what the mission was, she was on a team that didn't want her with them, and the living conditions on the ship were in the pits, so she did what any good Marine would do under the circumstances: she went to sleep.

****

Gracie grunted as she shoved and pulled on the mule tongue. The stupid thing wouldn't hook up to the battered container, and at 41 kilos, she didn't have the mass to horse it around. She wanted to call Ali, but that would sink her even further in the team's opinion.

She gave the tongue four good kicks, and finally, the green light of a successful connection appeared. A moment later, the mule started backing, pulling the container with it.

If I wanted to be a stevedore, I'd have joined the merchant fleet.

At least she now knew where they were. The mule was registered to the Pollux Port Authority. Pollux was an independent world, a major trade hub between the Brotherhood and the Confederation. Why the team was there was still a mystery to her, but given the planet's economic reach, Gracie was getting the feeling that this might have to do with some economic mission—although why that would take a SEAL team and a Marine sniper still escaped her.

Of course, this could only be a waystop to another location, made to throw off anyone bothering to notice this particular tramp freighter plying the space lanes. Gracie was a Marine, and while the Marines could and did use subterfuge as part of their strategy, what she was going through now was far beyond her field of knowledge.

Not that she needed much knowledge to play the part of a deck ape. She took a moment to look around at her companions. It was obvious to her that the five SEALs were not your run-of-the-mill merchanter deckhands. The team leader might fit the bill, with his slouched posture and easy movements, but the other four simply screamed out danger, like a coiled snake ready to strike. They may have on the same ratty purple overalls as she was wearing, they may be monitoring the offload of cargo like she was, but they carried themselves with a deadly grace that couldn't be hidden. Ali, in particular, might as well have a neon sign pointing at him with a flashing "DANGER: NAVY SEAL."

The men were killers, and she didn't think anything could hide that. The irony of her thoughts was not lost on her. Gracie had 58 confirmed kills, the most of any active Federation sniper, and she thought of the SEALs as "killers?" In her mind, though, she wasn't really a hard-nosed killer, just as she wouldn't consider a cannon cocker or a Navy gunners mate killers. Their killing was done at nice clean distances. These guys were the type to disembowel someone and strangle him with his own intestines while smiling in his face. Maybe their killing was more honest, in a way, but she hadn't come to grips with the moral ramifications of that, nor did she want to dwell on them.

She turned back to her mule. On a higher-end freighter, the offload would have been done by the ship's systems, taking an hour at the most with the station's docking facilities the bottleneck. On her ship, which she still didn't even know the name, it was the brute manpower of the six of them, along with the ship's captain, that moved the cargo. It took almost six hours to complete the offload, and Gracie was aching and dead tired when it was completed. She was in pretty good shape, and the mules did most of the heavy hauling, but this was a different kind of labor, one to which she was unused. She almost looked forward to getting back to their tiny compartment and into the rack, but no such luck.

"Good job, people," the ship's captain said. "Go get cleaned up. We'll meet at the Gecko's Perch down in K-town at 2000 local.

"We're on," Franz said quietly from beside her.

Gracie felt a familiar jolt of adrenaline. She still didn't know what their mission was, but just to know it would commence soon was enough to get her competitive juices flowing.

"Don't take too long in the shower, Grace," Dock said. "The local worm-grubbers will fuck about anything, so no need to make up."

Gracie felt her hackles rise. She knew Dock was playing a game on the off-chance that anyone was listening in—which there was a good possibility that there was at least a Pollux AI doing just that—but she thought he was taking it too far. The smile on his face while he spoke looked genuine.

He's enjoying this, she realized.

"Well, *you b*etter send some time with your make-up kit, Dock. I hear the billy-boys are a little more discerning on who *they* fuck," she replied.

Dock's face turned red as the others, even Wister, laughed. Dock looked like he had a retort, but Franz put an arm around his shoulder and led him back down belowdecks to the crew head.

Gracie wondered if she should have pushed his button like that. She still had a mission to do with them, and the fact that she hadn't felt welcomed had no bearing on what was expected of her. She'd show the almighty SEALs that Marines were there to accomplish the mission and not let petty egos get in the way.

Still, that felt good, she told herself as he left the cargo hold. *And fuck him if he can't take a joke.*

****

Three hours, a shuttle ride to the planet's surface, and a tram ride later, the six military and the ship's captain walked into the Gecko's Perch. It wasn't the skuzziest dive Gracie had ever seen, but it did tilt toward that end of the scale.

"You've got a room and grub for the *Dougie Blue*?" the ship's captain asked the barkeep.

So that's our ship's name. Glad we know in case it comes up sometime, Gracie thought, knowing they really should have been briefed on such a simple thing.

The barkeep motioned toward the back hallway.

"OK, let's go. Remember, four pitchers are on the ship. After that, you're on your own," the captain told them as they herded themselves down the hall, past the heads, and into a smallish room.

The captain never said a word but let himself out a small door in the back. Wister motioned to the seats.

A few minutes later, a rheumy-eyed waiter entered carrying a pitcher and mugs, which he put on the table, some of the beer sloshing out and splashing on the wood surface.

"Alcohol abuse," Kevin said by rote.

The man pulled out a small scanner and waved it around the room, his manner suddenly professional. He seemed satisfied with the results as he hid the scanner away back under his apron.

"Wait one," he said before leaving.

The six sat, looking at each other stupidly before Dock reached out, took a stein, and poured himself a beer. He passed the pitcher to Franz, who looked up at Wister, then when the team leader nodded, poured himself one.

It made sense, Gracie knew. The waiter-who-was-not-a-waiter had scanned the room, but if some sort of spy device was missed, then nothing screamed out that things weren't as they seemed than deckhands not helping themselves to beer. The pitcher had made its way to Gracie when the waiter came back in, two platters full of grilled sausages and potatoes.

The waiter scanned the room a second time, then placed a second device on the table, flipping a switch. He waited a few seconds until a small light on it turned green.

"Lieutenant O'Rourke, I'm your liaison," the man said, his voice firm and steady, belying his outwards appearance.

"O'Rourke?" That's his name? How the hell did they get "Wister" out of that? she wondered.

"Your mission here is simple, at least in theory. Executing it might not be as simple."

What else is new?

"Foreign entities have stolen Federation intellectual property. They plan on demonstrating what they have stolen two days from now here on the planet. Your mission is to see that the demonstration fails, and fails spectacularly."

He looked around at the six of them, but no one said a word. Beer steins and food were forgotten, and six sets of eyes bored into him. The SEALs might have exhibited a devil-may-care attitude in the ship, but now, their attention was locked on their liaison.

"The object developed with this knowledge is this," he continued, pulling out a small projector and flipping it on.

A very normal-looking truck appeared in the projector's field.

"A lorry?" Dock asked, breaking the silence.

"Yes, a lorry. A truck. It isn't the vehicle that's important, but what's powering it. You don't have the clearance to know just what that is, but suffice it to say that it's a technological leap, and they're introducing it before our own, well, more impressive demonstration of the new tech.

"There will be more than this one vehicle at the demonstration. You will need to spot and identify the correct target before you engage," he said, looking straight a Gracie.

Great, a BOLO mission. And how do we know which is the right truck?

"So, we—" Dock started before the man raised a hand, silencing him.

"You have the time and place here," he said, holding up what looked like a simple data drive, "as well as the identifying markings on the target," he added, as if he'd been reading Gracie's mind. "Lieutenant, I will give you the code for the access. Otherwise, all you'll get from this is porn.

"Staff Sergeant Medicine Crow, your weapon is here," he said, opening up a bench against the wall and pulling out the Bullmaster to the "ooh's" of several of the SEALs. "You've got six rounds, which have been slightly modified from what you've used before. That shouldn't affect their flight characteristics, but the pulse they put out will ensure that the target is destroyed."

Pulse? They've put a pulse charge in one of them? That WILL affect the firing solution, no matter what he says, Gracie thought, her mind snapping into sniper mode.

"What about our weapons?" Ali asked, leaning back in his chair to look into the bench.

The man returned the Bullmaster into hiding and took out what looked to be two small versions of a normal Marine Corps toad incendiary device.

"That's it? Mini-beads?" Ali asked.

"You will not be armed. These are to destroy the staff sergeant's weapon if you cannot get it off planet."

"No weapons?" Dock asked, his voice incredulous.

"That is correct. No weapons. You are on Pollux, and we are not a war. There will be observers from the Brotherhood and the Confederation, among others, and we are not at war with them. You will destroy the vehicle, and nothing else."

"This doesn't make any sense. We're here to take out a fucking lorry, and that's it. We're not even armed, except for the grunt here. So what if we take it out? They can just build another, right?"

The liaison looked at Dock, then turned the small sound suppression device on the table around as if checking to make sure it was functioning.

"Yes, they can make another, but we are sending a message to both them and those who might want to purchase from them. That message is that we will not stand idly by and let our own developments be stolen."

"That's fucking crazy," Dock started until Wister interrupted him.

"There is obviously a reason why the team is here with the staff sergeant," the lieutenant said, his voice calm, but instantly shutting Dock up. "I'd like you to hear you say it."

The slightest hint of a smile creased the corner the liaison's mouth, and he said, "Very well. While we expect the potential buyers will get the message, there will be some very upset people at you. Your team is particularly well trained in hand-to-hand combat. If some people attempt to extract revenge, if they try to stop you from getting off-planet, you will do all you can to prevent that—non-lethally."

"And if it takes lethal force?"

"If it takes lethal force, then you'd better be ready to justify your actions, Lieutenant."

"Fuck me," Kevin muttered.

The liaison handed the small data drive to Wister and said, "The details are on here, to include your extraction instructions. The *Dougie Blue* has a small problem with its port bay gate, which will be fixed by 2230 local in two days. If you are not back onboard, another crew will take your place, and you will be stranded here until, and *if*, we deem it feasible to recover you."

The "if we deem it" caught Gracie's attention.

"Do you have any questions?"

"Not until I read the drive," Wister said.

"I'm on shift here until 0200. You have until then. After that, you're on your own. If you need me, order two pitchers of Golden Rout, but wait until I have the suppressor field activated before you say anything," he told Wister, pointing at the small device on the table.

"So now, please give me your PAs."

There wasn't a sound as the SEALs gave up their personal PAs. They may be used to doing that in their missions, but Gracie wasn't. Her firing comp was on hers, and she'd need that.

She handed it over and said, "I need my firing comp."

"You've got a new one on this," he said, giving her a new PA—new to her, but looking rather well-used.

Gracie wasn't sure she trusted it, but it wasn't as if she had any choice in the matter.

"And now, gentlemen, your wrists, please," the liaison said, pulling out a small wrench-looking device from the edge of the sausage platter.

"Shit, I knew it," Dock said as he stood up, offering the inside of his right wrist to the man.

"What's going on?" Gracie whispered to Franz, a feeling of dread flowing over her.

"Plausible deniability," Kevin whispered back as the liaison put the device up to Dock's wrist and squeezed. "If we get caught, we've nothing to tie us to the Federation."

"But the Harbin Accords—"

". . .mean nothing to us now."

Gracie was stunned. Her chip was what identified her as a Federation Marine. If she was ever captured, it provided her with the protection afforded to all combatants by the Accords. Without it, she was . . . she was a criminal at best, a spy at worst, subject to whatever the local authority wanted to do with her.

"But they can do a DNA scan and find out who we are," she protested as Ali stepped up to get his chip removed.

"So what? The Federation says we deserted and joined a merc group. It's happened often enough. Like I said, plausible deniability."

"But that guy said they . . . *we* want them to know the Federation is taking action," Gracie said, grasping at straws.

"And they will. But this is how the game is played," Kevin said. "Welcome to Special Forces."

Gracie watched with growing dread as Franz, Wister, and Kevin had their chips removed. Finally, it was her turn, and she couldn't delay. Her arm was trembling as he held it out. With a swift move, the liaison placed the device on her wrist and triggered it, a lance of pain making Gracie jerk her arm back. A streak of blood formed on her arm.

"Shouldn't have moved," the liaison told her before turning to the rest. "Like I said, I'm here until 0200. You might as well enjoy the food while you get up to speed. It really isn't too bad. But I don't have to remind you, turn on the suppressor before you talk about anything concerning the mission. I'll leave it here for now, but keep it off until needed. No use advertising to any scanner that there's a suppressor field activated in here."

He picked up the half-empty pitcher, filled the steins to the brim, then took the empty with him as he left, ever the good waiter.

No one said a word. Gracie was in shock, her wrist feeling naked. Her identity of being a Marine was embedded in her. It was who she was. And now, she'd been cut off, and she really, really, *really* didn't like it one bit.

Finally, Dock reached over and grabbed a whitish sausage with his fingers and chomped on it.

"He's right, they're not bad," he said.

As the lieutenant started to insert the drive into his new PA, Dock added, "He said it's porn. Maybe we can take a look at that first?"

****

"Where's Dock?" Gracie asked, nervous as she stroked the stock of the Bullmaster.

"He'll be here, don't worry," Kevin said.

49

"I can't do any good without a barrel, you know," she replied, stating the obvious.

They had broken into two-man teams to make their way to the hide-slash-firing position Gracie had selected the day before. It was her second choice of a firing position, but Wister had nixed her first choice due to security issues. Kevin and Gracie had arrived first, and Wister and Ali not five minutes later. Now they'd been waiting for 40 more minutes, and Dock and Franz were nowhere in sight.

It wasn't the missing two SEALs that bothered her; it was what they were carrying. The Bullmaster was a massive weapon at 32 kg, and it was a little bulky to just tote around out in public. Unlike the Marine Corps M99, which was mostly composites with only the mag rings and barrel being metallic, the Bullmaster was a veritable hodge-podge of exotic alloys. Even the Windy (the Windmoeller and Holscher) and the Barrett, the two Marine Corps kinetic sniper rifles, barely tipped the scales at five and twelve kilos respectively.

But the Bullmaster came apart easily, and each two-man team was given a component of the weapon to get to the hide. Two-thirds of a weapon was on the ground in front of Gracie; the barrel was still missing. They had two hours before the demonstration was supposed to commence, and it would only take her a few minutes to run the diagnostics on the re-assembled weapon, but her stress level was rising.

Not having her weapon was stressful, but another part of that stress was undoubtedly related to the "new" Gracie. Before leaving that morning, Wister had given her inclined pads to put into her work boots, cheek pads for her face, and tacks for her ears. The pads were small, and they changed her gait, supposedly fooling any surveillance looking for stride patterns. The tacks that brought back her ears weren't much, but the cheek pads made her feel like a chipmunk, and they affected her speech. Whether all this spook stuff would really work was questionable to her, but they were uncomfortable, and Gracie was worried the pads would affect her cheek weld. Somewhat anal in her personality, Gracie liked things a certain way, and this wasn't that way.

Then there was the target. Gracie had never been on an actual BOLO mission, which was an old police and FCDC term for "Be On The Lookout." She had engaged anti-material, or "material-denial" targets, which were basically anything other than simple humans, like the vehicle-borne suicider who'd tried to blow up the checkpoint on Jericho, but those were targets of opportunity, not specific vehicles. To make matters worse, there would be at least five of the same kind of truck driving around: the target vehicle—referred to as the objective in sniper-talk—and four others there to serve as controls. Her target was supposed to have a small orange logo on the sides and the back—if the intel was correct. Wister and Ali were on the roof of their building, and Dock and Franz were supposed to be observing the demonstration from the next building over to help her spot the objective, but between the missing barrel, the spook disguise, and a BOLO target, Gracie was not going into the mission with a warm and fuzzy.

She rose to stand just inside and to the left of the open window. Raising her Zeis binos, she glassed the open area 1200 meters away where the demonstration was to take place. A few personnel were moving about, busy at something, but it really didn't look like a major demonstration was about to happen. Six stories below her, a scattering of people were going about their daily business, but this was towards the outskirts of town and hardly a hub of activity. There weren't even any of the bleachers out at the demo area as would be at any Marine Corps demo.

Kevin was a saving grace. As the team sniper, he'd helped Gracie set up the firing position, using scrounged material to hide them from prying eyes. The professional in her had to admit that he'd done a good job. She couldn't find any fault with his work, even if she ended up making some minor adjustments just for GP. He was eyeing the Bullmaster as Gracie scanned the area below. He'd admitted to her that he'd never fired the big gun, which surprised her—she thought the SEALs were given every known weapon with which to play—and she could tell he ached to take the shot himself. That actually instilled Gracie with renewed confidence. She'd been selected for the mission because she was the best there was, end of story. Missing barrel, weird spook disguise—none of that mattered. She was Gracie Medicine Crow, sniper extraordinaire!

At that moment, Wister re-entered the hide, Dock and Franz in tow. Dock was carrying the barrel out in the open, with a brush attachment on one end, a flexible tube to the other and leading to a contraption on his back.

He made it a vacuum cleaner? she wondered as he rushed to him, hand out.

"Really, Dock? Carrying it in plain sight?"

He popped off the brush attachment and handed it to her, the flexible hose stretching out.

"In case you didn't notice, Marine, it's a little long to hide," he said, pulling back until the hose snapped off with an audible pop.

"If you've damaged it. . ." she started as she held the barrel up so she could see down it.

It looked OK, she had to admit. But she wasn't going to confirm that until she'd checked out the assembled weapon. Without another word, she snapped the barrel in place, then hit the diagnostics. The small circle of dull red lights lit up, one after the other, completing the swirl. Gracie started getting concerned when the lights were still red after 20 seconds, and she glared daggers at Dock, but then the lights finally switched to green.

She sniffed dismissively, forgetting the SEAL, and then brought the weapon up to the firing position they'd set out. She'd be firing from an old table they'd pulled out of another room, but for the moment, she left the Bullmaster on the deck beside it. There shouldn't be anyone actively searching for them, but there was no use setting up a big hunk of metal in front of an open window.

"Unless you need anything else, we're getting into position. We'll do a comms check once there."

Gracie rolled her eyes at that, but a tiny smile made an appearance. As expected, a SEAL comms check was not the same as a Marine check. Wister was going to say something to the effect of going to get pizza wraps. Dock was to ask Wister to bring them six, and Kevin was going to pass on the offer. It was so . . . so . . . "un-military!" It was almost silly, but it made sense. Even a scrambled transmission could be picked up, and that would send alarm bells ringing in the city's AI monitoring. They could switch to scrambled if they needed to, but no use tipping their hand needlessly.

Ten minutes later, they played out their little performance. Gracie wondered if anyone was, in fact, listening in, but it did sound like a hungry work team to her.

And they settled in to wait, something SEALs evidently were as used to as snipers were. Gracie figured she'd spent a good portion of her career simply waiting. Sometimes, the waiting was for nothing, sometimes it resulted in a shot. For a while, Gracie wondered if the intel had been wrong, and this would be one of those wasted efforts, but after an hour, a bus came up and disgorged about 15 people who had the look of a work party. Gracie glassed them, and the evident leader, an older women with white hair, pointed this way and that, directing her worker bees. She looked on her map—the range to the woman was 1240 meters, if Gracie had positioned her correctly. She could log into the GeoSat and get an exact figure, or she could ping the woman with her scope, but one would alert the city AI, and the other could be picked up by surveillance. If her target were some government VIP, either would certainly alert security. No one thought that any security would be to those heightened levels for this, but Gracie didn't think it was worth the risk. With a vehicle as the target, she should be able to hit it blindfolded at this range, so a map read should be good enough.

Even with the work party, it still didn't have the look of a major demonstration. The area was once a university sports complex with five large practice fields. There was a fence around the area, but whatever structures had been inside had long been scavenged. What had probably been manicured fields had disappeared due to lack of sprinklers and fertilizer, reverting to dusty and worn patches of grass gamely struggling to stay alive. On the far side, old university dorms had been converted into public housing. Rooms there would offer superb fields of fire over the entire complex, but the buildings were occupied, and extracting from the firing position would be problematic.

The building Gracie and Kevin were using had once been an office building, but as with the defunct university, it had fallen on hard times. Pollux's economy was supposedly doing well, but evidently, that boom had bypassed this area. None of the larger buildings were completely occupied, and Gracie's was completely empty. There was a scattering of new-looking restaurants and bars in the lower stories of some of the buildings—gentrification in action—and a few small factories and warehouses looked to be hanging on. If the demonstration organizers wanted a degree of privacy, it could have done worse, but still, it wasn't like this was isolated territory.

"Lookie," Kevin said. "Here come the stars of the show."

Gracie swung her glasses over to where five trucks were entering the complex. They were in a column, each a bare five meters from the one in front of them. A ground guide led them up to a spot on the ground, and the vehicles stopped.

"Which one is the target?" Gracie asked as she scanned for the orange logo. "Can you see it?"

"No, they all look the same to me."

Hell, how am I supposed to know which is the demo truck?

"How're we doing on the pizza rolls?" Dock's voice came over the comms. "I still don't see my lunch."

"Dock and Franz can't tell, either," Kevin said. "I hope Wister can."

But the team leader was silent. Gracie didn't know if that was because he was moving to a different vantage point or what.

"I need to know which one to take out," Gracie muttered.

The drivers were getting out of the trucks, and the white-haired lady spoke to them, her arms waving again as she gave them instructions. If she was paying attention to one driver over the others, Gracie couldn't tell. Instructions given, the drivers went back to their vehicles to wait.

After five minutes of silence, Gracie asked, "Should we call Wister?"

"If he's got something for us, he'll say something," Kevin said, his eyes not leaving his binos.

A good twenty minutes later, the drivers perked up, looked back, and then hurried into their trucks.

"Looks like it's showtime," Kevin said.

"I still don't know what's my target!"

"I know! Maybe we'll see something as they move out."

I hope so.

Gracie swung her binos wide, and three black utility hovers entered the complex, followed by a bus. They drove up to where several of the worker bees and their leader were standing, and several people emerged from each of the black hovers.

"Military," Kevin said. "Those three from the second hover."

The two men and one woman were in civilian clothes, but Gracie knew Kevin was right. They positively screamed military—and high ranking at that. They hadn't come out of the first hover, so they were not leading this thing, but their presence was interesting.

"I'd give my left nut to see their IDs. Which force is willing to risk stolen technology?" Kevin asked.

Gracie lifted the Bullmaster to the table. If she was going to get a shot, she needed to be ready. She checked the scope AI one more time. The environmentals for Pollux were entered correctly, as was a basic firing solution for the drop and distance to the center of the fields. The kicker was how the modified round would react—she had to trust the programming. She'd spent two days on a Bullmaster, firing at least a hundred of the standard rounds, so she had a pretty good feel for it, but not as much as for a Windy or a Kyc, the Corps' hypervelocity sniper rifle. Even with a Barrett, she'd fired thousands of rounds. Where she might tweak her comp's firing solution for any of those three weapons, with the Bullmaster, she was going to stick with the firing solution worked out by her firing comp.

The bus was almost empty, a stream of lesser-noteworthies walking up to join the big dogs. What struck Gracie as odd was that there was no evident press present. At every dog-and-pony in which Gracie had participated in her career, the press was always evident, even if it was Marine press.

A dog-and-pony wasn't worth putting on if it didn't need to be recorded for posterity.

The mass of about 40 attendees stood on an otherwise featureless piece of ground. A man was speaking to them, but most of the group had their eyes on the vehicles. Gracie zoomed in close, hoping that she could discern which was the super truck from which one they were focusing on the most. From the way their eyes darted about, though, she was sure they didn't know, either.

Great. It's a frigging surprise.

"Can you take out all of the trucks?" Wister passed on the comms, but this time secured.

That meant that he couldn't identify the target either, and he thought it important enough to break into scrambled comms. If the airwaves were being scanned, it would probably take a while for any reaction—not from the AI's but for live bodies to take a look and decide on doing something.

Gracie had six rounds, and there were five trucks. She half expected that the special configuration of the rounds would throw off her firing solution and that she would have to take a second shot, but once she knew how the round would react, she should be able to apply that to subsequent shots.

Should.

"Roger, I think I can," she passed.

If anyone can, it's me, she thought.

"Be ready for that on my call."

The trucks came to life, and on some unseen signal, moved out, passing the group of observers and heading for the far side of the complex. Gracie tracked on after the other, mentally noting the distance as the trucks reached certain points. She looked for the orange logo, she looked for anything that would set the target vehicle off, but the trucks looked identical to each other. None started to fly into loop-the-loops, none took off into bubble space. All five just floated on their bubble of air as they cruised the complex.

They reached the far fence, and one after the other, started back.

"Gracie, just take them all out. Everyone else, get ready to beat feet."

"Roger that. I'll wait until they reach the center," she said.

They were a good 400 meters past the observers, and while that was still an easily doable shot, 1200 meters was even more of a slam dunk. She thought she'd take out the first truck as it reached its closest distance to her, then get the rest in the resulting confusion the best she could.

Gracie led the first truck as it came back towards the observers. She wanted to ping it once just as a precaution, but that could be detected by any surveillance, and she'd much rather have a quiet, uneventful exfiltration if at all possible.

There were two passive methods to determine an approximate range—well, three if you used the scope indices and entered the dimensions of the target. The two weren't extremely accurate, but they were good to a couple of meters, and that could validate what she had now as the range.

And it hit her.

What if the target vehicle was putting out different transmissions from the others?

She quickly switched the display to emissions mode. Most machinery put out vibrations, and they could be picked up. Her firing AI could read them, and then using deep-level math, determine a range based on more variables that Gracie could even grasp.

Her heart fell, though, when the ranges came in. She didn't care about the actual ranges, but she wanted to see a difference in the pattern, something significant enough to scream out that one truck was different. All five were within normal variations, though.

Her adrenaline spike over, she switched to the infrared mode—and where four trucks had hot, red engines, the third truck in line's engine was a deep, cold blue. Gracie stared in shock for a moment as she took it the significance of that.

"I've got the target. Stand by," she passed as she switched back to normal visuals.

"On spot," Kevin said from beside her.

She pulled the stock into her padded cheek, forgetting her earlier misgivings. Her Bullmaster didn't care if she had some disguise on; the round would go where fired.

The vehicles picked up speed as the neared the observers, the gaps between them opening up just a bit. Gracie calmed herself, lowering her pulse rate as she entered the zone. Although she had vowed to trust the AI, she raised her crosshairs to just over the hood—her gut told her the new round needed that—and lead it by four meters. She started squeezing the trigger before her target reached the observers, and the big gun went off, a mule kick to her shoulders.

Gracie never felt it. She was locked onto her scope, and she watched a beautiful bullet trace arc up, then down. She knew immediately that she was spot on, and a second-and-a-half later, the round plunged to penetrate the engine block.

"Hit, center mass," Kevin said.

For a moment, nothing happened, and Gracie chambered the next round, ready to fire again, but then the engine erupted into beautiful sparks, shooting a good five meters into the air. The truck dipped down, the far skirt hitting the dirt and creating a pivot that jerked the truck towards the observers.

People dove out of the way, but the truck, now a Roman candle, was too quick, smashing three or four of them, leaving them in crumbled heaps. The truck continued until the hover fans failed and it slid to a stop on the ground, engine still shooting out fireworks.

"I guess that was a special round after all," Gracie said, still on the scope.

"I guess so," Kevin said in awe. "That was freaking wicked!"

"Are you sure that was the target?" Wister asked.

"Roger that. I'm sure."

"We're on our way. Break down."

Gracie took one more look at the burning truck. Some people were beginning to rush to it; others were tending those hurt. Sliding off the table, she released the scope first. The rifle was valuable, but the scope was six months of her salary. She slid it into her overall chest pocket. It might make her physique seem a little unnaturally lumpy to anyone looking closely, but with her light work jacket, it shouldn't be too obvious.

The barrel of the Bullmaster was still hot, even after firing only one round, but she smacked the release lever, and it fell with a clunk to the table. The receiver went into Kevin's toolbox, under the top tray. She'd let Dock pick up the barrel, but she held the stock assembly to give to Wister and Ali.

"Shit! We've got company!" Kevin said as he glassed the area.

Gracie raised her binos, and six men in security uniforms were running down the road right towards them.

"Where did they come from?" Kevin asked.

Gracie didn't wonder. She'd hoped for an easy egress, but she'd feared this. The 880-grain round might as well have been an artillery shell. Any city's AI would have picked it up. The bullet trace had only been icing on the cake. Gracie had never been on the receiving end of a round that left a visible trace, but it wouldn't take a genius to back-track along the trace to see where it originated.

"Six security, heading our way. Four-hundred meters out and running fast," Kevin passed.

"Burn the gun and move. Option C, I repeat, Option C," Wister passed.

Immediately, Kevin pulled the receiver out of his toolbox.

He placed it on the barrel when Gracie said, "On the deck. It'll last longer."

He nodded, then took both off the table and placed them on the floor. Gracie handed him the stock, which he placed next to the other two components.

Pulling out his mini-bead, the small SEAL incendiary device, he said "Fire in the hole" before thumbing it on and putting it on top of the pile. A moment later, a small sun erupted, making Gracie avert her head to protect her vision. An acrid smoke started to fill the room, and both of them rushed towards the door.

Gracie knew she should have put the scope on the pile as well, but if push came to shove, each scope had a small self-destruct sequence that wouldn't destroy the scope, but would wipe it clean beyond any hope of recovery. Snipers revered their scopes, and she just didn't quite have it in her to destroy it yet. Kevin either forgot about it, or SEAL snipers felt the same.

"Nice shot, by-the-way," Kevin said as he stopped to make sure the Bullmaster was being consumed. "I guess that's why you were assigned to the mission."

It wasn't much, but Gracie appreciated the comment.

"OK, it's burning. We've got to move," he said.

The Bullmaster wasn't going to be totally destroyed, something that was reflected when after bounding down one story, they could hear a crash as the mass of material burned through the floor above to plunge down to the next one. The weapon didn't have a serial number, and by melting most of it, it would be even harder for the forensic investigators to get anything useful from it. Possible DNA any of them might have left would be crisped.

Gracie was right on Kevin's ass as they bounded down the ladderwell. They reached the bottom floor just as somebody crashed into the front door.

"Glad we blocked that," Kevin said as the broom he'd stuck in the door handles bulged with each slam from outside. "I'm going to go out on a limb here and suggest we take the back way out of here," he added as if they had a choice.

"Yeah, not a bad idea. Lead on," Gracie said with a small snort of amusement.

She took one last look back at the front door as they ran through a back office and out a broken window, landing on the hard parking apron just as the snap of the broom and the doors being flung open reached them.

The two of them took off at a dead run, crossing the old parking lot and under a fence as shouts reached out to them, ordering them to stop.

They didn't.

Several small alleys cut through a block of buildings across the street. Dodging past two men coming out of a restaurant, they bolted down one of the alleys. They counted two cross-alleys, then entered the next building. Also abandoned, the front of the building opened up to a larger street, one on which they hoped they could mix in with the afternoon crowd and be lost.

"OK, calm down. We're just two workers looking to get a beer before going home," Kevin said, waiting a moment for Gracie to catch her breath before opening the door.

"OK, I'm good," she told him. "Let's go."

"Kevin, where you at?" Dock passed on the comms. "Wister and Ali are going to be in the shit in a moment in Purple."

"Purple" was the name given to one of the alleys leading through the block.

"Close. What about you?"

"We're still in Frankfurt, up high. Too far to do anything, but we've got eyes on them."

"We don't need help," Wister said. "All of you, keep going."

"Bullshit, Wister. I can see you, and I can see who's coming. You're not going to make it."

Kevin looked at Gracie, his eyes questioning.

Gracie was a sniper, a damned good one. But a sniper without a weapon can't accomplish much, especially a sniper weighing 41 kilos dripping wet. But more than a sniper, she was a Marine, and Marines don't leave other Marines in the lurch— or SEALs.

"Let's go," she said.

Kevin was in action before she finished speaking, running back the way they came. No one was in the alley they'd used, but the sounds of fighting reached them from the next alley. He didn't hesitate, and with Gracie right behind, raced around the corner. Two steps later, Gracie rounded the corner to see Kevin launch himself at the back of a jimmylegs, punching him in the back of the neck and dropping him like a sack of potatoes.

Wister and Ali were back to back, facing six jimmylegs— five now that Kevin had taken one out. Another was prone at their feet.

Kevin's arrival threw the party into a mix. Two of the jimmylegs turned on him while another two rushed Wister and Ali. Like all Marines, Gracie had been through MCCMAT, the

63

Marine Corps Combat Martial Arts Training. She immediately moved into a sidekick against the knee of one of the jimmylegs attacking Kevin—and got knocked to the ground by an almost casual swing of the man's baton. She struggled to her knees, trying to clear her head.

Kevin was a kicking fool, not so much connecting but keeping the two men at bay as he maneuvered to his team leader. Ali had one of the men in a guillotine, the man's face red, as he weakly struggled, but that left him defenseless as another jimmylegs darted in to give him smack on the head with his baton which he couldn't entirely avoid.

Their liaison had said the SEALs were picked for their hand-to-hand skill, and Gracie could see why. This wasn't the Hollybolly martial arts of flying combatants, twirling and dodging. This was a cross between an MMA match and a street brawl—and the SEALs were winning. Two more jimmylegs were down.

They had been briefed that if they were spotted, while the police might escalate any confrontation, the security forces would try to capture them with non-lethal force so they could be interrogated. Evidently, at now-even numbers, one of the jimmylegs never got the memo. From his knees, he drew a small energy handgun and started to bring it up to take Kevin in his sights.

Gracie was still wobbly, but she surged to her feet. Pulling her scope out, she brought it down in a decidedly non-Marine Corps sanctioned manner and hit the man on the side of his head, sending him sprawling just as he fired. Kevin stiffened up but kept his feet. Gracie had knocked the weapon off target enough so that Kevin had only been caught in a side lobe. He was still mobile, but limping. The "tingles" could be temporary, but they could also last a few days.

And suddenly, it was over. Gracie's head was throbbing, Kevin had the tingles, and Ali had a gash on his head that was bleeding, but seven jimmylegs were down, three down hard.

"Thanks, Gracie," Kevin said, nodding at the scope in her hand.

With sudden dread, she looked down at it. Marine sniper scopes were high tech, but they were not designed as clubs. Gracie immediately knew that this scope would never sight in on anything else again. She popped out the AI cube. With that, she had a visual record of her shot. On a regular mission, with Marines around her, she could upload it, but here on Pollux, she had to carry it. She armed the wipe on the cube, ready to be initiated with a touch, then slipped it into her side pocket.

"Boss, there's a whole posse of police arriving to your east. Looks like 25 or more," Dock passed.

Wister looked at the two SEALs with him.

"I'm out," Kevin said, shaking his head.

"I'm not feeling too good, either," Gracie said despite knowing that she wasn't considered by him as part of their fighting strength.

"Where are they entering?" Wister asked Dock.

"Some are hanging back, but it looks like Red. I'd say they know where you are. Four are moving south, probably to block your exit. They're moving cautiously, but still, four minutes and they're on the other side of you."

"Can you make it?" Wister asked the two of them.

"Four minutes? I can try," Kevin said.

"Yes, sir. I can," Gracie said, trying to sound confident.

"Go. Now."

"I've got the chokepoint," Ali said. "Go with them."

Wister looked at Ali for only a moment before he nodded, command decision made. He gave Ali a clap on the shoulder, then took Kevin's arm around his neck and to help him down the alley.

"But . . . Ali!" Gracie said as the SEAL took a moment to knock out the conscious jimmlylegs with a puff from what looked like an asthma inhaler.

"Sorry about this, guys. You'll wake up in a couple of hours," he said before heading farther down the alley.

"Gracie, come with us, now," Wister ordered.

The team might call the slight man by his first name, but there was authority in his voice that brooked no argument.

In a moment, they were around the corner and out of Dock and Franz' sight. That bothered her. The two SEALs might be out of reach, but she'd felt good that they could see them. Now, the three of them were on their own again.

"Come on, Kevin. Just a little farther," Wister coaxed.

Kevin was struggling, sweat beading on his brow, his right side not responding to his commands. But he was not giving up. They entered the building and made their way to the front.

"Wister, don't exit the building. You've got ten cops coming up," Franz passed. "Wait one. Dock's got a plan."

"Oh, shit. Just what we need, Dock with a plan," Kevin said with a laugh, which seemed like a good sign to Gracie.

"What's the plan?" Wister asked.

"Hold on, Boss. I just need to get to where we can be seen," Dock passed.

"Do you have a bug-out route?"

"Affirmative, Boss," Dock said, followed by a grunt and an "Oh, shit. That one sucked."

What sucked? Gracie wondered, not following what was happening.

"OK, I'm popping a mini-bead. If they take the bait, Franz'll tell you to go."

Gracie suddenly knew what Dock's plan was. He was going to try and draw the cops off. It was pretty transparent, and Gracie couldn't imagine it would work, but she held her breath.

"He's popping now," Franz passed.

"They'll leave a security team here if they go investigate," Gracie said.

She served her first tour as a regular grunt, and that would be standard SOP.

But Pollux police were not Marines, because a moment later, Franz was passing, "Go, now!"

Noises from outside the building behind them were more than enough goad, and the three opened the door and stepped out. Gracie looked to their right to see the backs of a couple of cops running down the street. If the cops looked back, the three of them would be spotted.

"Give me him," Gracie said. "You're too obvious."

Wister didn't hesitate. Once again, his command-centered mind realized she was right, and without any sense of ego, surrendered his charge, a Navy lieutenant essentially taking orders from a Marine staff sergeant.

"There's a bar up there," she told him. "Get me a beer. Something strong."

"Now you and I are lovers, hooking up after work before we go back to our boring, loveless families," she told Kevin as the lieutenant hurried down the street.

"And we are drunk, I assume?" he asked.

"I don't know why else we'd be holding each other up. Let's get moving."

Kevin leaned heavily on her as they made their way down the street. Three cops ran from around the corner, and Gracie pulled Kevin's head down into a sloppy kiss. If the seven jimmylegs had passed their appearances on before they'd been taken out, the two of them were sunk.

Kevin's tongue felt weird in her padded mouth—which was an exceedingly odd thing for her to notice with three cops running at them, she realized. She kept kissing him, though, raising one hand to her breast, and the cops rushed passed them.

"Holy crap!" Kevin muttered as they faced forward again. "I thought I was going to shit my pants."

"You and me both."

They managed another 50 meters before Wister came back out. He handed Gracie the beer pouch. She took a swallow, gave it to Kevin, then took it back and squeezed beer in her hair and under her top. She gave Kevin a squirt, too.

"Three's a company, Wister. Back off, but keep us in your sight."

Gracie felt like she was in a spy movie, and she was sure Wister had been trained in this kind of thing, but he didn't argue. He crossed the street and fell behind. Gracie could feel his eyes burning into the two of them, but she didn't dare turn to look.

"OK, we're drunk, and going home."

"It's a little early to be drunk," Kevin said.

"Not when love's in the air, *mi amore.*"

Kevin leaned heavily on her, his right side balky and uncooperative. A few times, they had to stop, and they went through their groping and kissing until the spasms quit and they could continue.

"What's going to happen to Ali?" she asked after they'd managed to make it a klick or so.

"With one against that many, they'll beat the crap out of him. He'll be thrown into a cell for interrogation. If he holds out for another four hours, we're in the clear."

"And he's going to stay here?"

"For a week, for a month. Who knows? He'll get traded for one of theirs, and that'll be that."

"You don't seem too concerned, Kevin," she said, almost breaking their charade as she challenged him.

"That's what we get Special Ops pay," he said, then when he felt her stiffen, added, "It's happened to me twice. That's more than most, yeah, but not that unique. We know that when we sign up. I was zombied for one of them, so maybe that doesn't count."

Gracie looked at his face, trying to see if he was putting her on.

He died on a mission? He was zombied and finally returned in that condition?

She'd just spent several days with the team, and it was only now that she was beginning to realize just what made them tick. Many Marines thought the SEALs were arrogant prima donnas. Well, maybe they were, but they walked the walk, too.

She hugged him a little closer, and not entirely due to their play-acting.

A long—and excruciating—hour later, Kevin said, "This is it up ahead. If you can, take a look for anyone watching. I'm about finished," he added, his voice tense with strain.

They hadn't even been acting amorous for the last 30 minutes. Most people gave them plenty of room, and disapproving glances had been the norm. The smell of beer had become their disguise.

Gracie, with Kevin's arm around her neck, looked around. For the first time, she saw Wister, pacing them 40 or 50 meters back and on the other side of the street. His gaze lingered on her for only a moment, but in that instant, he gave the barest of nods.

Gracie didn't know what she was looking for, but Wister's nod gave her a boost of confidence.

"It's clear," she said.

Covering the last 100 meters seemed to take way too long, but at last, they stumbled up a set of steps and into an apartment building. At least they were on the ground floor—the steps up might as well have been the trail leading up to Mount Motherfucker at Camp Charles. The door to 1C opened to Gracie's palm-print, and the two almost fell inside. Gracie helped Kevin to the ground, then rotated her aching shoulder upon which Kevin had been draped for the last two hours.

Gratefully, she pulled out her cheek pads. Her mouth felt flabby for a moment as she stretched her jaw.

"I'm going to take a shower," she told Kevin, who hadn't moved. "Then we need to get you cleaned up and changed. We don't have that much time."

"Sorry I can't take one with you, lover of mine," Kevin said with a weak laugh.

"In your dreams," she replied, but with a smile on her face.

****

Four hours later, the six crew members of the *Dougie Blue*—Wister, Dock, Franz, Kevin, Gracie, and a new man whose size and jet black skin might be close enough to pass as Ali—left a spaceport bar and took a shuttle back to the commercial port. Gracie didn't help with Kevin, who was reeking of an alcoholic binge. Wister had given him a shot of Adrenalboost, but the damage was to Kevin's nerves, and the boost was not that effective. Once again, alcohol became a field-expedient disguise.

Franz and Dock had shown up at the safe house almost an hour after Wister. Dock sported a few bruises, but Gracie hadn't bothered to ask why. Ali never showed up at all. Just before they left, the new guy had appeared. Gracie never got his name.

Back in their ship's overalls, and without their disguises, they looked like a crew who'd had an unexpected holiday while the ship had been repaired. The question was if their "other" selves had been different enough that scanners would alert on them now.

Security was visibly heightened, but to Gracie's relief, they were passed through to the commercial lounge. She sat, waiting for their shuttle, trying not to fidget. She didn't know how long Ali could hold out—if he was still alive.

Gracie had been on many missions, more than a few being quite dangerous. But she'd always expected to make it out alive and in one piece. Ali had knowingly sacrificed himself to make sure she and the others made it back.

Finally, their shuttle was called. She loaded along with the others, waiting for the warning klaxon to sound, for port police to come rushing in. Even when the shuttle lifted, she couldn't shake the dread.

She couldn't shake it when the shuttle docked. She couldn't shake it as she walked down the terminal to the ship. She couldn't shake it as she entered the welcomed confines of the *Dougie Blue*.

Twenty minutes later, the *Dougie Blue* undocked and moved into open space, and Gracie finally relaxed. She let out a huge rush of air, and suddenly, she felt elated. This wasn't a normal Marine Corps mission. She hadn't had Marines on her side, supporting her. But she had the same rush of a job well done.

She hadn't had Marines with her, but she had a SEAL team. No matter the service, they had entered the fray together. They were her brothers in arms.

As she looked at each one in turn, Kevin caught her looking at him.

"Not bad, for a grunt, Gracie," he said with a smile.

"Yeah, you guys are all right, too, I guess."

"You guess? Ha!" Dock said. "The thing is, Gracie, I'd be happy to have you with us any time," he added.

She raised her eyebrows in surprise. Each of the team was looking at her, and each nodded their agreement.

"Well . . . well, thank you. And I'd be happy to serve with you guys again."

She'd meant to say it just to be polite, but to her even greater surprise, she realized she meant every word.

HIGH VALUE TARGET

And here is the third Gracie story.

****

Staff Sergeant Gracie Medicine Crow knew the centipede was trouble. She had seen the brown, 12-centimeter-long creature crawl up, antennae questing in the air for whatever centipedes sought. "Animals won't attack a human for no reason," her mother used to say, back at along the Greasy Grass Creek in Montana. This centipede had obviously never heard that bit of tribal lore, because it crept up to her, stopping just half a meter from her face, before disappearing down her right side and out of view. Gracie had waited impatiently, knowing what would happen next.

Sure enough, a few moments later, a searing lance of fire struck her right thigh. Evidently, her bones (the armor inserts that provided protection by instantly hardening when struck by a projectile) didn't consider a centipede's massive pinchers noteworthy.

Who the hell introduces centipedes onto a planet? she fumed as she tried to keep still. *Do they really fill some vital ecological niche?*

Gracie had been in her hide for over 22 standard hours. That was only after a three-day insert and a fifteen-hour stalk to get into position, so she was not in the best of moods. Having a centipede take a chunk out of her thigh hadn't improve that any.

And for what? She could observe nine SevRev terrorists lazing about their camp some 750 meters in front of her, but they didn't look like a group waiting for the number-two priest of the entire Seventh Revelation sect. The SevRevs were a doomsday cult, anxious to bring about the End of Days, and they had perpetrated some horrendous acts of terrorism, so this was a priority mission—but a mission that Gracie was now pretty sure was going to be a bust. She hoped that one of the other three members of the operation was having better luck, if for no other reason that if one of them registered the kill, she could retrograde and get the hell off of this dust-ball of a planet. Gracie was competitive to a fault, and she wanted the kill for herself, but she'd cede it to one of the others if it would bring the mission to a close.

Without turning her head, Gracie's eyes flicked off the SevRev camp and out past them to the north. Three klicks beyond the camp, Rancine would be in position, overlooking a SevRev security outpost. Rancine was her spotter, still just a PIG—a "Professionally Trained Gunman"—without a kill to his credit. He was a good kid, eager to learn, but she wasn't sure he was ready to be off on his own. Without rock-solid intel, however, both Shaan Ganesh's sniper cell and hers had to be broken up to widen the sweep. For the hundredth time, she wanted to break comm silence to check up on him, biting back the urge. At some point, every Marine sniper had to sink or swim on his own.

The fire in her leg simmered down to a dull ache as her nanos rushed the spot. They'd close off the bite and neutralize any venom, but they wouldn't do much for the pain other than secrete some barely effective local painkiller. She couldn't accept any system-wide meds if she wanted to be able to accomplish the mission—if it ever came to that.

She hadn't felt another bite, so either the centipede didn't like her taste, or it had merely been letting her know that this little piece of the planet was its kingdom, and Gracie was trespassing. If Gracie had to bet, she'd go with the taste. She was beginning to reek, despite the efforts of the best antiperspirant nanos the Corps could buy. It was a wonder the terrorists couldn't smell her all the way down to their camp.

To most people, it would have been a wonder that the terrorists couldn't see her as well. The SevRevs' camp was well placed. With a lake at their backs and almost barren land to their sides and front, the terrorists had superb fields of observation, and the tiny fold in the dirt where Gracie lay didn't seem large enough to offer any concealment. But at 750 meters, with a skill developed over years of practice and with the tarnkappe covering both her and her weapon, Gracie was virtually invisible to anyone at the camp. Any mistake, though, any sudden movement, could reveal her.

The tarnkappe was a great, if low-tech, piece of gear. It was passive camouflage, the type she favored. It essentially bent light, channeling it over and around an object. Gracie's tarnkappe had light fibers running both lengthwise and widthwise, so she couldn't be easily seen from head on or directly from the sides, but with any sudden movement, she could be spotted.

Gracie knew she could have stalked closer to her FFP, her Final Firing Position. However, the SevRevs, although not known for their investment in technology, still had rudimentary sensors that could be able to pick her out at up to 500 meters or so. With her M-23 Windmoeller .308, the Marines' standard-round Sniper Rifle, she was confident of a kill out to almost two klicks.

Gracie had her Windmoeller's bipod extended, buttplate resting on the ground, so she was not expending any energy supporting it. At 750 meters, her Miller Scope could just about read the labels on the SevRevs' uniforms. If it ever became go time on this mission, Gracie thought it would be child's play to take out the target.

She took a small sip from her water tube. After so much time in the field, she was used to the reclaimed water. It wasn't much different than on ships, where all water was reclaimed, but as with a ship's reclaimed water, the flat, processed taste did nothing to hide the fact that it had been urine only an hour ago.

Something brushed by her shoulder, and she almost startled. The centipede was making its way back up Gracie's side. She had to will herself still.

Gracie could feel the centipede climbed over her right elbow. She tried to relax—her mother also told her that animals could sense fear, and that would make them aggressive. True or not, she didn't want to take the chance. The creature was near her right hand, and she couldn't afford to have her trigger finger affected by another bite.

Gracie's discipline in a hide was one of her strong points, but she tilted her head up and over the stock of her Windmoeller, losing her cheek weld. She had to see what the centipede was doing. It kept crawling, a hundred or more pairs of legs working in a weirdly fascinating wave. It followed the barrel of her rifle, out towards the opening in the tarnkappe. Gracie let out a breath of relief as the centipede emerged from the tarnkappe, only to hold it again as the creature stopped to lift the front thirds of its body off the sand and rotate, its antennae going crazy. It turned to face back towards Gracie.

Don't even think it!

But it did. The head section came down as it doubled back.

What is it with you? You want piece of me? Tell you what, big boy, that isn't going to happen!

Supporting her weapon with her left hand, she thumbed the bipod lever, retracting its two legs. Slowly, trying to balance the chance of getting spotted with the ability of the centipede to scurry out of the way, she lowered the barrel of the Windmoeller. She pinned the centipede to the sand, her left hand too close to it for comfort. With its back pinned against the ground, the centipede rose back to attack the rifle. Gracie could hear the click of its mandibles as they tried to dig into the ceroplast handguard.

Gracie hesitated a moment. She didn't consider herself a violent person—even with 51 confirmed kills to her credit—if that made any sense at all. The centipede was not her enemy. It was just trying to go about its life.

But Gracie was a professional, and anything that could affect her mission had to be addressed.

Plus, her leg was still aching something fierce.

She pressed down on her rifle, smashing the centipede. The front part of it, the section not trapped by the Windmoeller, spasmed once, then fell still, legs curling up beneath its segmented body.

Gracie glanced at the dead creature for a moment, then gave a mental shrug. Looking up, she couldn't see any sign that her movement had been noticed. Ever-so-slowly, she raised her Windmoeller again and re-deployed the bipod. Using her scope, she checked each of the SevRevs in the camp. Nothing had changed.

Staff Sergeant Gracie Medicine Crow settled in for a long wait.

****

Five hours later, as the late afternoon sun beat down upon her, Gracie was still at her FPP and still under the tarnkappe. She took another sip of water, getting half a swallow before the tube collapsed in her mouth, empty. She had two more liters in her assault pack, but she'd have to wait for nightfall before risking being seen as she took one out and emptied it into her camelback. She'd have to wait for dark to break open a couple of energy bars as well. Hunger was a constant companion, but the emptiness in her gut was getting severe. Despite being on "butt-pluggers," (which slowed down the digestive track), Gracie preferred to minimize her bulk intake on an extended mission like this one. When she was a PICS Marine during her first deployment, she hadn't had to worry about human waste; the armored combat suits took care of all of that. As a sniper, though, human waste was a major consideration. . . and this was already the longest kill mission in her career.

It was pure coincidence that Gracie and Shaan's two teams had been on a training mission with the Galeland militia when the op was called. Galeland was a sparsely-settled planet, barely terraformed, and with only a small and poorly-trained militia force. SevRev pockets were known to be on the planet, but they had never moved on any of the Galeland population centers. Still, both the Marines and the FCDC—the Federation Civil Defense Corps—had been trying to train up the militia so they could attend to their own security, so all four Marines were there on site when the mission developed.

Gracie had been rather enjoying the original training mission. As the senior Marine at the small militia base, she was in charge, and being out from under the flagpole back on Tarawa was a welcome respite from the daily grind of garrison life. The militia snipers they were training were a fun bunch, and Gracie liked their laid-back attitude. She was also acquiring a liking for their local "desert nectar," a brew with a powerful kick that could sneak up on a person. Less than three weeks into the training, however, Federation Intel had somehow found out that the SevRev number two had arrived on the planet, and the mission was born. Gracie had immediately snapped from training into go mode. She was given four hours until they would be flown to the wastelands on the other side of the planet, almost an hour of which was wasted on the meson comms with Lieutenant Spicer, the battalion assistant intelligence officer and nominal sniper platoon commander. The lieutenant was a decent-enough guy, and he seemed to try hard, but even with the two-week scout-sniper platoon commanders' course back on Tarawa, he obviously did not totally understand what it took to be a sniper. Gracie gave all the appropriate "aye-ayes," but this was her mission to run—the first multiple-team mission in her career. The lieutenant was half a galaxy away, and that gave her some leeway to do as she deemed fit.

Her hardest decision was when she chose to break up the four scout-snipers instead of leaving them in their two-man teams. With the intel they'd received, she knew they had too many potential areas to cover unless she sent each of them out solo. Even as it was, they only had a 66% of being where the High-Value Target would arrive as there were six identified locations. Gracie hoped the two potential spots that were left uncovered were the least likely.

With no action so far, Gracie was beginning to second-guess herself. If the intel was good and the HVT had not only arrived on-planet but was heading for a meeting in this particular area, had she selected the right four positions? She'd been pumped up to be the mission commander, but now the weight of command was weighing heavily upon her.

She glanced down at the body of the centipede. With her rifle back on the bipod, the body was fully exposed. The smashed back half was leaking a yellowish gunk that was drying on the sand. An ant had discovered the body, and while Gracie watched, it latched its mandibles on a leg and somewhat heroically tried to drag the huge carcass off. The centipede's leg shifted in the ant's grip, but the body didn't move. It tried for over a minute, straining, its little legs sliding in the grains of sand as it pulled.

I know how you feel, she thought. *Biting off more than you can chew.*

The ant let go of the centipede's leg and turned away. Within a moment, it had scurried under the edge of Gracie's tarnkappe and disappeared from sight. Gracie knew it would return and with enough of its friends to haul the body away.

For some reason, that bothered her. She'd killed the centipede, and she'd admired the ant's attempt to haul it away. But it didn't seem right to her that the centipede would get cut into pieces and hauled down some dark hole.

She slowly dropped her hand from where it had been resting on the top of her rifle stock, just aft of the receiver group. Reaching out, she scrapped away a shallow hole in the sand. Once it was deep enough, she grabbed the dead centipede by the head, pulled it over, and dropped it into the hole. With a few slow sweeps of her hand, she covered it up.

Gracie figured the ants could come back and dig up the centipede, but still, she felt better.

She brought her hand back up, leaning her cheek on the fingers hooked over the top of the stock, and looked back to the SevRev camp—to see activity. She dropped the hand to the trigger assembly, leaning forward to be able to see through her scope. Three of the men were hurriedly taking down a makeshift awning they'd erected to give themselves shade. The rest had lost their air of relaxation and stood fidgeting with their hands and the tensed posture of soldiers waiting for something.

Gracie's heart skipped a beat.

Could it be. . .?

Intel has designated the SevRev camp as a potential location of their HVT. That hadn't made much sense to Gracie because the camp was out in the open, kilometers from anywhere else. The only unique terrain feature was the salt lake at the camp's edge. The lake wasn't a valuable resource; the water was almost toxic for any normal human usage. Intel had given it a 35% probability though, the highest on their list, and now, Gracie wondered if they had been right. Something was definitely happening.

By habit, Gracie picked up her firing cues. The planet's constants of gravity, atmospheric make-up, and Coriolis figures had already been entered into her scope AI. She could go active and get current temperature and humidity, but she didn't trust the convention that the SevRevs did not usually have passive sensors that could pick that up. "Not usually" could get a Marine killed. She could guesstimate the environmentals, and at only 750 meters, she thought that would be good enough.

If she fired and missed, she could go active for a second shot. Wind-speed would be more important than temperature, though. The intervening distance was mostly sand with very little vegetation. There wasn't much to act as a telltale. Still, a few tufts of dead grass barely shifted near her, while at the camp, the sleeves of a military blouse stuck on a pack fluttered slightly in a breeze. One of the terrorists ran up from the edge of the water, zipping up his fly. He grabbed the blouse and put it on, but Gracie didn't need to see any more. Near her, she figured there was less than 5 kph of right to left wind. At the camp, there was about 10 kph coming straight off the water.

SevRevs didn't usually have full military gear. Still, the men at the camp straightened each others' uniforms, as much as the hodgepodge of clothing could be so-called. Gracie felt more confident that they expected someone important.

She was feeling less confident when no one had arrived almost two hours later, and the men started to relax, sitting on the ground, sucking on stimsticks. Gracie had given up using the scope—her eyes could only take that for a limited time—and was back to leaning her cheek on her hand while she watched the camp with her naked eyes.

At some point, the mission had to be scrubbed. As the commander on the ground, she could take that action, but she wasn't ready to yet. As long as there were terrorists at the camp, or at any of the other three positions, she was going to keep at it. Canceling the mission would be the call of whoever on high was running the show. As this mission was not initiated by the Marine chain of command, she didn't even know who that was.

Despite the inner discipline that drove her to excel, Gracie's mind had started to wander as she watched the camp, and it took a few moments for the change in the SevRevs attitude to register. The stimsticks were put back in pockets as they stood up and looked to their right, clearly on the alert.

Gracie took her eyes off her scope and glanced to her left, trying to see what had caught the SevRevs' attention. The tarnkappe blocked her view, so she had to reach up and lift the edge.

Her heart lurched in her chest.

Bouncing down the dirt trail that served as the road alongside the lake were two old AR-Tracs, immediately recognizable from being depicted in almost every War of the Far Reaches flick ever made. Cheap and reliable, the armored vehicles were churned out in the millions during the war. They hadn't offered much protection against determined enemy fire, but they could move troops efficiently, and mounted with various weapons, they could pack a decent punch.

Of the two vehicles making their way down the path, only the first had a mounted weapon. It was an energy weapon, that much was obvious, but Gracie couldn't tell just what kind. Gracie wanted to swing her rifle around so she could scope the vehicles and see exactly what it was armed with, but that could give her position away. She wracked her brain trying to remember what the AR-Tracs carried, but the vehicle was made by so many different manufacturers and on so many different worlds, it could be almost anything.

She mentally urged the two vehicles to speed up. Her anxiety was rising along with her competitive juices, but anxiety was the enemy of a sniper. They had to be the cool, calm, and collected soldiers of popular culture. A calm sniper could make the shot; a nervous sniper would pull the round off-target.

They're just coming to pick up their fellow SevRevs, she told herself in an effort to remain calm—even if she didn't believe it.

Her senses told her Mr. Big was in one of the vehicles. Why he'd be coming to some God-forsaken meeting place out in the middle of nowhere, she had no idea. Maybe one of the bozos she'd been watching for the last day was another bigwig, and with all the surveillance arrayed against them, they thought a face-to-face was more secure. But out in the open, if it were him, they'd be in full view of any Federation Navy ship in orbit.

There wasn't a ship of the line in system, though. However, the Galeland government had drones and satellites of their own, so a meeting in the open would still seem to be risky.

Maybe there's something to the rumors, she thought, considering the persistent whispers about the central government being paid off by the SevRevs to look the other way.

That could explain why no Galeland population centers have been hit by the terrorists.

The waiting SevRevs were standing at close to attention as the lead vehicle reached the campsite, a puff of black smoke belching out its tail end as it came to a halt. Gracie quickly scoped it.

She still didn't recognize the weapon, so she captured the image, then risked a quick link to her AI. Her scope was reasonably shielded, but not enough to escape possible detection from a sophisticated enemy. The SevRevs were not sophisticated, though, so she felt reasonably confident that they wouldn't pick up the slightest milliamperes necessary to make the query.

Energy weapons were very effective in the vacuum of space, but in an atmosphere, the energy beams quickly ablated and dissipated. Gracie was 750 meters from the campsite, and that provided some protection, but there were more than enough mounted weapons that could reach that far. Without shielding, Gracie was more than a little vulnerable. There were weapons with less power could throw a jacketed energy charge, much like a grenade launcher that shoots the grenade long distances before it detonates. The energy-release of those rounds were limited, with an ECR from as little as five meters to as much as fifteen or twenty meters, but the weapons systems could throw those shells up to four or five thousand meters downrange.

The results from her AI were both good and bad. The trac was armed with a Gentry UE-113. The good news was that it was pure energy, a two-kilojoule plasma cannon, so at least it couldn't fire a charged shell for longer distances. The bad news was that it was a powerful beast, and at 750 meters, Gracie was still at risk.

She now regretted choosing this FFP. She'd had another choice, a good 400 meters back that might have been out of effective range of the SevRev weapon. That was still well within her ability to make the kill with the Windmoeller.

It is what it is, she thought as she watched the back hatch of the trac open.

Five terrorists crawled out and stretched. Since it was a ground vehicle, not a hover, Gracie knew that the ride in an AR-Trac was rough, and that dirt road was not the smoothest surface possible, so Gracie couldn't blame them for needing to get the kinks out.

She carefully scoped each one; none of them was her target—she thought.

Gracie might be the most celebrated sniper within the Corps, but she had never been on a live-mission with a specified target. She'd had several in training, to include her final stalk to graduate from Scout-sniper school, but in each case, she'd had an image of her target downloaded into her scope AI. For this mission, she was going in blind, or nearly so. With a nod to the suspicion that some in the local government could be in the pockets of the SevRevs, no image had been sent to her to disseminate to the other three Marines. She'd received a hand-written physical description on a piece of plastisheet, nothing more.

Gracie couldn't even capture an image from her scope and upload it for confirmation before taking the shot. Her scope AI didn't have interstellar comms capabilities, and there were no Navy ships in system. If Gracie was going to pull the trigger, it would because she saw someone who basically fit the description.

One of the waiting SevRevs, the man Gracie had nick-named "Potbelly," suddenly became the group the alpha, striding forward to the five who'd just debarked. With arms out, he hugged one of the men, then pounded his back. The rest of the men, both from the trac and the camp, gathered around those two.

Potbelly had never shown any indications that he was the top dog in the camp, but he radiated a command presence now that the others had showed up. Gracie looked again at the man Potbelly was hugging, but since he was tall and lanky, that man did not fit the description of her HVT.

Lanky broke their hug, then pulled on Potbelly's upper arm, pointing beyond Gracie's scope's field of view. She immediately shifted her gaze to the second trac, just in time to see several men slip around behind it and out of her view. The briefest glimpse of white hair caught her attention. She shifted her sight to the front of the trac, ready to pick up the SevRevs as they emerged from behind it, but no one appeared. Potbelly and Lanky walked into view for a moment before disappearing behind the trac as well.

Gracie's scope AI was recording everything. She ran the recording back fifteen seconds, then froze it just as she reached the spot where she had swung the scope to the second trac.

There! she thought.

Most of the man was blocked by another SevRev, but that white hair was bright enough to be a beacon. With the image frozen, she could see more of him. Judging against the trac itself, he was about 1.9 or 2 meters tall and cadaver-like skinny. He had to be the target.

Who is now behind the trac!

Gracie shifted the scope back and forth. The other men from the camp had stopped and were standing uneasily about 20 meters from the second trac. Four of the men who'd debarked from the first trac with Lanky were standing between the campers and the second trac with weapons lowered, but the alert posture that screamed bodyguard.

The entire situation was obviously tense, not what Gracie would expect from comrades. She wondered what it all meant. She was sure the spooks would be able to glean lots of information from her scope AI's recording, but she didn't have a clue.

Her mission was the HVT, however, not on whatever internal conflicts might be going on within the sect. She swung her scope back to focus on the rear of the trac. If this was a quick meeting, the HVT would have to make an appearance there to get back aboard his ride.

She went through her firing solution in her mind, three, then four times. She'd previously set up a range card in her mind, so she knew the range to a large, rust-colored rock at the edge of the water was 773 meters. The trac was forward of the rock, but offset to her left by about 20 meters.

That would make the aft end of the trac . . . about 788 meters, she calculated. *Wind at the target coming from my 015 at 10 kph. . .*

She'd already been locked onto where the SevRevs had previously put up their sunshade, but she re-calculated her firing solution. It wasn't much different; she right-clicked her scope twice, glad to have made the adjustment before her HVT re-appeared. With her scope's crosshairs centered just aft of the trac's back ramp, she settled in to take the shot when it presented itself.

Only he didn't show. After 20 minutes, her right eye began to water, and she had to pull back and blink. Leaving the Windmoeller locked on to where she hoped the HVT would appear, she looked alongside the scope, both eyes open. Which was fortuitous. The men from the camp suddenly became alert. They started forward, carefully moving past the security team and then stepping up to the trac. Gracie shifted her aim to the front of the trac just as Potbelly and Lanky emerged from behind it, Potbelly with one arm out beckoning his men in. Just at the edge of the trac, her HVT stopped, more than half of him still behind the bulk of the vehicle.

Come on, one more step, she implored silently, hoping for a better shot.

She was pretty sure she could still hit the HVT, but she needed a kill shot, one that put him past resurrection. With the SevRevs' dedication to death and eagerness to suicide, Gracie wasn't sure they would be philosophically able to justify resurrection, but her orders on that point had been clear.

But as the saying went, he who hesitates is lost, and Lanky stepped in front of the HVT, effectively blocking her shot. She caught brief glimpses of her target as he reached forward to shake hands, but even if she got a clear shot, at 788 meters, it would take her round slightly less than two seconds to reach the target, which was more than enough time for him to randomly step back or for someone else to step in front of him.

Keeping her cheek weld in place and her right finger on the trigger, she reached under her blouse collar and pulled on the plain green cord that hung around her neck. Hanging from it was a short-chambered .308 jacketed round collected by her spotter after her first confirmed kill, back on Wyxy— coincidentally another SevRev terrorist. She'd tallied six kills that day, but the important one was the first. Tradition was that all snipers had a round with their name on it, but by wearing her "HOG's tooth," collected from her victim when she first became a "Hunter Of Gunmen," she controlled that round, and it couldn't ever be used against her. It made her invincible. It was superstition, she knew, but that didn't stop her from raising the round to her lips and kissing it.

And the God of Snipers must have been pleased with that moment of obeisance—for a moment, Lanky stepped away just as the HVT stepped forward into his last handshake. With his upper torso exposed, and knowing he'd be there for a couple of heartbeats to finish the handshake, Gracie squeezed off the shot, aiming for center mass. She cycled the next round and squeezed off another round just as her first tore into the HVT's chest.

The Windmoeller normally fired a .308, 172-grain tef-sleeved round. This round packed a pretty good punch, still lethal out to possibly 3,000 meters if the shooter could somehow hit a target at that extended range. It was designed to punch through a body, though. The bullet expanded some upon impact, but a through-and-through torso shot might not cause enough damage to preclude resurrection. That didn't matter on the battlefield, and in fact, it was probably desirable. Two soldiers evacuating a wounded soldier meant three out of the fight, whereas a permanent kill only removed one.

This mission was a kill mission, though. The powers-that-be wanted the HVT permanently erased from the picture. If the Marines had brought their Barrett light-fifties on the training mission, with their wide variety of tactical rounds, Gracie would have used one of them. But even with the Windmoeller, there was still a handful of different choices.

Gracie liked the mass and trajectory characteristics of the basic M21 round. But the M43 round, at 175 grains, wasn't much different in external performance, and it had the added advantage of disintegrating into tiny shards that made hamburger of the human internal organs. The chances of coming back from that were far less than with the M21 round.

But still, that chance existed. To be sure, Gracie needed a headshot. Gracie had aimed her second shot on the ground where she thought her HVT might fall, hoping to luck out and hit his head. Instead, her round hit Lanky in the leg as he lunged to catch his falling boss. Falling over her HVT, he essentially became a human shield as the security team sprang into action.

Should have kept the M21, she told herself as she fired at Lanky, this time on purpose.

With the greater penetration of the M21, she would have had a good chance of punching through the SevRev and reaching the HVT underneath him. She hit Lanky in the middle of his back. She was pretty sure, though, that if the M43 round was doing what it was supposed to do, it had fragmented into tiny shards that chewed up his organs, but failed to pass through him to the HVT.

The few seconds since she fired her first shot were enough for the HVT's security team to react. They were on top of her target as quick as any FCDC security troopers, pulling him towards the trac. Gracie snapped off one more shot at his limp body, but missing him, hitting and dropping one of the men holding the HVT's legs instead just as they disappeared from sight.

Gracie switched her Miller to fully active mode. Range and environmentals flashed on the scope's display. She changed her point of aim back to the rear of the trac, figuring the SevRevs would try and get the HVT back into the supposed safety of the armored vehicle.

Not supposed, she admitted to herself. *Actual safety. My Windy can't penetrate even that piece-of-crap armor.*

Gracie *did* have a naga strapped to her weapons harness. The tiny rocket had the power to knock out a AR-Trac with a well-placed shot, but 788 meters was over three times the rocket's effective range.

Her scope registered 787.2 meters. She'd been off with her calculations by less than a meter. The reports of rifle fire reached out to her. The SevRevs were firing wildly, and with nothing hitting near her, she didn't think they had a lock on her position.

When the first two of the security team came rushing from behind the trac, weapons at the ready as they scanned for a threat, Gracie withheld her fire. She didn't want *them*. A moment later, two of the SevRevs, holding the arms of the limp, face-down body of the HVT, appeared into her sight. They halted and pivoted as one more SevRev, holding the HVT's legs, wheeled around to give them a clear run up to the rear hatch.

Stupid mistake, there, geniuses. You should have just shoved your boss in the hatch feet first, head first, butt first— whatever it takes.

Gracie fired at the closest of the two on the arms just as they moved to lift Mr. Big through the hatch. The shot took him a little lower than she'd intended, but it didn't make a difference. He dropped like a rock. His buddy stumbled over him and dropped his grip on the HVT's left arm.

This was her chance. Gracie could hit a ten-centimeter round target at 1,000 meters ten times out of ten—on the range back on Tarawa. This was not the range, however. This was on another planet, with different gravity and other environmentals. All of those environmentals were uploaded into her scope AI, so from a pure exercise in physics, the shot should be just as easy. But this was not simple physics. If it was, then anyone could become a sniper. Being a sniper was part mathematics, part physicist, part zen master, and more than a little part artist.

Combat was never the same as the training ranges. Forgetting the fact that thirteen or so SevRev terrorists were doing their best to locate her and take her under fire, Gracie had to deal with her own emotions and adrenaline, and these were the Achilles' Heel of being an effective sniper. Excitement caused missed shots.

Gracie knew she had only moments before they SevRevs would untangle themselves and get her target into the trac. She willed herself to calm down, and holding the crosshairs of her scope about twelve centimeters high and to the right of the

HVT's head, squeezed the trigger, cycled, and squeezed again, slightly shifting her aim to the left.

She'd just recovered enough of her sight picture to see the first round skim the HVT's head and into the hip of the SevRev who'd been on his left arm. A moment later, the second shot hit the HVT's head dead-on. Given the nature of the M43 round, there wasn't the blast of pink mist favored by the Hollybolly flick-makers, but that wasn't necessary. Gracie knew there would be no chance of resurrection.

Rounds stitched the dirt in front of her, not five meters away. Gracie ducked back, trying to get some cover. One of the SevRevs had spotted her, either by skill or luck.

Gracie switched on her active comms and said, "Murgatroyd."

Her AI recorded her command, then relayed it out in a pulse to the other three Marines. Comms silence was broken, but it didn't matter much to Gracie now. The SevRevs knew where she was.

Having given the order to commence extract procedures, Gracie had to figure out how she would comply herself. There wasn't much in the way of cover for a good 300 meters behind her; beyond that, a series of washes could give her the cover and concealment she needed to exfiltrate. Gracie could low-crawl the 300 meters, but if the SevRevs pursued her, they could cover the intervening distance at a run before she could crawl any significant distance. She knew she had to either discourage them or at least slow them down.

Gracie popped her head up just enough to take a head count of the terrorists firing her way. Ducking back down before she was hit, she thought she'd seen 12 SevRevs. One was moving forward, yelling at the rest, his arm pointing right at her.

Gracie switched magazines to load the M21s. After chambering the new round, she gathered her legs under her, then rose for an instant, sighting in on the man and taking the shot before dropping back down. She hadn't waited to see if she'd hit him, but long experience with the Windmoeller let her know that her aim had been true.

She shifted a few meters to her left, then rose again. Sure enough, her first target was down, another man rushing to his aid. Gracie acquired a new target and took the shot. This time, she was pretty sure she'd missed, but even a miss could make an enemy hesitate. She moved another few meters to her right and rose one more time.

"Poppy-Three, do you need assistance?" Rancine asked over the net, breaking his own comms silence.

Gracie knew that at only three klicks away, he could probably hear the sound of gunfire. Three klicks was a long distance to cover on foot, however, even if Gracie thought he could somehow help her without putting himself in danger. And by coming live on the comms, he had just let the SevRevs know there was another Marine out there. She had to get him off the air. She bent over and paused for a moment to respond.

"Negative. Murgatroyd," she passed on the command net. "Murgatroyd."

Suddenly, a mule kicked her hand, and her scope burst into a million fragments. The Windmoeller was knocked out of her hand and to the ground.

Stupid!

Either one of the SevRevs had enough time to acquire her and take a shot, or he'd just been pretty lucky. The round had been off-target to her, but it had hit her weapon.

She reached out for her rifle, gasping at the sharp pain in her arm, and pulled it in. The scope was a loss, shattered beyond repair. She released it from the rifle, letting go of what had been a 35,000 credit piece of gear, more than she made in eight months as a Marine staff sergeant.

It fell to the dirt as just so much junk.

She gave the Windmoeller a quick check. The weapon could be fired without a scope. It had a rudimentary set of iron sights, but the max effective range had just been reduced from over a klick to possibly 100 meters. There was a slight bend in the barrel, too, which Gracie would have thought was nigh on impossible. It did not portend well.

Several more rounds peppered the ground around her while she considered her options. She still needed to give the SevRevs something to think about before she tried to boogie out of there. And before heading directly to the extraction point, she had to break contact with them completely so they couldn't follow.

She worked the action on her Windmoeller. It was still functional. She steeled herself to fire off a few more shots, hating the fact that each shot would be essentially blind. The old adage of "one shot, one kill" no longer was a possibility, and that pissed her off to no end.

But she didn't have a chance. The SevRevs forced the issue.

Gracie hadn't forgotten the UE-113, but in the press of taking out her target, then with the incoming fire, it had faded in importance. It moved to the forefront of her attention when the air around Gracie ionized as a bolt of plasma shot past her off to her right, missing her by a few meters.

If the trac had been armed with a meson canon, Gracie would be dead or incapacitated even though she wasn't hit directly.

Immediately, she rolled to her right, stopping in the smoking earth. Two or three seconds later, another plasma beam blasted where she'd just been laying. She saw the smoking mound of what had been her Windmoeller, dropped when she rolled.

She knew from the data pulled up previously by her AI that she had 15 seconds before the UE-113 could fire again. So she was up and running, ignoring the kinetic rounds chasing after her.

I've got to get more distance between us and fast!

The UE-113 had a dual capacitor system that allowed for an initial two-shot volley, three seconds apart. After that, charging took progressively longer, with a second volley about 15 seconds later before slowing down to over a minute to recharge.

Forty meters behind her, away from the camp, there was a tiny ridge of sand, barely 30 centimeters high. That was Gracie's target. She hoped she could make it, running in full battle rattle, before the trac could fire again.

Gracie hadn't figured getting shot into the equation. The blow to her back sent her stumbling to the ground where she ate a face full of sand. She struggled to her feet, spitting out the sand as she lurched forward.

Her bones had hardened as designed when she was hit. The round hadn't penetrated, but the full force of it hadn't simply disappeared contravening the laws of physics. It was just spread out. Gracie was still in one piece, but a piece that would be pretty sore if she managed to survive the situation.

Gracie searched for the tiny wrinkle in the sand, wondering if she'd been knocked off course by being shot. She expected to feel the hot blast of the plasma finger reaching out to her at any moment. Finally, she saw the ridge and lurched over it, diving to the ground. She lay there breathing hard for a moment before the sky above her lit up and the ionization burned her nose. She could feel the superheated air as it expanded over her.

She waited for the second shot, and waited. . . and waited. Off in the distance, she could hear a transmission change pitch. Either the trac with the plasma gun or the non-armed one was moving. Maybe to retreat.

Most likely not. It was probably coming for her.

Gracie waited for another ten seconds, hoping to see another shot so she would have some time to move while the trac's cannon recharged. She knew she had to move as the trac's big engines got louder.

"Mother save me," she whispered, as she jumped up.

Instead of running straight away from the trac, she took off at an oblique angle.

Not two seconds later, the plasma gun belched out another finger of fire, superheating the air behind her. Gracie was sure the hair on the back of her head was singed as she tried to speed up into sprint while cutting back to her left again. She could hear shouts and gunfire behind her.

Gracie was a hell of a sniper and a hell of a Marine, but at 1.4 meters and 45 kilos soaking wet, she wasn't the most physical Marine in the Corps. Her semi-annual physical fitness tests were an ordeal to her. But a dozen pissed off SevRevs and two AR-Tracs chasing her gave her wings. She flew towards the first of the washes, rounds zipping past her as she ran.

Somehow, Gracie survived the gauntlet to plunge into the first wash, a two-meter deep dry crevasse. She knew that the series of washes converged in the dry river bed a klick to the west, which in turn fed the salt lake after each heavy rain. She could follow the washes as they joined each other, but they led in the wrong direction away from her extract point. The SevRevs also knew where they led, and they could easily cut her off.

Instead, Gracie had to travel up the washes, losing their protection in another 600 meters or so as they got progressively shallower.

She wished she had a Navy ship in orbit to tell her exactly how many of the SevRevs were on her.

Hell, if I had a ship, I'd just have them zero anyone following me. Might as well wish for a PICS platoon, too, for good measure.

Gracie was too short to see over the lip of the wash, and where she'd jumped in was too difficult to climb, but the wall had collapsed about 20 meters away, so she ran to it and carefully climbed up just far enough to see who was on her ass. Back at the camp, one of the tracs was already 500 meters down the road, black smoke pouring from the exhaust as it retreated. The HVT's body was probably inside with the SevRevs hoping for a resurrection. Gracie didn't care about them—it was a futile hope, she knew, and that meant one less vehicle to run her down.

Of more concern was the armed trac over halfway to the washes and the four SevRevs following behind it.

If she still had her Windmoeller, Gracie would take the time to zero each of the running SevRevs. They were in the open, and the distance was well within her capabilities. But once again, she might as well wish for a Wasp to come sweeping out of the sky to blow them to kingdom come.

Gracie took stock of her situation. She had her Ruger, of course, in her thigh holster. She had two toads, the small incendiary grenades. Either one could completely waste the trac's engine block, but that would require a pretty accurate throw that Gracie had little confidence she could make. She had four frags, a tiny knee-popper anti-personnel mine, and the one naga. She felt naked.

Gracie was a sniper. With a rifle in her arms, she was invincible. No other sniper had as many kills as she had over the past ten years, supporting her deeply-set belief that there was no one better in all of human space, much less just the Marine Corps. But without her weapon of choice, she was just an ordinary Marine, and not a particularly effective one.

What the hell am I thinking? There's no such thing as an "ordinary" Marine!

The trac was more than half-way to her. She figured she had a minute, maybe a minute-and-a-half before it reached the wash. She turned and slid down the wall on her ass, hitting the ground hard. She ran across the bottom, then scrambled up the other side. Keeping low, she squirmed her way behind a mid-sized rock as the trac's engine noise got louder and louder.

Gracie pulled the little naga from her harness. Snapping the tube out, the fins deployed. A naga was just a 4mm rocket and it looked like a toy in her hands. But it had the power to take out a full battle tank if it hit the right spot. Gracie just had to hit one of those spots.

She flipped up the sights. Gracie hadn't fired a naga since boot camp, more years ago than she wanted to admit. She was a firm believer in proficiency through continual firing, but other than qualifying with her Ruger and the Marine M99 Assault Rifle, her mission-centric mindset meant she fired with all sniper weapons in as many situations as possible. That did not include a naga or any other infantry weapons.

With the engine noise getting still louder, Gracie risked a glance around the rock.

The trac was heading right at her. If it tried to cross the wash, it would be ten meters from her. Not firing since boot camp or not, she should be able to hit it at that range. She felt a surge of confidence.

Shit! What's the arming range? she suddenly wondered.

She'd known it at one time, of course, but a lot of water had gone over the damn since then. She pulled it up on her AI.

Twenty meters.

If she waited until the trac was ten meters away and then fired, all she would do would be to piss off whoever was inside. The naga would hit but simply bounce off, little more than the child's toy it resembled.

And she had no time. The trac, so close it looked immense, pulled up to the lip of the wash, probably 15 meters from her. It edged forward, and the driver, with only his head poking out of his turret as he craned his neck, was probably calculating his ability to drive the beast into the wash. On top, the UE-113 slowly traversed back and forth as the gunner sought Gracie out.

Without consciously making a decision, as soon as the plasma gun was pointed to the east, Gracie stood up and bolted to the west. She took five strides before wheeling around and going down on one knee. She swung the little rocket up, right arm outstretched, left hand locked on her right elbow in her best boot camp firing form. The driver saw her—his eyes growing round with shock, his mouth open to shout—as Gracie pressed the release.

Like a hornet, the naga took off and flew across the wash, impacting right at the front skirt. There was a flash of light as the driver scrambled out of his turret. Gracie pulled her Ruger, and as he fell on his butt in his efforts to get away, she put three 2mm darts into his chest.

You should have ducked back into your trac, buddy.

Gracie had half-expected an explosion. Instead, there was a horrible clanking screech of broken metal and a gush of smoke and flame coming out of the exhaust, followed by silence. The trac was dead, but not destroyed.

The turret gunner inside was still alive. The UE-113 started to track back to her, and Gracie took off running. Sprinting to the west, she crossed over the finger of ground and down into the second wash. The plasma gun didn't fire. She wasn't sure if it was damaged by her naga or if the gunner hadn't thought he had a good enough shot.

Gracie jumped into the wash, hitting the ground in a soft section of sand. That gave her an idea. She stepped heavily, making obvious footprints towards west before hopping up to the harder center of the wash. Doubling back, she ran to the east, towards the shallower end of the wash. She'd crossed the series of washes on her initial movement into her FFP, but that had been at night, and she hadn't paid too much attention to the full breadth of the terrain feature.

Evening was approaching, but there were still a good two hours before dusk. Gracie wasn't sure about the SevRevs' night vision capabilities, but after the washes petered out, the land was a featureless pan for at least two klicks. If she emerged during daylight, she'd be certain to be spotted.

Which was why she hoped the SevRevs, if they remained after her, would assume she fled to the west.

With her Ruger at the half-ready in her right hand and a frag in her left, she trotted up the wash, nerves on full alert. When on a normal mission, Gracie had learned to control her stress, to remain calm. This was so far out of her comfort zone, however, that none of her tricks worked. She was as nervous as the proverbial long-tail cat in the rocking chair factory, ready to jump at the slightest alert.

She didn't get far. Gracie had assumed the washes ran for at least 500 to 600 meters to the east before disappearing. Either she'd gotten mixed up, or this wash was one of the short ones. Within 200 meters, the bottom of the wash started to rise.

Within another 100 meters, she could see it end, merging with the flat pan above.

For a moment, she considered crawling across to another wash, but she decided that was too risky. If she were spotted, she'd be trapped. And with the trac still sitting there like a pillbox, she couldn't climb up into the flat pan to the east.

Instead, she turned back to the west, keeping low until she came to a small protuberance in the wall she'd passed a few moments earlier. She carefully backed up into the tiny corner, pressing her back against the dirt and knowing that anyone walking the wash on the high ground on the opposite side would easily spot her. But it was the best she could do.

Her best hope was that the SevRevs thought she had gone west. If that would occupy them for two hours, she could try and escape under the cover of darkness. So she stood there, thoughts running wild, as she willed the sun to go down. For the first 30 minutes, she expected to see a team of SevRevs come running down the wash at any moment. She mentally choreographed who she would take out first with the frag, then how to follow up to take out the rest with the Ruger. After an hour, she began to hope that they'd either given up, or they were so far down the washes to the west that they'd double back to the camp. She allowed herself to relax a bit, trying to conserve her nervous energy. After 75 minutes, she finally started to hope she was safe.

Which, of course, was tempting fate. She was doing a couple of deep-knee bends to keep her legs from going numb when the tiny sound of a skittering rock caught her attention. She froze in place, trying to identify the source of the sound. A few moments later, she heard another quiet rattle.

Galeland had been fully terraformed, so even if this corner of the planet seemed desolate, she knew there was animal life. She'd already killed a centipede and now wondered if one of the creatures was large enough to create the sound she'd heard, even as quiet as it was. There were rabbits back at the militia camp, but Gracie wasn't a zoologist by any stretch of the imagination, so she wasn't sure if a rabbit could survive in a desert.

The next faint whisper banished that line of thought; the very evident sound of a footstep reached her. Someone was carefully making their way down the wash.

Gracie thumbed the safety off of her Ruger and tried to melt into the wall. The same geological force that had formed the little lip behind which she hid had created a sister lip directly across the wash. That lip was larger than the one Gracie was hiding behind, but it curved more and offered less concealment from the west. Gracie stared at it considering her options, Ruger held tight to her chest.

She heard soft crunching near her, but when the muzzle of a UKI edged out into her view, only a meter or so away, she almost jumped. A moment later, a body followed, training the muzzle of the UKI on the space behind the other lip opposite Gracie.

It was obvious that there wasn't anyone hiding there, but when the SevRev turned back to the front, he couldn't miss Gracie.

Act, don't react!

She lunged forward, reaching up to grab the long hair on the back of the SevRev's head just as he realized his mistake. She yanked back with all her strength and brought the muzzle of her Ruger to the base of his neck, firing three times. Most of the sound of the hypervelocity darts was absorbed by his flesh, making a soft "thwock" that Gracie hoped no one else heard.

The SevRev didn't even shudder as he fell. Gracie tried to hold him up, but his body slipped from her grasp and hit the ground with a thud and rattle of gear. Gracie froze, but there were no shouts of alarm.

Breathing heavily, she grabbed the heavy body, pulling it to the side. He was too big to hide behind the tiny lip of rock, especially sprawled out in a limp pile of what had been living flesh.

Finally, she gave up trying to jam him in there. Anyone coming down the wash now would see him from at least 40 meters away, and there was nothing she could do about that. She grabbed the SevRev's UKI before slumping to the ground, trying to catch her breath. It wasn't anything close to her Windmoeller, but she felt better having a long gun in her hands.

As the sun went down, the soft rustlings around her became more numerous as the desert denizens started to stir. Another centipede, even bigger than the first one, slowly made its way across the floor of the wash, crawling over the dead SevRev as it went along its way. Gracie didn't bother it.

She listened and waited, but no SevRevs made themselves known. About twenty minutes after sundown, Gracie stood up, and—ignoring the dead SevRev—with one more glance down the wash to the west, turned around and started walking in the opposite direction. Five minutes later, the wash had gotten so shallow that even crouching would no longer keep her hidden.

It was now or never time. If the trac was still manned *and* it had night vision capability, *or* if the SevRev security teams were still watching for her and had the capability, they would see her. There wasn't any way she would know until she tried. Gracie took a deep breath, stood up straight, and jogged out of the wash and onto the hardpan.

She imagined a neon target squarely on her back as she ran, expecting a flash of plasma to light up the night sky as it burned her into gray ashes. It wasn't until she'd crossed the two-klick-wide shelf and reached the low hills on the other side that she finally felt safe. Her extract point had been downloaded into her AI, which was in gyroscopic position mode. She had another 15 klicks to go.

Almost two hours later, a tired Gracie slowed to a walk and activated her telltale. That speed wouldn't pass her semi-annual fitness test, but she'd been up for almost three days, had fought for her life, and was beyond exhausted.

Three blue avatars immediately appeared on her monocle. Gracie felt a surge of relief that everyone had made it back and were waiting for her only 200 meters ahead. A couple of minutes later, she strolled into the rally point as the other three Marines gathered around.

Shaan gave the UKI a pointed stare that Gracie ignored, so he asked her directly, "So, how did it go?"

"You know. The usual. Killed me a centipede, though. That was exciting. Now how about activating the beacon so we can catch our ride out of this friggin' desert?"

"You look like shit, Staff Sergeant," Rancine said.

She rolled her eyes. Her left arm still hurt, and her back was beginning to ache from the round that had caught her. More than that, she was bone tired, and she didn't need any of his crap.

I'm getting too old for this stuff, she thought, not certain if she believed it.

She was pretty satisfied with herself. Gracie was far from humble, but even with a critical eye, she knew that not many snipers could have completed the mission and made it back alive.

But now, her body protesting the abuse, she had to get some rest. Gracie sat, taking off her assault pack and using it as a pillow, lay down on her back, UKI clasped to her chest.

"Wake me up when the bird's five minutes out," she told the other three scout snipers.

Within a minute, Gracie Medicine Crow was fast asleep.

Jonathan P. Brazee

CHECKMATE

Checkmate is another story written for Craig Martelle, this time for The Expanding Universe 4. I'd been toying around with this concept for quite some time, and I hope I did it justice.

****

"Come on, Lettie," Jorge muttered as he popped up out of the fighting hole and snapped off a burst at the advancing Valks.

He ducked back as return fire showered dirt and debris over the three in the hole.

"What the hell is taking her? The damned Valks are closing in!"

"Lettie's on top of it," Military Tech 2 Isaac Stein said, gripping his Compton-3 to his chest.

He raised his rifle over the edge of their fighting hole and blindly emptied his mag, exposing only his hands for a few seconds. He knew he hadn't hit anyone firing like that, but hopefully it would give the advancing Valks pause.

"What are you worried about, Jorge?" MT3 Anatasha Dela Cruz asked, only half-facetiously as she pushed up the snakeyes. "PrimeMil takes good care of us. Only the best medical care for their miltechs."

"Easy for you to say. You don't have exes and kids to support. I can't afford to get zeroed."

"If you'd just keep your dick in your pants, you wouldn't have to worry about that, lover boy," Tasha said as she examined their field of observation through her commercial fiberoptics tube.

Jorge rolled his eyes at Isaac, hoping for moral support, but Isaac was having none of it. Jorge was a horndog, pure and simple, and that was why he'd signed on with Prime Military Contractors, Inc. Seven kids by three women and court-ordered child support meant he needed the money.

"Better zeroed than ghosted," Tasha said as she adjusted her line-of-sight.

"Tell my exes that," Jorge retorted.

Aside from inconsequential fact that he'd be dead, there was a degree of truth to what Jorge had just said. If he was ghosted, his beneficiaries would receive a two-million-BC payment, courtesy of the United Alliance of Military Workers. If he was wounded and required anything over a Class 2 treatment, however, his entire financial holdings were subject to confiscation, leaving him with a big fat zero as his bottom line. Incentive, the contracting companies said, for miltechs to fight. Utter bullshit. They were on the hook for all medical costs for injuries, and they just wanted recourse to recoup at least some of that.

Three jobs ago, Jorge had tried to run a backdoor to protect his earnings, having his new girlfriend open an account and transferring his money into it. Said girlfriend had left him a week before this job, closing the account and disappearing.

"I'd be better off with the Valks," Jorge said, firing off another burst. "Looks like they'll be getting the winners' share this time."

"Ha! Fat chance of them taking you," Tasha said.

As in zero chance. The Valkyrie Brigade was a top-of-the-line, professional company, but one that only accepted female apprentices. They were expensive, but claimed they were worth it. Maybe they were. They boasted a superb win-loss ratio, at least. Isaac hadn't been overjoyed when he found out the GMI had hired on the Valks for this trial, but if he'd refused to fight, he'd lose his union card. Lose the card, and not a single Tier 1 company would hire him, leaving only the gray-market companies, which fought nasty, semi-legal trials in the shitholes of the world.

"Skipper, I'm counting a full platoon coming up the west side of our pos," Tasha said into her throat mic.

"A platoon? Shit," Jorge said as he overheard her. "Where's Lettie?"

"Charging the beast," Isaac said.

At least, that was what he hoped she was doing. Military Engineer 3 Lettie Patel was young, gifted, and very aggressive. She had a habit of pushing the envelope, which had paid off so far. But living on the razor's edge meant failure was only a millimeter away, and that failure could be catastrophic.

"The skipper says hang tight," Tasha, their team leader, relayed.

Debris showered them as automatic rifle fire ate up the edge of their fighting hole. Tasha's snakeyes took a direct hit, flinging the top portion to the rear of their fighting position.

"Son-of-a-bitch," she snarled, pulling it in and examining the ruined lens. "A hundred-and-a-half BCs gone."

Tough on Tasha's pocket. More pertinent to Isaac was that now they had no eyes on the Valks, unless they exposed themselves. Each of the three had the latest and greatest helmets from Anodyne, and they should protect their heads from whatever the Valks could throw at them, even their J4, but *should* was the operative word. Two missions ago, Kofi Ocloo had taken a .221 round that cracked his helmet and ghosted him. "My bad, so sad," was crux of the Anodyne rep's response to the union complaint.

Their position was rapidly becoming untenable. Gryphon Company's 2nd Light Chasseur Platoon was trained for quick, rapid movement. Comprised of smaller miltechs, chasseurs were lightly armed and trained for hit-and-run action. They were not organized nor trained for static warfare, and Isaac hadn't liked being split up and on their own in what was essentially a three-person observation post. With a Valk platoon on them—and from the chatter of the big J4 gun, a heavy dragoon platoon—the three of them didn't stand a chance unless Lettie came through. Despite sticking up for her a minute ago, Isaac was beginning to wonder if this time she'd gone too far and left them hanging out to dry. PrimeMil didn't have a rep for wasting techs, but sacrificing three to score a win over the Valks might pencil out, especially with regards to booking future trials.

"Hey, PeeEms!" a voice shouted out from below them. "I hope your union dues are paid, 'cause you're about to get ghosted."

"Did you hear that?" Jorge said, firing another wild burst over the edge of the fighting hole.

"The bitches are just trying to panic you," Tasha told him.

"They're doing a good job at it," he muttered.

Isaac glanced at his wristcomp, checking the time. Surely the beast's capacitors were charged by now. But nothing, not even a hint.

What's Lettie doing? She's got to see what's happening.

The longer this went on, the closer the Valks came to overrunning them, and the more being a sacrifice sounded like the game in play. That sucked big time. Within the union, there was an unofficial policy of limiting casualties when all was lost, but the Valks had a reputation of going all out all the time. Isaac had almost saved enough to buy into the navigators' guild, and getting zeroed would set him back to square one. He was getting too old for this shit, so getting zeroed might be all she wrote with his career.

"Princess Lettie's finally overreached. Too bad it's you grunts who have to pay the price. Come on, just surrender. We promise we won't hurt you," the voice called out.

"Much, that is," another voice, sounding very young, shouted out as laughter rolled up the hill—laughter that was getting very close.

Jorge looked at the other two. Surrender would forfeit their union cards, never to work again. But they wouldn't be zeroed. They could simply cash out. Isaac was tempted, but Tasha's scowl made her opinion known. Besides, although time was running short, Lettie could still save their asses.

"Think Beaker Ag will pull the plug?" Jorge asked, his voice hopeful.

"We're the only ones in contact, Jorge," Tasha said. "They aren't going to give in to GMI that easily. 'Sides, they haven't tallied up much in broadcast credits yet."

The financial incentive for a company or state to order a stand-down was significant. The fewer miltechs wounded, the less they'd have to pay for medical treatment and rehab. Even with the miltechs themselves contributing their entire savings, costs almost always exceeded that by far. More than a few companies and/or their insurance companies had gone bankrupt after keeping a hopeless fight going too long. But the corporate or government heads were humans, with all their foibles, and some just couldn't bear to see a hated rival win. So they made stupid decisions . . . and the miltechs in the field paid the blood price.

"So, we can crouch here like cornered rats and wait, or we can go out with a bang," Tasha said. "Maybe get the fan vote."

"Why the hell not?" Jorge said with a sigh. "Might as well give it a shot."

"OK, then. Let's kick a few asses. On three: one . . . two . . . THREE!" she shouted as she popped up along with Jorge and Isaac.

With most of the fire coming from the front and keeping the three pinned, eight Valks were moving quietly out in the open on their left flank to envelope them, not 20 meters away. The shock on their faces was almost comical as they dove to get out of the line-of-fire, but they were too close to miss.

"Get some!" Jorge shouted as he sprayed fire on them.

Isaac was a little more deliberate, targeting vulnerable legs. He hit a Valk in the back of her knee as she ran pell-mell back down the slope. She tumbled spectacularly, ass-over-head before sliding to a stop a good ten meters from cover. Isaac let her be as she curled into a ball, clutching the back of her leg. He followed union practices, even if rumor held the Valks did not.

Two rounds hit him from the Valk base-of-fire, one pinging off his helmet, the other smacking him right in the chest. Luckily, neither were fired from the Valk's JP4 machine gun, and the smaller rounds didn't penetrate his armor, but they were enough for him to duck back down into the fighting hole.

"Oh, man, did you see them?" Jorge said, breathing heavily as he laughed like a maniac. "Running like rabbits. That might be enough for fan-favorite, don't you think?"

Isaac *didn't* think. Sure, it could hit the highlight reels, but it probably wouldn't be enough. Not that he wouldn't appreciate it if it did get the vote. Ten thousand BCs were nothing to sneeze about, and that was untouchable even if they did get zeroed. But he nodded and said "Sure." Jorge was flighty as a butterfly, going from despair to exultation in the space of a few heartbeats, but at 5'4" and 131 pounds of solid muscle, he was one of the more physically imposing members of the platoon and could be a good soldier when they were in the shit.

"How many did you get?" Tasha asked, ever the professional.

"One for sure. Took out her knee," Isaac answered.

"I got three or four," Jorge added.

Which wasn't true. Isaac had seen only one Valk go down. Jorge might have hit three or four, but body shots that didn't penetrate their armor meant nothing. He didn't say anything. Better to have Jorge on a high.

"Medevac!" a Valk's amplified voice rolled up the hill.

"Five minutes!" Tasha yelled back, relying on pure lung power.

All three popped their heads up to watch, hoping to better spot the disposition of the Valks facing them. Only two appeared, rushing out to the Valk Isaac had shot. Her groans were clearly audible as they lifted her, one on each side, clasped hands making a seat. Within a few moments, they had carried her out of sight where she'd be shot up with painkillers and left until the end of the battle. No one would be wasting power to get her off the battlefield before then.

"Honor to you," the voice called out again, the standard thanks for the truce, and the signal that it was now over.

"See anything?" Tasha asked the other two as they slid back into their fighting position.

"Just those three," Isaac said.

"Yeah, I got her good, didn't I?" Jorge said, slapping the stock of his Compton. "That's what you get when you take on PrimeMil, bitches," he added, drawing out the "beetches."

"Think they're going to try a frontal assault again?" Isaac asked Tasha, ignoring Jorge.

Tasha was a MT3 with 18 campaigns under her belt. She'd been zeroed three times and was considered a hard-ass soldier. This was only Isaac's seventh campaign, third with a Tier 1 company, and he respected his team leader's experience.

"I don't know," she said, eyebrows scrunched up as she thought about it. "They've still got that JP4 with them to provide a good base of fire, but it would still be costly. They might bring a squad, but the power draw . . ." she trailed off.

"Could they bypass us?"

"Sure, and maybe they will. But with the other five teams, they need to take some of us out before they go after the skipper and the rest of the company. And I think we're the most vulnerable."

Isaac had been afraid of that, but it was still sobering to hear Tasha confirm it. While the two forces felt each other out, the Valks hadn't revealed enough yet for the skipper and Lettie to know what they were up to, but it was obvious that they'd have to take out at least a couple of the OPs. The fact that the platoon facing them had a JP4, with all the weight penalties that entailed, was proof enough that the Valks knew that, too.

The Yellowstone Military Arbitration Reservation was noted for peaks and long fields of vision, and with Lettie emplacing six teams into selected high grounds, the advantage had shifted slightly to the PrimeMils. Great for the company, not so great for the 18 miltechs of the 2nd Chasseur Platoon who manned the positions.

Most companies would have played it safe, keeping the unit together while each side feinted and probed until an opening presented itself, but most companies didn't have Lettie. "Princess Lettie," the Valks had called her with disdain— but Isaac knew with more than a little jealousy, too. Lettie had hit the scene on the run, with six impressive victories in a row. Isaac thought that this time, however, she might have bitten off more than she could chew.

"Skipper," Tasha asked MT6 Merrill Listrom, their company commander, "I don't think we can hold on much longer. Anything from Lettie?"

Tasha bled PrimeMil black-and-copper, so for her to even ask was telling. She listened to the reply, for a moment, then placed her hand on her throat mic and told the other two, "He's checking, but he said Lettie's not keeping him in the loop."

The skipper was a Level 6 and technically the commander, but he was still a MT like the rest of the miltechs. Lettie was only a Level 3, but she was an ME, a military engineer, so once the battle commenced, she had all the power—literally, as well as figuratively.

Tasha's eyes lost their focus for a second as she listened, and then she said, "OK. Understood. Can you at least tell us what the Valks are doing?"

It wasn't the skipper who answered but rather the Valks. The J4 opened up again, chewing at the top of the fighting position, showering the three miltechs with dirt. Isaac tried to scrunch his 5'2" frame even deeper into the bottom of their position. Over the din of the firing, they heard the unmistakable pop, pop, pop of displaced air on the backside of their position, in defilade to the incoming Valk fire.

"How many?" Tasha shouted as all three spun to face the rear. "I counted nine."

"I got ten," Isaac answered, his Compton raised, ready to engage the first head that appeared.

Which probably meant a Valk squad of 13 had just appeared on the other side of their fighting position.

"Come on, Lettie!" Jorge shouted.

The incoming fire ceased, and Tasha said, "Get ready to ghost the assholes." A Valk J2 Carbine, held aloft, appeared over the edge of their fighting hole and fired, hitting the dirt walls just over their heads. "Jorge, right; Isaac, left. Don't let them enfilade us."

Isaac swung his Compton to the left, ready to fire at anyone who came into his field of view. More J2s popped up in front of them, once again without the Valks wielding them exposing more than their hands, firing without aiming. But an unaimed round sucked just as much as an aimed one if it got lucky and hit them.

An undulating battle cry sounded from the right, designed to instill fear—and doing a pretty good job at that—as the Valks commenced their final assault . . . and pain wracked Isaac's body, as the very atoms that made him were torn apart.

"About fucking time," Jorge shouted, firing a final burst from his Compton.

Through his agony, Isaac barely registered the Valk who appeared at his side of the firing position, J2 raised to fire at him as his world went dark . . . before coalescing again a microsecond later—or an eternity, he was never able to decide on which—in the same body position as if still in their fighting position. But instead of on the military crest of the high ground they'd been occupying, they were down on the banks of what had to be the Yellowstone River.

The intense pain was gone, as if it had never happened—"ghost pain." Isaac sprang to his feet, orienting himself as Tasha and Jorge scrambled up beside him, Comptons at the ready.

"Nothing like cutting it close," Jorge said, his voice sharp and angry. "I was already shitting myself."

"Stop bitching. Just be grateful that she got us out of there," Tasha said, breathing hard from the adrenaline rush. "Either of you hurt?"

Isaac had to check, remembering the flash of the Valk's muzzle just as he ported. He patted himself down, relieved to find nothing. Jorge was fine too, if still fuming.

"So, what—" Isaac started to ask before Tasha held up her hand to stop him.

Isaac never understood the company policy of limiting comms to command freqs. If Tasha went down, his comms would kick in the command nets, and the skipper could pass to all hands when he wanted, but for the most part, the grunts were kept in the dark, relying on team leaders to pass the word. Before he'd made the jump to PrimeMil, he'd been with Absolute Military for four battles, a third-rate outfit at best, but they'd all been on connected nets during a fight. There had to be a reason that PrimeMil did things differently. But he was damned if he knew what it was.

"OK, we're to stand by," Tasha relayed to them. "The Valks just ported half their company to Fountain Flats, like we thought they would."

First Dragoon Platoon had been emplaced at the edge of Sentinel Meadows where they had extensive fields of fire for their Sakura .30 cal heavies, the most powerful weapon in the Gryphon's arsenal for this mission. Lightweight for their punch, they still took an exorbitant amount of power to port, so once emplaced, they tended to stay put until the battle was over, and they tended to attract a lot of attention as a target. Only this time, they were a feint. The platoon's position was good, but not optimal, and the Valks probably thought they saw an opening in an unmarked trail that paralleled the treeline.

The skipper and Lettie had decided to sacrifice the two real guns there to entice the Valks to expend power porting one or both heavy platoons to Fountain Flats. The other two Gryphon Company guns were elsewhere, being held in reserve for the actual Gryphon assault. When the Valks hit the platoon—which was more of a squad playing the part of a platoon--Lettie would port the miltechs out but leave the power-sucking guns behind.

"That's right," Jorge said. "Keep porting all around the reservation. Use up your power while we dance around you."

Angry just minutes before, Jorge had undergone another sea change, as usual. Isaac suspected that had a direct correlation to his money woes. Going from the possibility of getting zeroed to a nice winners' share had that effect on someone.

"Any indication on which options we might take?" Isaac asked Tasha.

"Not a one."

Which was to be expected. The company had been given a detailed operations order, as usual, by PrimeMil's Director of Strategic Planning herself, which was not the usual for a one-company job. The board was probably chomping at the bit with the opportunity not only to win one over the Valks, but at their share of an expected inflated viewer royalty pot as well. Given by the director or not, no ops order Isaac had ever received survived past first contact. Too much in any fight depended on the maneuver/counter-maneuver by the MEs.

"Don't matter none. Lettie'll take this one to the bank," Jorge said, walking to the edge of the river while unclasping his armor codpiece and opening his fly.

And the agony of porting hit him again, the second time in less than ten minutes. The experts said that multiple ports over a short period of time didn't intensify the "discomfort," as they referred to it, but miltechs swore just the opposite. The "discomfort" set every nerve in his body alight as the beam took hold and broke him apart. He knew he'd forget the pain as soon as he arrived, but that didn't affect the here and now, and he wanted to scream. Of course, he couldn't. He was frozen in time and space as the beast disassembled him at the river, then . . . the pain was gone as he was reassembled, good as new, as if the agony had never happened.

Tasha was beside him, and a few feet away, Jorge was still answering the call of nature.

"Hell, that wasn't cool, Lettie!" he shouted to the sky as he fastened his fly.

They weren't alone this time. The entire platoon, not only the six teams that had been sent to man the OPs, were materializing around them in a clearing, surrounded by evergreens, the crisp smell banishing even the ghost pain from his thoughts.

MT5 Abodaca, the smallest member of the platoon at 4'5" and 80 pounds, and their platoon commander, shouted out, "We're going hunting!"

"That's what I'm talking about," Jorge said as the rest pumped their fists in the air.

"Chasseur" was an old French military term that meant "hunter," and hunting was what they'd been trained to do. With a few succinct hand-and-arm signals, the platoon took off through the trees, ready to harass the Valks. They were part of the subterfuge, one more layer in leaving a false trail, but that didn't mean they couldn't bloody some Valk noses in the process. That would make the subterfuge even more believable.

They glided like silent wraiths through the forest, the needle litter acting as sound dampeners. Chasseur units ran incessantly during training, first because it kept their weight down, but more importantly, at least from a combat standpoint, because it kept them in superb physical condition. Now all those miles were paying off as they closed with the Valks.

Firing broke out somewhere ahead. The Valks would be thinking that they'd flanked what they believed was a full Gryphon dragoon platoon.

Third team was taking point, and they were the first to initiate contact with the rear Valkyrie miltechs. As they opened fire, the other teams flowed around them as they had a hundred times during training. Isaac's heart threatened to burst out of his chest in anticipation. This was what they were supposed to be doing, not hiding in a fighting position like a chipmunk in a hole.

He glimpsed motion through the trees and fired, hoping to get a seeing-eye round through to strike flesh. Needles fell around him, torn free by the Valks' return fire. He didn't care as his warrior-self took over.

He caught sight of a Valk through a gap in the trees, firing somewhere to his right. He pulled up against a tree, and using it as a support, targeted the Valk's right arm. He was breathing heavily, and his sights rose and fell with each breath. He shut out the noise and commotion around him, exhaled, then squeezed off two rounds. At least one hit in a burst of pink mist as she spun around and dove for cover.

That's two of you I nailed!

In his previous seven fights, Isaac had never taken out an opposing miltech for certain. He'd fired, and he'd undoubtedly hit others, but he'd never seen someone go down. Now, he'd dropped two. Civilized people didn't hurt others, and Isaac thought of himself as a nice guy, but here in the reservation, where everyone was there by choice, the human veneer cracked. Two wasn't enough, and he wanted more.

He wasn't going to get more now, though.

"Break, break, zero-six-zero," Abodaca pushed through their comms.

Isaac fired one more burst at another Valk he could barely see before breaking off, running at the designated heading. He'd been right beside Tasha and Jorge when they moved to contact, but he'd gotten separated as he engaged. He could see four or five others as they ran, but not his team. It wasn't until MT5 Abodaca halted 500 meters back for a head count that he married back up with them.

Lassie Grundwild had taken a round through her upper arm, but she was still combat ready. No one else had been hit, much less wounded.

"Again, but we're hitting their J4s this time."

"Do we take them out?" Tasha asked.

"If they'll let us, sure," Abodaca answered. "But they'll be protected, and we're not to become decisively engaged."

A Valk J4 opened up in the near distance, taking the First Platoon's dragoons under fire.

"That's our cue," Abodaca said. "Platoon wedge, guide on Singh."

MT2 Singh's face broke into a toothy grin, basking in the honor as he took off. Abodaca would keep him on course, and it was up to the rest of the platoon to guide on him. They were close, and within a minute, the platoon was receiving fire. Rounds zapped past him like angry hornets, but Isaac didn't have a target. Even with caseless ammunition, the weight issue limited him on his combat load, and he'd expended quite a few rounds between the fight up at the OP and the clash a few minutes ago. He wanted concrete targets before he wasted any more ammo.

He saw movement and snapped off a shot, but his intense focus was almost the end of him as a J4 opened up, the big rounds reaching out to him. He dove behind the tree as splinters filled the air. His body armor might be able to stop those rounds, but then again, it might not. Getting hit in his legs or arms could take them right off, and that was for sure a Cat 4 or 5 medical treatment.

On his belly and keeping his head low, he peered around the tree trunk, trying to spot the J4. When it opened up again, the muzzle blast gave it away. Isaac fired five rounds at the spot, not knowing if he'd hit anything or not.

"You OK?" Tasha asked, on her belly ten meters to his left.

He gave her a thumbs-up, then pointed in the direction of the J4, using the hand-and-arm signals for "heavy gun," "assault," and "interrogatory." She nodded, and got to her knees just as the whumps of collapsing air of people porting reached them.

Isaac wanted to rush forward to catch any laggards, but that was inviting a J4 round in the face. It was a common deception: simulating a full unit port, but leaving a defense force to surprise anyone following.

Cautiously moving forward, they found nothing. No Valks, no guns. They must have realized that the supposed full dragoon platoon was a diversion.

"At least they're bleeding power," Tasha said as she put her finger in the furrows left in the forest floor by the J4's spades. "They won't be able to port much more."

"So, now what's for us? Are we done?"

"Ask Lettie," she said automatically, then added, "I mean, it depends on what goes down. She's still going to try and lure them into one of the kill zones, and we might be needed to help nudge them along."

Being ported three times in a day, twice within 20 minutes, was not unusual, but the final clash in a trial was usually between dragoons or heavy infantry. The 2nd Chasseur Platoon might very well be finished, at least with the fighting.

They rallied around Abodaca before sweeping the battlefield, searching for casualties. Lance Ithaca, one of the new joins, was down hard, a good chunk of his femur gone from a J4 round. He was cursing up a storm as they inflated the temporary traction sleeve and gave him a shot of Be-Happy.

Normally, people drifted off pretty quickly after that, but Ithaca was evidently made of sterner stuff, and he kept up his invectives for a good two minutes.

"That's pretty impressive," Jorge said as the MT1 finally quieted. "He'll be a good'un."

Three of the 1st Platoon dragoons were down hard, as were two Valks. All five were treated and flagged for medevac out of the AO as soon as the fight was over.

"Look at that. The Sakuras aren't even operational," Tasha said as they did a last sweep.

"Of course not. They're just tree trunks and rocks," Isaac said.

"No, not them. The real ones. Look."

There had been two of the company's Sakuras in the position. As Isaac took a closer look at one, he realized that not only were there no ammo packs, the heavy breech assembly was missing.

"Son-of-a-bitch," he muttered as he stepped in for a closer look.

A Sakura was light-weight for a .30 cal, with most of the mass in the breech assembly. He knew that the two guns were to be sacrificed, but he hadn't imagined that they would be stripped down to the minimum while still showing up on Valk sensors. Without the breech assembly, they were nothing more than big paperweights, however. The dragoons playing decoy had been sent in without their main weapon, all to save power. And as a result, three of them had been zeroed before Lettie ported the rest out to join the main effort.

Sometimes, a chessmaster sacrificed their pawns in order to gain an advantage which would eventually lead to taking the opposing king. Good strategy, but it still sucked if you were the pawn being sacrificed. His four fellow miltechs were zeroed and faced long and painful rehabilitation.

I hope it was worth it.

The platoon gathered under the trees with the wounded. This wasn't the Amazonian jungle where triple-canopy would hide them from prying eyes, but no one was too concerned. With things rapidly coming to a head, their little light infantry platoon would be way down on the Valks' priority list. However, this was still a live battlefield, so they took defensive positions as they tried to follow what was happening with the rest of the company. Move and counter-move, the two opposing MEs maneuvered their miltechs, seeking an advantage.

"Standby!" MT5 Abodaca shouted.

"What? Again?" Jorge asked.

A moment later, Abodaca shouted, "We're joining Second Dragoons. They're being hit hard! Listen up for orders!"

The beast, circling high over the reservation in its dirigible, reached out its tendrils, and for the fourth time today, Isaac's body was disassembled, the molecular bonds mapped and then broken. This was the worst, and despite his training, he wondered if something had gone wrong. He knew the beast was broken, and he'd never come back from whatever hell he was in now, living . . . no, *existing* . . . forever in torment . . . and then the pain was gone, the memory of it fading as he oriented himself. Second Dragoon Platoon was in heavy contact. Ten meters to Isaac's right, one of the Sakuras chattered away, sending the big .30's across a meadow dotted with hot mineral pools, the sulfuric stench overpowering the bite of the rounds' propellant.

Abodaca was everywhere, grabbing miltechs and plugging holes in 2nd Dragoons' lines. Isaac was hit three more times before he went prone. One round struck high on his shoulder, numbing his arm, but it didn't penetrate. There wasn't any J4 fire from the tree line, which was a relief, but the sheer mass of J2 rounds made up for it. Walter Simms, the Sakura gunner, in heavier armor, was getting peppered. Isaac could see the rounds hit him. He kept up a steady stream of fire while Lindsay Han, his a-gunner, readied the next box magazine. He signaled to Lindsay for the mag when he slumped, head lolling back.

Both the dragoons' and chasseurs' armor were STF, or shear thickening fluid. Very effective against the smaller caliber rounds, but it could be defeated with multiple shots in the same spot one after the other. The Valks had put enough rounds into him to defeat his armor.

He didn't know who had taken down Walter, but as Lindsay scrambled to take over the Sakura, Isaac emptied his second-to-last magazine into the tree line to give her cover. He dropped the mag and slammed in his last one when the opposing fire stopped. The PrimeMils kept firing for a few more moments before Abodaca and MT5 Harris, the 2nd Dragoon Platoon commander, ordered a cease fire.

Silence hung heavy over the meadow while sulfur and propellant mixed, making Isaac break out coughing, his throat raw.

Don't just sit there, he told himself, jumping up to help Lindsay with Walter. He was alive, but had taken a round to the belly.

"Put pressure on him," Lindsay said as she pulled out Walter's #12 flat from his cargo pocket.

As Isaac leaned into Walter, Lindsay ripped open the pack, pulled the cover layer, then activated it.

"OK, now!"

Isaac released his pressure, and Lindsay slapped the flat over the entry point. The flat expanded, stopping the blood flow.

"They're gone. Ported," Jorge said to Isaac, looking over his shoulder at Walter, who was out cold but seemed to be breathing better, at least.

"Hell, how much power do they have left?" Isaac asked, trying to go over in his head how many times the heavier Valks had already ported.

"That has to be about it," Tasha said. "For us, too."

With porting out of the picture, the fight was going to come down to an old-time slugfest. The time for the engineers playing chess with their pawns was over, and the knights had to battle it out.

Isaac sat down, pulled off his helmet, and wiped his brow with his forearm. The adrenaline that had kept him going had evaporated, leaving him tired. Whatever happened would happen without him.

Never assume anything.

"All hands, drop your armor," Abodaca shouted out, running along the line while MT5 Harris echoed her.

"What?" Isaac asked stupidly, confused.

"Chasseurs in the first wave. You've got twenty seconds. Drop your armor now!"

"Oh, hell," Tasha said. "We're getting sent back in, and Lettie's short on power."

She was right. The company had to be in deep shit, and all resources were going to be sent to reinforce—all resources that Lettie could port. That meant without armor that would weigh them down. The lighter, smaller chasseurs would port first, and if there was any power left, the bigger dragoons.

Isaac snapped into action and hit his armor releases, kicking free just as the beast grabbed him for the fifth time. Pain? Yes, pain. Agony. Yes, agony. But Isaac's thoughts were on what was awaiting them. They were going into battle without their armor in the hopes of saving the company.

Getting zeroed suddenly seemed to be the preferable alternative. Without armor, their chances of getting ghosted rose tremendously.

His body came apart and reassembled under ten-meter tall trees, a roar behind them. He recognized the place as the Upper and Lower Falls, one of the areas into which Lettie had hoped to lure the Valks.

"Don't just stand there, Stein," Abodaca shouted, grabbing his arm and yanking him to a position behind a fallen tree trunk.

With Tasha beside him, he rose to look over the trunk. Out across the road and the fields on the other side, he could see at least 150 Valks forming up. As he watched, more winked into existence.

Two 2nd Dragoon miltechs ported to his left.

"The beast is out of power," Tasha said when no more appeared. "This is who we've got to the dance, I guess."

"How many do you think?"

"First Dragoons, us, First Chasseurs, some cats and dogs. Maybe eighty all told."

Isaac tried to count the Valks, who were forming just out of Compton range, before asking, "Any Sakuras?"

"Nope. Too heavy. But we've got cover, while they have to cross a sweet killing field. We can do this."

More Valks joined the main body until there were at least 200 out there, 200 to face 80.

"I've only got one mag left," he told Tasha.

She sighed, then pulled out one of hers and tossed it to him. "How about some fire discipline, huh?"

"You got any more?" Jorge asked. "I'm out."

"Here," Isaac said, tossing him the one Tasha had just given him. "Like she says, fire discipline."

The fives were running back and forth, adjusting position, checking fields of fire. Isaac didn't know if that was just their commanders' nervous energy or if they were really improving the company's chances. Probably a little of both.

Isaac ran scenario after scenario through his mind. With their Sakuras, the company would be sitting pretty, but they didn't have any. With the 80 miltechs they did have, it was probably going to be touch and go, to see whatever client blinked first.

Eight minutes after Isaac had ported in, the Valks started forward in line. Their undulating cries reached them but were muted from the roar of the waterfalls. Dwarfed by nature, they sounded like children.

They won't fight like children.

"Eight hundred meters," the skipper passed on the open net. "At six hundred, weapons free."

"You two ready?" Tasha asked.

"Bring them on," Jorge answered.

At 700 meters, the sound of heavy gunfire swept over the line at the same moment as the Valks broke into a run.

We've got Sakuras? Isaac wondered for a moment.

But it wasn't PrimeMil Sakuras. The unmistakable report of a J4, then another, then two more echoed from the ridgeline above as the ground around the PrimeMils erupted with rounds chewing into dirt, trees, and bodies.

To their front, the Valk line shifted to their left, so they could concentrate their forces and break the PrimeMil line. They had to shift to meet that threat, or the battle was lost. It was probably already lost anyway.

It was a trap all along, Isaac thought. *They outsmarted Lettie!*

They were pinned down under heavy plunging fire as the J4s rained death and destruction upon them. If they maneuvered to meet the onrushing Valks, they'd be zeroed at best, ghosted at worst. Yet if they hunkered down, they were just waiting for the Valks to overrun them. They had the numbers, and the PrimeMils no longer had their armor.

"She blew it," Jorge said bitterly. "That freaking child genius couldn't keep her numbers straight."

Isaac wanted to argue, to stick up for Lettie, but he couldn't. Jorge was right. She'd played it too close to the razor's edge, and now they were going to pay the price. If he'd been the Valk ME, he couldn't have picked a better place for their ambush had he tried—better for the Valks, disastrous for the PrimeMils.

And this time, there wasn't going to be a rescue. The Valks were out of power, but so were they. Without porting, it was down to old-fashion military tactics, and the terrain and troop disposition left only one logical conclusion. All they could hope for was for Beaker Ag to pull the plug before too many of them fell.

"Sucks, right?" Tasha asked him, her face just a foot from his while rounds kicked up around them.

Someone called out in pain as one of the heavy rounds hit home.

"Yeah. But we gave them a good run, huh?" Isaac said as he popped up and fired into the mass of charging Valks.

"If Beaker Ag doesn't call it, the skipper wants us to charge the Valks, hit them on the flanks."

"Two hundred of them and eighty of us? With those J4s pounding us?"

"If we're in among them, the J4s are out of the equation, right? And if I'm getting zeroed, I want to take some of those assholes with me."

"Me, too!" Jorge said.

"So, what? We wait?"

"I think it won't—"

The familiar pain, for the fifth time in two hours, sixth time today, wracked his body.

How . . . ?

The beast was out of power. Lettie hadn't been able to port the entire company, which was why they were in this mess. She had mismanaged the power consumption while the Valk ME had calculated hers correctly. But there was no doubt about it. Somehow, he was porting.

He felt a surge of relief, then guilt. He might survive the fight, but that was not going to change the inevitable, only that he would still have his bank account. His fellow miltechs would suffer.

An instant/eon later, he coalesced under the bright Wyoming sun.

"Take them out!" Abodaca passed on the net. "All of them!"

Isaac turned around. Ten meters away, a very surprised J4 crew looked over their shoulders as six chasseurs appeared. A hundred meters down the ridgeline towards the falls, six more from the platoon had ported by the second gun.

Isaac didn't need a repeat order. He moved before he consciously thought to, covering the ten meters in a second. The Valk gun crew were all big women, as were most Valks. But these weren't the Valk shock troops, used to close-in fighting. The six Gryphon chasseurs hit them hard, using anger and days-upon-days of training, their instincts taking over. They were not a unit, operating in conjunction with each other, but were rabid dogs, ready to rend and tear.

The gunners didn't have a chance. Isaac threw himself at the woman who had a moment before been firing a steady stream of rounds into the company—his company—below. He came in low, swinging his empty Compton up, the stock hitting her in the chin and dropping her bonelessly to the dirt. He looked for the next one, but the other three were already down: unconscious, for sure, ghosted possibly.

Isaac stood there, breathing heavily. His Compton, never designed for hand-to-hand combat, was demolished. He let it drop to the deck.

"Turn the guns on the Valks!" Abodaca shouted over the net.

Hell, of course!

Isaac pushed his victim out of the way and took her place. He'd never fired a J4 before, but it didn't take a rocket scientist to figure it out. He swung the muzzle to aim down at the advancing Valks, then depressed the trigger, sending a stream of rounds high.

"Lower," Tasha said.

The shoulder support was set for someone a little taller than him, but he stepped up on the body of the Valk he'd taken down, depressed the muzzle, and fired again, this time sending a stream of fire into the enemy. One, then another, and then a fourth J4 opened up, tracer fire reaching out and touching the Valks who dove for cover. But where the PimeMils had been in the sparse trees by the falls, giving them a tiny bit of cover, the Valks were out in the open. From above, they were totally exposed.

A shout that grew into a roar reached up to them, overpowering the sound of the falls. From the downed trees, from the nooks and crannies, Gryphon Company was rising and charging. These were the dragoons. Isaac was proud to be a chasseur, but there was something awe-inspiring about seeing the heavy infantry charge.

The four J4s continued to wreak havoc among the Valks. Their advance was broken, and with the charging Gryphons, a handful started to retreat. A few tried to form a line to stop the charge, but Isaac and at least one other J4 pounded them. More Valks began to retreat, and that trickle became a torrent. But by running, they lost whatever slight cover they had, and the four J4s extracted a heavy toll. Isaac saw them drop, yet he still fired. There were too few Gryphons there to oppose the Valks, so it was up to the teams on the four guns to keep them from realizing it.

His J4 clicked empty, and he called out "More ammo!" when the blessed recall sounded in every miltech's earbud. Isaac could hear if from the earbud of the Valk he was standing on as well.

The battle was over. Somehow, someway, the Gryphons had pulled it off despite Lettie's blunder. Training and force of will had saved the day.

Tasha pulled him off the Valk, and brought him in for a bone-crushing hug, laughing so hard she was crying. Jorge hit them like a bull, almost knocking them over.

"We won. We fucking won!" Jorge said. "I swear, I thought we were goners, for sure!"

"Me, too, Jorge. Me, too," Isaac said, just letting it all sink in.

****

Four hours later, they were pulling into the old Yellowstone Lodge. Chairman Waanstadt himself was there, along with Director of Strategic Planning Lim and other bigwigs Isaac didn't recognize. All wanted to be part of this. On the ride over, the driver had said the ratings were off the charts, and he asked for autographs. This was a big win, no doubt, one that would raise PrimeMil's reputation (and fees).

A team from Beaker Ag was there, too, all smiles as they shook the hands of each miltech as they exited the bus.

"Think we'll get a bonus?" Jorge whispered as they filed through the impromptu receiving line. "Look at all of them. If they do, I'm gonna get me that new Razorback coupe."

"What about your exes?" Tasha asked.

"Screw them."

"That's what got you into your mess in the first place," she said with a laugh.

They went through the line of bigwigs, then formed up out-of-the-way on the side of the lodge while the next bus pulled up. A PrimeMil flunky met them, all smiles.

"OK, if you can listen up for a moment, I've got some word to pass, then we've got a nice spread inside the lodge for you."

Isaac's stomach growled. They didn't take food into battle. Extra weight and all that. Always on a strict diet, weighed every three days by the nutritional staff, an eating binge after a win was tradition and one of the things that kept them going.

"First, Beaker Ag has authorized a fifteen percent bonus," he said to the cheers of group. "In addition, they will not be attaching anyone's personal account for medical care."

"What's the count?" someone behind Isaac asked.

"Well, it looks like twenty-nine Class 2 or higher," he said, his enthusiasm toned down a few notches.

"Could be worse," Tasha whispered to Isaac.

"How many ghosted?"

The flunky brightened and said, "None. No one!"

Isaac was shocked. Relieved, but shocked. When the J4s opened up, he'd seen miltechs fall, and he'd been sure some had died. Immediately after recall, the air ambulances had arrived and bodies loaded, Valk and PrimeMil alike.

"And more good news. The ratings were through the roof. Best in a year. Most were mid-joins."

Which meant the word was being passed through the ethernet that a good fight was in the works.

"No word on the fan-favorite, of course, but I'm sure it's going to be from PrimeMil."

There was more good-natured cheering, then a voice called out, "Where's the food? We're starving!" to even louder laughter.

"OK, OK. You need to turn in your weapons at the armory truck parked in the lot, and then come back to the side entrance. Your dinner should be ready in another twenty minutes or so. If any of you need to see a medic, one will be there as you eat."

Everyone was feeling good, more than good, and no one really minded lining up to turn in their weapons. Some bitched because it was a God-given right, even expectation, for soldiers to do so, but their hearts weren't into it. Isaac gave his ruined Compton to MA4 Tong, expecting a rebuke, but the normally surly man said nothing as he entered the return into the system.

Along with Tasha and Jorge, he walked back around the lodge to where a line was already forming for chow. They joined the tail end, Isaac's mouth watering as the smell of BBQ filled the air.

"Hey, look," Jorge said, pointing back to the front of the lodge where the VIPs were still waiting for the last of the miltechs to return. "She's got some balls to show up like that, after all the stuff she fucked up."

ME3 Lettie Patel was rolling up on her chair, tiny body held in place by straps that crisscrossed her torso. Without them, she couldn't sit upright. With all the Gryphon miltechs being in superb physical condition, and where fitness was almost worshipped, it had seemed odd to have someone with an untreatable condition in uniform with them, but as a military engineer, all she needed was a sharp mind, not a robust body.

And until today, she had proven not only to be up to the task, but to be an expert.

As she rolled up, all of the VIPs turned to her, gathering round. People posed for holos as if she was a star. Maybe she was. There were enough fanboys and girls who followed the trials that they knew the MEs, but the VIPs, those used to the rich and famous, were fawning over her.

"Don't they know she almost cost us the win?" Jorge asked. "Look at them."

The chow line finally started to move as the VIPs still crowded Lettie. It wasn't until the next bus arrived that they broke off—reluctantly, it seemed—to go greet the returning heroes.

Just before the three climbed the steps into the lodge, a single person who'd been waiting at the fringes of the VIPs stepped up to her, a woman in a Valk uniform with the white engineer tab on her shoulders.

"I think that's the Valk ME," Isaac said, elbowing Tasha.

"I bet she's pissed. She did it right, but we won," Jorge added. "I wonder if she's gonna punch Lettie."

Isaac didn't think so. The Valk ME had the slumped shoulders of the defeated, not the carriage of someone about to go to town on someone, even someone confined to a wheelchair.

"Next, let's move it," the woman at the door said. "People are waiting."

Something kept Isaac back, though. He looked at the two MEs deep in conversation. He wondered what the Valk had to say to Lettie. To his surprise, the Valk shook Lettie's good hand, then leaned in to hug her. Valks and PrimeMils might not be enemies in the old sense, with countries going to war with each other, and they both belonged to the same union, but Isaac was not about to go seeking out Valks to hug them for a battle well fought.

And Lettie hadn't fought well. The Gryphons had won despite her.

Then it hit him. The VIPs. The Valk ME. How they seemed to defer to her.

No, not won despite her. *Because* of her. He was sure of it. Lettie had planned it all. She knew how the game would play out, using feint within feint to get the Valk ME to act as she wanted her to. The grand chessmaster had moved her pawns around the battlefield, always thinking five moves ahead. In the end, checkmate had been a surprise, not only to the Valks but to the PrimeMils.

"Son-of-a-bitch," he said, quietly to himself.

Isaac was smart. He was brave. He was in tip-top condition. But he knew his place in the company. He was a pawn. A well-paid pawn, but a pawn, nothing more. The real warrior was the young woman over there, trapped in her chair. She was the chessmaster, the one who determined if they won or lost, if they got paid a winner's share, or if they got zeroed.

If he was going to be a pawn, he'd just as soon it was Lettie making the moves.

As if feeling his thoughts, she lifted her head and turned to him, catching his eye. She smiled and gave him a slow, deliberate wink.

Isaac drew himself up to his full 5'2" and saluted.

"Hey, you going to eat or not?" the woman at the door asked. "If you ain't, then let the others go past you."

Lettie gave him a nod before someone else came up to shake her hand. Behind her, in the distance, Old Faithful started its show, just as it had done for centuries. Isaac smiled, then turned to go through the door.

"No, I'm going to chow down. I've worked up quite an appetite."

DUTY

I now have twin baby girls, but my wife and I tried for five years before they were born. During my research, as I read about how infertility is rising worldwide, I began to wonder what was the end game for that trend.

****

Tyler Bemeny lay on his bed, staring at the cracked and peeling ceiling. He'd been awake for two hours, unable to drift back to sleep. And from the absolute stillness of his wife, he was pretty sure she wasn't asleep either. He turned his head to her, just able to make out the curve of her body under the sheet as she lay on her side, back towards him. He slowly reached out and put his hand on her wide hip, but there was no reaction.

He hadn't expected one.

Tyler and Liosha had been married for 75 years, tying the knot the day before boarding the *Porter Union 3*, the brand-new colony ship heading out of St. Teresa for the newly commissioned Sangfroid Hope, deep into the Spiral Arm. She'd been so lovely, he remembered, with her close-cropped hair and bright, laughing eyes. That hair, now more gray than black, was still as short, but the light in her eyes had long-since faded, and that tore at his heart.

They'd been so full of hope back then, knowing the universe was theirs for the taking. Mankind kept pushing outwards, populating the stars, reaching for its manifest destiny, and the two of them had been no different. They'd left warrens on Cygni 3 to reach for the stars. Upon arriving on Sangfroid Hope, they'd received a Series 3 land grant and through the sweat of their brows, had turned the raw, newly-terraformed five hectares into fertile, productive farmland, earning a free and clear Series 1 after only 17 years.

They knew they'd been lucky to pull Sangfroid Hope as a destination. It had been close to Earth-normal even before the TEG wizards had gotten to work, and when they were finished, people said it was even more conducive to humans than the over-crowded mess that the homeworld had become. Far, far from most of humanity, the planet had become their home.

The soil hadn't been the only thing that was fertile: he and Lisosha had eight children, their blessing and their curse. The first two had been natural-born, which had been something of a rarity, but with starting the farm, they'd neither the time nor funds for the normal crèche-banks. Three of their children had their own grants surrounding theirs, and the other five had settled in Montpellier and Graves' Landing, the two largest cities in the governate. Between their eight children, they had 16 grandchildren and 22 great-grandchildren.

Tyler took his hand off Liosha's hip but inched his foot closer under the light sheet until it was touching hers. After another long minute, he let out a long and noisy breath of air, but still, she didn't move.

The clock on the wall kept blinking as if doling out their remaining time in this life, second by second, minute by minute. Sometimes he hated that clock with a passion that he couldn't muster for anything else.

He watched the clock, wanting it to stop so he could stay in bed, but wanting it to hurry up to he could get lost in his normal routine. Tyler knew he could just get up now, but they'd spent the 72 years in their home rising exactly at 6:00 AM. Liosha might have given that up over the last two years, but he couldn't. It was as if he was grasping for the past, anxious to hold onto whatever of it he could. It made no sense, he knew, but that didn't keep him from his routine.

As the clock switched to 6:00, he turned one more time to his wife, then with a real sigh, slid his legs over the edge of the bed and sat up. Tyler was just into his second century, relatively hale and healthy yet, but age was still taking its toll. His knees creaked as he stood up, and his lower back cried out in protest. He was not looking forward to his appointment that morning and hoped it wouldn't be too taxing on him.

Shuffling over to the bathroom, he grabbed his toothbrush and scrubbed the stale out of his mouth. They'd been back to manual toothbrushes for almost 15 years now, but that wasn't anything he minded. There was something almost mesmerizing about that simple act. Liosha had laughed when he'd first mentioned that to her.

If I could only hear her laugh again, he thought as he spit out the last of the water and carefully put the brush, handle down, in the clay cup on the sink.

He turned on the water in the shower, not bothering to fire up the heater. He was pretty sure the contraption was venting into the air, and neither he nor Liosha needed to be breathing in those fumes. He made a mental note to remind June again that it had to be fixed. The council was supposed to take care of all those things now, but what with everything else going on, they weren't much in the way of responsiveness.

Now let Tyler slide in his duties, and they'd be at the house immediately, finding out what was wrong, and when he admitted that nothing was, sit him down for a two-hour lecture on why he couldn't slack off, and that if he forced them, they'd take more aggressive measure to ensure his "contribution," as they called it, was given. Tyler had tried refusing several times before, but it just wasn't worth the effort. It was far better to meekly go to his appointments, do his duty, then come home to his distant and silent wife.

Liosha hadn't been so distant when he was first called upon by the council. She understood duty as well as he did, and she'd been supportive. But over the intervening years, after hundreds of appointments, she had shifted her views, rarely overtly complaining, but expressing herself by pulling away from him. It hurt him to see her suffer like this, and he wished things were back to the way they were before, but this was their new reality.

He reached into the stream of water, almost changing his mind about firing up the old heater. The planet's fall was in the air, and the water was cold. It would take at least 45 minutes to get the water even up to warm, however, so he just took a deep breath, then stepped into the stream. Whatever lingering wisps of sleep still muddled his brain were instantly washed away as the cold torrent washed over his aging body. He took in a deep breath of air, then hurriedly grabbed the soap and lathered up, the water washing away the suds, and he hoped the old man smell, off of him and into the drain. He scrubbed the best he could, then stepped out, toweling himself vigorously. Despite his previous mood, the cold water had shocked him back to life, and he found himself humming as he rubbed the scratchy old towel down his legs.

He broke out into the oldie but goodie "Down by the stream, my love—" before quickly cutting himself off. He leaned over to look into the bedroom, but Liosha still hadn't moved. He was pretty sure she'd heard, though, and that filled him with guilt. She didn't deserve that.

Leaning back, he put the towel down, and for a moment, as the morning light filled the bathroom, he looked at the reflection of his naked body in the mirror. Years on the farm had made him strong up until his seventies or eighties. Now, he looked gnarled and bumpy. He could still put in a day on the tiller, he knew, but then he'd probably have to spend the next two days in bed recovering. He sucked in his gut, but when that didn't turn him into the young man he'd been, he let it back out. This is who he was, and no matter how hard he tried, this is not what a "hero" looked like. This was not what a savior of humanity looked like.

With another sigh, Tyler pulled on a clean pair of robin pants—no underwear of course. He'd been going commando ever since his change in status. He'd never bought robin pants when they were in fashion, but their baggy fit was just what the doctor ordered—literally what the doctor ordered. They did a pretty good job of hiding his chicken legs, so he didn't mind wearing them. At least he could wear whatever shirt he wanted, so he pulled out the first clean one in the drawer and slipped it on. He took one last look at Liosha, but she might as well have been a statue. She hadn't moved a centimeter since he'd woken two hours ago.

Wandering out into the kitchen, he put a pot of water on to boil, then looked inside the cooler to see what they had to eat. The council made sure he had all the right foods, but his appetite had faded in recent years, and nothing in there caught his eye.

He opened the bin and pulled out a handful of the herb mix that had served for coffee for the last ten years. He wasn't even sure what was in it anymore. After the last of the prepared coffee mix had run out over a decade ago, he'd graduated to chicory, dandelion, and Morseweed 301, but this was a mix put together by Falls Foods and delivered to him every week. He knew it was probably doctor-approved, and it didn't taste at all like he remembered real coffee tasted, but it was more of the routine than the taste that mattered to him anymore.

This is what their life had become since the Quiet, cobbling together substitutes for the equipment and premium products that they'd always received in trade for their rare earths and agricultural bounty. Without trading partners, there wasn't much use for the rare earths within their still limited manufacturing capabilities, and the 12,000 or so farms produced more than enough food for the planet's population, so the bulk of the people spent their time and effort in recreating the past with varying, and usually lacking, degree of success.

He took a sip of his coffee and frowned. Yes, it was usually with a lack of success. He didn't understand why the original settlers, himself included, hadn't thought to try and grow real coffee beans. The climate in the governate wasn't tailored for coffee plants, but there had to be GM plants that would grow there. But the cartel had made coffee essence so cheap that it hadn't make much sense at the time, just as the large food fabricators had made growing basics such as wheat and corn commercially impractical.

Still, he didn't put the cup down as he walked up to the schedule posted by the front door, the schedule at which he'd been avoiding looking. He could put it off, but that was just delaying the inevitable. He'd heard the little elves open the door and come in last night to make the entry, as they always did.

His eyes drifted to his appointment: Felicity Evans-Kim.

So soon? he thought. *We've already had two appointments.*

Felicity was a 30-something machine-operator in Graves' Landing, and she was far from his favorite meeting. She could be dismissive and abusive at the same time, and he'd complained to June about her, but this was business, nothing more, and June wouldn't relent. Their previous success damned him to more appointments with her.

He slowly opened the front door, trying not to let it squeak on the hinges, and stepped out onto the porch, stretching for a moment before sitting on the old bench. He'd probably spent a year on the bench if totaled up, and the seat on the left side had worn away to fit him nicely. It had been the first piece of furniture he'd made after raising their initial bubble-shelter, long before he'd built the house. And as they'd prospered and bought or bartered for better furniture, the bench had been relegated to the porch of the then-new house. He'd sat on it watching the children play with Liosha beside him. It had become part of who he was.

Liosha didn't sit on it with him anymore. And he only sat on it while waiting for his ride, just as he'd done every other morning for the last two years.

His coffee had grown cold, but he didn't bother to get up and refresh it. The time between sitting down until the taximan came had become his time for contemplation and remembering. Remembering all they had lost, and contemplating the future.

The Quiet had descended on them 17 years ago. Even to this day, no one knew what had happened, although theories abounded. Tyler didn't know what to think. One day, Sangfroid Hope had been just one planet, albeit a remote one, in a large and scattered spread of humanity. Ships arrived each week to bring in the necessities of life and take their rare earths and specialty crops in trade. Communications, entertainment, and government rulings and regulations kept them abreast of what was happening throughout human space and kept them connected with the rest of humanity.

Until one day, it all stopped. No more ships. No more communications. There was only a deafening blanket of silence. They waited, hoping, for contact to be re-established, but after five years, even the most optimistic of them had come to the realization that they were on their own. Some calamity had befallen the rest of humanity. Still, the trans-station was manned around the clock, sending out questing messages in the hopes that some other outpost had survived as they had. There had been pushback to that for fear that if another race had wiped out humanity, doing so would bring that race to the planet to finish the job, but the fear of being alone simply grew too strong.

Tyler took a last sip of his cold coffee, draining the cup. He remembered when the last distribution of the essence had been made. From the reaction of most of the people, this was as bad as the day the universe was cut off. Not everyone, though. Tyler and Liosha were of the 21% of the population who'd been born off-planet. Life on Cygni 3 had been no cakewalk, and doing without had been part and parcel to their very existence. That was why the two of them had entered the lottery and why they'd married the day before debark despite having met only that morning.

And like many of the Immigrants, he thought the Sangfroids had a feeling of entitlement merely because their parents had braved the far reaches of space. Sangfroid Hope had turned into a benevolent mother, but people had to reach for that golden ring, not simply have it dropped into their laps. So when one thing after another ran out, the Immigrants made do while the native-born Sangfroids complained.

The lack of news and entertainment had hit people hard at first. The Universal Cup had just started the first round when the Quiet descended, and for many, that seemed to be the ultimate catastrophe. Opinions started to shift when one after the other, foods and equipment thought to be God-given rights ran out or broke down. Cottage industries cropped up, repairing broken-down appliances, machinery, and equipment, but some were simply too high-tech for their capabilities. Everything was online, of course, but if a repair started with using an ephemeral-wave analyzer to get the initial readings, and there wasn't a working analyzer on the planet, that did no one any good.

Some items, like the fusion engines that powered everything from landcars to Tyler's tillers and harvesters were almost indestructible. Other things, such as fabricators, medical and reproductive equipment, and molecular printing broke down or ran out of supplies to run them.

Reproductive equipment, Tyler thought. *Therein lies the rub.*

If Tyler was a young man again, then perhaps his contribution wouldn't be so onerous. But he was in his last decade or two, and it was a burden on him, mentally and physically.

Ever since the 20th Century, medical science had fought to combat infertility, and they'd become quite good at it. Anyone could have a child if they so wished. People whose infertility would have removed them from the gene pool reproduced, spreading their infertility to their descendants.

With ancient methods such as IVF, IUI, EUP, and a host of other, more modern processes, there was no longer the absolute need for human intercourse in order to reproduce. Doctors continued to delve into the human DNA to try and solve the root problems, but with the shameful population scourges of the late 21st Century, where the masses of the poor were unknowingly "infected" with infertility via viral transduction, it just became easier to treat the symptoms rather than the underlying causes, a one-size fits all solution. The introduction of the first crèche-banks, where the zygotes were transferred to develop into healthy babies further separated humanity from natural conception and childbirth. A couple could go into their appointment, have sperm and ovum removed, and a day later, have a developing child in the crèche-bank with no need to go through the physical burden of pregnancy and childbirth. Most humans, like the over-manipulated turkeys and other livestock of the 21st Century, could not naturally reproduce.

Which had made his and Liosha's first two children something of a local happening. It wasn't that rare of an occurrence—there were 117 natural births on the planet the year Liosha gave birth to Axel. But with the crèche-bank up and running shortly after the arrival of the first wave of settlers, it was considered quaint and unnecessary. They might as well have been using horses to till the fields and gas lamps for light.

The two of them weren't in one of the retro-groups that dotted humanity where natural childbirth was considered godly. No one from any of those groups had been allowed to emigrate to Sangfroid Hope, and with the infertility bred into most of the population at large, these retro-groups didn't have birthrates to organically keep their numbers going. And when he and Liosha gained their Series 1, the first thing they'd done was to have Janinie-Ann, their third child, in the standard fashion.

Tyler had never given the reproductive system another thought until several years after the Quiet. The Council of Primes had seen the problem coming, of course. There were only so many crèche-packs, the artificial amniotic baths, nutrients, and other materials necessary to grow a healthy fetus. The physicians had attempted to recreate what was needed, and while they might have succeeded with the amniotic baths, the rest had been beyond their capabilities. That they had gotten as far as they did was something of a miracle, given that these were practicing physicians, the technicians who manipulated the medical appliances, not the research physicians on the larger worlds who furthered human medicine.

"Hi, Tyler," Gregari said as he walked up, interrupting his thoughts.

"Oh, sorry, I didn't see you," Tyler answered, willing to let the young man think old age instead of memories was affecting his mind.

But maybe that was what old age was, when memories became more real than the present.

"Anything special today?" Gregari asked.

As always, Gregari's question had two meanings. The young man was fascinated with Tyler, happy to be assigned by the council to take care of the farm. He'd asked before for the details of Tyler's duties, which Tyler had refused to give, but the young man kept asking, hoping that he could slowly wear down Tyler's reluctance.

Tyler chose to answer the base question, though, saying, "I think the Morseweed is about ready to harvest. Wait until the sun dries off the dew, then make sure you get it down and into the shed before sundown."

He really didn't need to tell Gregari that. Whatever else he was, he knew farming, probably better than Tyler did even after all these years. But the farm was his—his and Liosha's—and no matter what the council had him do, he was still in charge here.

Gregari nodded, then stood for a moment, silently staring at him.

"Is there anything else?" Tyler asked.

"Who?"

"None of your business, boy. You know that."

Disappointment spread over his face, but Tyler didn't care. It was bad enough that he was forced into this position, but he wasn't about to satisfy the young man's prurient curiosity.

He settled back into the old bench as Gregari left to get on with his day's duties. Behind him, the house remained silent. He wished there was something he could do to bring life back into it, but he knew by now that was a lost cause. His Liosha just wasn't able to accept the new reality any more. There'd been talk of him moving on to Montpellier for a while, exchanging places with one of the contributors there, mixing up the pool as it were, and lately, he wondered if that might be a good idea. Without it in her face every other day, maybe Liosha could grow to, if not like it, at least accept it again.

At long last, his ride appeared down the road, turning down the drive and coming to a stop in front of the house. Harris Harimoto stepped out from the driver's seat, waving at Tyler. Harris was a good taximan, all business, and never gossiping. He would have preferred a normal self-driving ride, but he thought the council sent a live driver to make sure he actually left for the job.

"Hey, Tyler," Harris said as he climbed up onto the porch. "You about ready?"

Tyler held out his arm, and Harris put the cuff around it. It took the small scanner about ten seconds to determine that Tyler was alive and healthy enough for his mission.

"OK, Tyler. You've got Felicity Evans-Kim today. She's . . . oh, hell, Tyler, I don't need to tell you about her. You've been with her before. She ovulated at 11:48 last night, and given your past success with her, she was moved ahead of the other two candidates.

"As always, I have to ask if you've had sexual relations since your Monday appointment."

Tyler glanced back through the front door, but he said nothing.

"All right, Tyler, I'm going to mark this down as a no. And there's one more thing. June asked me to ask you that if you're up for it . . . sorry, bad choice of words. She asked me that if you agree, she'd like you to try with one more candidate," he said, his hand patting the small case at his side, which carried the PDE5 inhibitors. "She's young and was just identified, and the docs think she's got a high potential of conception. She would have been your appointment this morning if Felicity hadn't ovulated. As always, though, a second attempt is your call."

He wasn't going to do it, Tyler knew. He'd do his duty, but a second try on the same day just wasn't going to help, and it could lower the chances for Friday's appointment. Harris' little pills would allow him to perform when his heart wasn't in it, but they wouldn't affect his sperm count, something June well knew.

It was ironic that his age was one of the things that rendered him a contributor. He was at a time in his life where his physical passion had faded, but he was born further back along the genetic family tree to where infertility was still rampant, but not as severe as it was today, particularly among the groups that had populated the planet.

His "harem," as people joking referred to it, encompassed a population base of almost 5,000 women, even if most would never be considered due to known infertility or simply because they refused to participate. Those that were willing were ranked by their potential, and over the last two plus years, he'd had intercourse with 312 of them: some, like Felicity, more than once. That had resulted in 17 children. And that was more than most of the other contributors on the planet had managed.

Seventeen children, who hopefully had inherited the mother's and his fertility. Seventeen of the 2,065 so far who had been born planet-wide through the contributor program. Another 514 had been born through a crude, homegrown IUI, although the medical techs were working feverishly to improve that method's efficacy. Other's not in the official program kept trying, of course. Humanity was an optimistic species, after all. And six children had been conceived outside of the program with four living long enough to emerge crying and squalling into this Brave New World.

"So, that's that. If you're ready, we can go now."

Tyler slowly stood up, walked to the car, and sat in the front passenger seat. Harris started the motor, and as they started to pull out, Tyler looked back at the house he and Liosha had built together. At the bedroom window, the curtain had been pulled back, and he saw her silhouette within as she watched him get taken to his appointment.

SEMPER FIDELIS

"Semper Fidelis" was my first short story, written in 1978 and sent off to Analog, where I receive a polite, but firm rejection. I put the story into my drawer until I was asked by readers to publish it so they could see my starting point.

****

"OK, Khan, you should be nearing the hill. There'll be four men on the gun, but probably no Weres. I want you to circle uphill of them and come in from the rear. Do you understand? There'll be four, " Manny's voice came over the receiver deep in Khan's ear.

"Four men, yeah, four men. No worry, "Khan rasped into the surgically implanted mic in his throat.

"Good boy, go get them. You're on your own now."

Khan glided effortlessly through the dense jungle growth, muscles rippling beneath his skin as he moved. He was at home in this environment, and at first glance, it was hard to distinguish him from his ancestors of not so many generations ago. All of his senses were trained forward, straining to identify his objective. At last, the low murmur of voices ahead pinpointed their position. He circled moving through the darkness until he was just beyond them, and then cautiously crept forward to a point fifteen meters from the emplacement

Just as Manny had told him, there were four men there. Three were in back of the gun playing cards, and the fourth was manning the gun itself, staring sleepily off into the distance.

Four rifles were stacked just out of reach from where the men were sitting.

The adrenalin began to flow throughout Khan's body as he tensed, the tip of his tail lashing back and forth. Instincts surfaced as forces seemed to take control of him, with the desire to kill becoming over-powerful. Just as one man gave a triumphant cry and began to sweep in the chips, Khan sprang.

With a tremendous sweep, Khan struck the winner across the head, instantly breaking his neck. Before the other two could react, Khan's hind legs disemboweled one, who gave a surprised look as he watched his blood and guts slid out onto the ground before he toppled over. At the same time, he raked the other's throat open, leaving him to gurgle out his life where he fell. The final man, just realizing what was happening, tried to swing around the big gun, but Khan was just too fast. Ninety kilos of muscle hit the soldier in the chest, knocking him down as Khan's jaws closed around his throat. The hot, salty blood filled Khan's mouth, triggering other ancient instincts, but Khan released his hold, letting the head thud against the dirt.

Khan stood back and viewed the scene with a glow of satisfaction. He walked over and batted the soft sides of the throatless man, but there was no movement, so he sat down and began to clean himself: Ten minutes later, he remembered that he was supposed to report in.

"Manny, this is Khan. I take care of."

There was a short pause, then the speaker came to life. "Khan, listen. Did you' 'take care of, or are you
going to? Answer. "

"Did Manny, did," Khan managed to prolong the answer into a whine.

"Did? Good boy, good boy. OK, come on home now."

Khan bounded off, anxious for dinner and Manny's attention.

Increased Intelligence Organisms, or "Weres, " as they were called in reference to the creatures of legend, were developed by the Federation States during the "Civilized War." They were animals that had, by genetical and surgical means, a vastly increased intelligence. Able to speak thanks to massive reconstruction of the larynx and tongue, they were organized into teams, which led by a human operator, carried out various assignments during the war.
Encyclopaedia Universalis 2064, p. 1612.

Khan belched and moved back from his dinner of raw liver. The morning sunlight gleaned off his jet black fur. He stretched out on the ground, basking in the warmth, feeling quite satisfied. Manny had heaped the praise on him upon his return, and then had given him the treat of the liver. Khan decided that he felt like a nap, so he rose and languidly moved off toward the Were-camp, the small, enclosed area near the latrines where the Weres made their homes.

"Hey Khan, you pussycat. Come here. I've got the cutest little she-leopard for you here, " a voice called out. Khan paused and swung his head around, trying to pinpoint the speaker. He emitted a questioning whine, and laughter surrounded him. A half-eaten apple flew out from behind a tent and struck his back.

"Go on, get out of here, stupid. Go back to the weirdcamp, where you belong." More laughter echoed out.

Khan finally realized that he was being teased, and with a warm glow of contentment, continued on. He was grateful that he was with friends, and while he really didn't understand just what was so funny, he enjoyed their play. They were always asking him questions he couldn't answer, or pulling his tail or something. It amazed them that such an awesome fighting machine could take such treatment and not strike back, but Khan would just sit there, basking in the attention.

He reached the Were-camp, and being the largest Were there, he took his customary position on the rock in the center of the area. Lazily, he viewed the other off-duty Weres through half-closed eyes. Knife, the wolf bitch, whose sense of smell had saved the team on the last offensive; Kyla, the falcon; and Sheera, the ocelot who was by far the most intelligent of the Weres.

Khan realized that Sheera was much smarter than he was and wistfully envied her. He tended to classify her as a human, and often followed her around the camp until she would get annoyed and swat him across the nose. This would almost always be followed with laughter from the humans, who enjoyed the sight of the petite ocelot man handling Khan. He would leave her alone for a while, but half an hour later, he would be back, dogging her footsteps again. Today, however, he was content to leave her be. He basked in the sun, and as his consciousness started to drift off, his body started to slide off the rock. Farther and farther he slid, until he finally fell off with a thud. The other Weres looked, up with a start and the few humans around howled with laughter. Khan stayed where he had fallen and started to clean himself, as if he had planned to get off the rock. After a few minutes, attention drifted away from him, so he gingerly stepped back onto the rock and warily drifted off to sleep.

Due to a fervor among the Federation citizens after the development of INO's, the animals were conditioned not to eat their kills. During tests, the animals starved to death before they would eat anything unless it was personally given to them by their handlers. The INO's were proven to lack the integrated intelligence to carry on mass attacks; they performed much better as scouts or reconnaissance patrols.
Encyclopaedia Universalis 2064, p. 1612.

Khan awoke to the briefing calls, so he dutifully trotted to the command tent and over to Manny. He rubbed his head against Manny's leg, then sat down beside him. He didn't pay much attention to the ops briefing as the CO informed the troops of the expected United Forces offensive. The major was visibly nervous, and he kept wiping the sweat from his forehead with a meticulously folded handkerchief. Against his one-hundred and forty men and six Were teams was what Intel described as a full enemy division. He stuttered and stammered for an hour giving general instructions before rounding it up.

"I don't need to tell you how important this is, men. We 've got to do our best if we want to survive. We've got to hold on until headquarters can evacuate us. Were teams, wait up. I want a word with you."

The bulk of the soldiers stood up and filed out. With only the ops officer and the handlers, and ignoring the Weres themselves, he said, "Team handlers, remember, we 're using your animals differently than they're used to being employed. They don't usually work well together, but that's the way I want it this time. We need to maximize shock value to give the enemy pause and make them hold up. Don't expect too much out of them, just try to get them to understand what we want. You handlers tend to consider them as humans, but you have to realize that they're animals, tools to be used, and boy do we need to use them now."

Sheera's upper lip wrinkled slightly at the comment, but Khan ignored the commanding officer. He'd been bred big and powerful, but his language abilities lagged behind some of the others, and it was just easier for him to pay attention only to Manny.

The major paused to look around the tent for a moment, then said, "OK, gentlemen, that's all. Good luck!"

Manny took his team to his tent to brief them on their missions. Before starting, he looked at each of his four team member in his or her his eyes: Khan, Benson, a doberman, Pecos, an overweight jaguar, and Knife .

"OK, there are going to be many men coming today," he said, carefully enunciating in his handler mode. "You will go out on the trails in teams of two. I know that you like to work alone, but you will be working together tonight." He paused to let this information sink in. "If you see movement, call me, then, attack." It is very important that these men don't get through. Khan, I want you and Knife to take the point on the trail below the gun you took last night. Benson and Pecos, you two take the creek. OK?" The animals growled their assurances. "Well, better get going then, I guess, " Manny said before reaching out to stroke each Were on the head.

The two teams split and went off in their separate ways. Khan and Knife loped the main trail, then headed up, Knife trotting with her tongue lolling out the side of her mouth and Khan following effortlessly. Khan's black coat and Knife's dirty grey rendered both of them practically invisible against the jungle trail in the darkening evening. Before long, they reached their position and melted into the undergrowth on either side of the trail. The smell of death was still strong as the bodies up the hill had started to decay. The smell started the adrenalin flowing through going in Khan, but he overcame the urge to roar a challenge at the approaching enemy and settled down for the wait.

"They come," Knife's growl drifted across the trail, five hours after taking their positions. As usual, her nose enabled her to detect the enemy first. "They have a dog. " She activated her mic and repeated herself to Manny.

"Knife! How many are there, how many? "

Knife tested the air, then shook her head slowly. "Many men."

Knife was almost as intelligent as Sheera, but numbers larger than five or six tended to give all Weres problems.

Manny gave an exasperated sigh, then continued, "OK, good girl. You did a good job. Now I want you two to wait, then attack them as they pass you. Understand?" When both acknowledged, he followed with a "Good luck! "

Both animals broke off concentration and let instincts take over as the adrenalin began to flow again. Khan's claws slowly started to extract and retract, drawing deep furrows in the decayed matter of the forest floor, and the tip of his tail began to lash. Knife kept licking her jaws in anticipation.

Suddenly Khan could hear them, too. Their number was more than Khan could easily discern as they filed wordlessly down the trail. He could pick out the nervous tread of the dog, signifying that it had detected them, too. The dog was not a true Were. Because the United Forces had very few Weres in their forces, they often used ordinary dogs to detect the presence of Federation Weres.

As the first man finally came into view, gun ready and peering into the dense growth, Khan emitted a muted growl and softly shifted his weight, readying himself to leap. When the third man passed, Khän could contain himself no longer, and he sprang among the men, dropping the first with a rake across the face. As she was waiting for more of the men to pass, Khan's attack took Knife by surprise, but she quickly jumped in to whirl and slash among the line.

As the two Weres attacked, the hyper-alert men immediately faced them and started firing. The darkness and the quickness of the Weres' movements caused their shots to go wild or to hit each other. Two men went down with lethal burns while neither Were was more than slightly singed. Knife had managed to open the throats of two men, leaving them to lie with their life flowing out, and was mid-air in a leap for another when the man fired his gun, hitting her full in the chest. She died instantly, burned through, but her body continued the leap to crash into the soldier, knocking him to the ground.

Khan lept again, caving in the ribcage of another as the man's shot went wild, ionizing the air as it went. The dog, an English setter, made a half-hearted rush on Khan, halted, and tried to wheel around when Khan's front paw descended on his back, breaking it in two.

A young soldier, really not much more than a boy, had frozen for the first few seconds of the fight. He suddenly wheeled and started to run back down the path. Khan leaped after him, hooking one claw into his back and yanking him to the ground. He sprang back as two beams sizzled to where he had just been, striking the still-alive boy twice, burning holes in his head and chest.

Khan bolted for the underbrush, and using the dense growth for cover, he circled around and by crossing the trail just around the bend, he ended up directly behind of the two soldiers who stood with guns ready, peering uncertainly into the vegetation.

Khan sprang once more, knocking the two men down. He ripped open the sides of one man, and as the other started to struggle to his feet, he sprang at him. Just before Khan reached his throat, the man threw a tremendous punch right at his nose. Khan screamed with rage as he heard bones crack and, his nasal passages started to fill with blood. He shook his head, then charged the man again, bowling him over and slapping the side of his head as he fell. Khan sneezed several times, and when he looked back up, the soldier had gotten up and was charging him, swinging a rifle by its muzzle while screaming at the top of his lungs.

Khan gave a puzzled whine and retreated, darting out of his way. As the soldier lunged for him, he tripped over the body of the boy, and with a surprised cry, fell, arms outstretched. Khan whirled and jumped on the man, closing his jaws on the soldier's neck. Incredibly, the soldier almost regained his feet with Khan on his back, but after a tense moment, he sank back down to his knees and then fell to his face. His struggles got weaker and weaker, until finally, with a soft gurgle, they ceased altogether. Khan held on for a little while longer, then let go, gasping for air. His snout was throbbing, and it was hard to breathe with all the blood in it.

Khan shook his head again, stepped back, and put a paw on the body. He was about to roar when movement over by Knife's body caught his eye. The man that Knife had knocked down had only been dazed. He had managed to pull himself out from under Knife's body and was now reaching for his weapon.

Khan launched himself for the soldier as the man grabbed his rifle, crashing into him a split second after the weapon fired. Pain burned through his left side as the beam sliced through skin and muscle. Khan's momentum, however, carried him into the man sending them both crashing to the ground. Khan clamped his jaws around the soldier's throat, cutting off his air, before the pain and shock took over and everything faded before Khan's eyes.

****

The war between the Federated States and the United Forces, or the so-called "Civilized War," is chiefly known for its loss of life along with its indecisiveness. At the end of the five years of conflict, both sides had lost over 20,000,000 men and women, and untold amounts of material goods, yet the boundaries of both sides remained the same as they had existed prior to the outbreak of hostilities. One point of historical interest is that the loss of life was almost military. The banning of the "dirty weapons" and the locations of the campaigns provided for a minimal loss of civilian life.
Encyclopaedia Universalis 2064 p. 4379.

Khan slowly awoke to a myriad of different impressions. A dull throb signified the location of the burn in his side. His nose also throbbed, and it felt much larger that normal. The sunlight burned through his eyelids and the cloying sickly-sweet smell of the bodies around him implied that many hours had passed since the attack. His mouth felt funny, as if he were being gagged, but then the realization hit him that his jaws were still locked around his last throat. He carefully opened them and let the dull-eyed head fall back. He twisted to disengage the pale hand still clutching the folds on the back of his neck, but a searing lance of pain stopped him, forcing a snarl. Slowly, he backed away and tried to stand. His hind legs seemed to be capable of some movement, but the pain precluded their use for the time being. Khan gave the equivalent of a mental shrug and dragged himself under a large, leafy bush using his front legs. He lay down in the shade and started to drift off to sleep when he remembered to report.

"Manny, Manny, this is Khan. " He waited for a reply, then tried again. "Manny, this is Khan."

There was a short pause, then suddenly Manny's voice came through. "Khan, old boy, where are you?"

Quite a bit of noise was coming through the comms as if there was a large commotion going on back at camp.

"I take care of enemy. All dead."

"You did? Really? Good boy, good boy. Where's Knife?" Manny's said, sounding was faintly incredulous.

"Knife dead, shot. I want water."

"Knife's dead, too then. That only leaves you. OK, Khan, I want you to get back to camp right now. Come in carefully, we're almost surrounded, but get here quick. Do you understand?"

"Manny, my legs no good. Nose hurt. I hurt. No can go home. You can come here?"

"You're hit? Oh great, just freaking great." There was a pause, then, "OK, listen to me now. Find a place to hide, because you might have to wait a while. "

Manny's voice was interrupted by another, slightly fainter as if the speaker was farther back from the microphone. "Manny, come on. It's time to get off this stinking island. Bring your set and get to pad number three. "

"But I've got one Were left out there."

"So, what? I know you guys get attached to them, but in the end, it's only a dumb animal. If you want to die over some mangy ball of fur, that's your problem. But if I were you, I'd get the hell out of here. Headquarters will give you some new pets. Come on!"

There was another long pause, a sound like an intake of breath of someone getting ready to say something, and then the set clicked off, leaving nothing but silence in Khan's receiver.

"Manny?" Khan settled back down and began to lick his wounds.

He knew Manny wouldn't leave him--Manny was his friend. He'd just wait here until Manny came to take him back home. Manny would take care of his burns and maybe give him some fresh liver, then he could rest for a while. No matter how long it took, he'd wait. Manny was his friend, and friends always stayed loyal.

This story was expanded to a full novel, Animal Soldiers: Hannibal. You can find the novel on Amazon.

SECESSION

This is what started it all. This was my first published story, written as a final project for my creative writing class at the United States Naval Academy.

****

Well, I've done it, I thought as I took the tube home.

After all the time and effort I'd spent throughout this, my last year at school, sneaking out for appointments and interviews, I'd finally gone and taken that last step. I just wondered how they're going to take it. No, not wondered, but feared. I was pretty sure this wasn't going to go over well.

The capsule whispered to a stop and the pneumatic door opened. I almost wished that the tube had taken me to some other sector, but the tube is maddeningly accurate, and I found myself in our all too familiar station, with its inane "Buy Seasonal Commuter Passes, Save Credit!" flashing just above my line-of-sight.

I sighed and walked up to the ramp, riding it up to my level. I had to fight for my balance as a small horde of basic school kids swarmed by. Watching them and hearing their shrieks of laughter made me feel much older than my meager years. They made me feel like an adult, at a level far above their childish concerns. I toyed with the thought—me, a full-fledged adult. I decided I liked that.

I stepped off the ramp at J-level and turned down McDavitt corridor toward our hatch. Hesitating for a second as I reached it, I flipped on the speaker switch.

"Yeah, it's Matt." I waited the ten seconds before placing my palms against the lock, opening the portal. Mom was in the living area poring over a report or something. She glanced up as I entered.

"Hello, son, have a good day?" she asked absently, returning to her reading before I could answer. Mom is like that—always putting up the correct front like a mechanized receptionist, never really expecting an answer.

Mom is the chairman of the Secession Movement, so she is actually the de facto leader of Luna. She is still a striking woman, and her competent looks framed by her long brown hair probably got her as much support, from most of the men, at least, as her ideological views. And she did have support. She would plead, cajole, bully, or do anything to get someone over to her side, and very few people could stand up to her pressures. Right now, she was just shy of the two-thirds vote needed for secession.

Mom constantly told us that she doesn't bring home her work, but while she rarely had guests over, she almost always would bring home administrative work and communications, and she could constantly be found buried underneath it. Most people don't realize just how time-consuming politics is. I know I've done my share of typing and running errands for her. Many times I've wondered how she can keep up with it all.

I walked on into the dining area and found Dad setting three places at the table. "Where's Teri?" Actually, I was relieved that my younger sister wasn't around. It would make things easier when I told them.

"Oh, she decided to stay overnight with Mage. I trust you had a productive day?"

I glanced up quickly, but he wasn't looking. There was no way that he could know, but you never could be sure with Dad. He seems to know everything that's going on, and he knows what you are going to do before you do yourself. It was rather convenient that Teri chose tonight not to be at home, but if Dad knew anything was up with me, he wasn't showing any indication of it.

Dad sort of keeps the family together and running smoothly. With Mom always gone or worrying about a new political crisis or something, we need a strong central figure to rely upon, and Dad is it. He is a farmer by choice—an "agricultural engineer" (Lunarians love to re-title things like that). His aptitude quotient is much higher than farming requires, (in fact, he is a F-1, the unlimited level), but he enjoys working in the tunnels, reclaiming soil and growing crops. Because of his work, he always has an earthy, wholesome smell, something rare in our antiseptic world. As kids, Teri and I used to go with him to work where we would play in the moist soil. At first, Mom didn't approve, but Dad in his own quiet way, convinced her that it was all right.

"Yeah, Dad, I got a lot done," brushing past him.

I grabbed a stick of celery and walked over to my cubicle, dialing the aperture open and entering. Sitting on my bed, I started to make a mental inventory of my belongings. I could see I was going to have to get rid of a lot. I had waited until the very last minute to accept, and I hadn't done any sorting yet. As usual, my eyes faltered as they passed over my model rocket collection. Those rockets were my prized possessions. From the intricate Sputnik model to the 1/10,000th scale Gyron class star voyageur, I had over 151 different models. Reaching out, I picked up my Apollo 11. It was my basic school graduation present. I remember Mom saying that it was too complicated for me, but I proved her wrong. Thirty painstaking hours of work went into that model, but I finished the module without help from anyone.

I held the command module at arm's length over the lunar surface of my bed. I wondered what it must have been like to be there, with Armstrong, when history was made. I brought the model in for a landing, notwithstanding the fact that it was actually the Eagle lunar module that made the landing.

"One small step for man, one giant leap for mankind."

God, I wished that I had said that. I could just imagine me being the first man on the moon. But Neil Armstrong got the glory for that. I'll just have to do something else. The ticket in my pocket was my guarantee that I'd have my chance.

The bell's chime snapped me out of my reverie as Dad's voice told me it was time for dinner. With a sigh, I put down the Apollo and went out to eat.

Dinner was unusually quiet. Mom had brought her screen to the table, and I was trying to figure out how to broach the subject. Dad noticed the quiet, too.

"Honey, put down that report and eat your allotment. Whatever you're doing can wait for half an hour."

She looked up at him for a second, then sheepishly put down the screen.

"You're right, it'll wait. You know that I don't like to bring my work home, but with the Americans and the Russians both agreeing to use force if necessary to keep us a colony, things are getting pretty hectic. We're trying to get the Asian states to support us, but so far it hasn't been working."

She picked up her spoon and started to eat.

Dad started to give me odd looks as I toyed with my food throughout the meal. I almost told them once, but I backed off at the last second.

Finally, Mom pushed herself back from her plate. "That was delicious, honey, thank you." She started to rise from the table when I interrupted her.

"Mom, Dad, I've got something important to tell you." Mom sat back down, glancing at her screen again before looking back at me. I took a deep breath, "I'm joining the Navy."

There, I've done it, I thought, glad that it was out in the open.

Mom's mouth dropped open as the room became deathly silent.

An eternity later, Mom sputtered, "You're. . .you're what?"

"I'm joining the Navy. I got an appointment at the Academy, and I'm going to accept it."

I realized that I was playing with my food again so I put down my fork and looked up at her. The shock was wearing off, and she was getting mad.

"No, you're not!" She said, standing up and glaring down at me.

"Mom, the matter isn't in your hands. I'm joining." I stood up to face her.

"No son of mine is going to join the imperialistic forces of Earth. I will not stand for it!"

"Mom," I pleaded, "I'm not joining some sort of decadent system. I'm just joining the Navy."

"After all I've taught you, how can you say that? After all I've worked for, you can't do this."

"Not only can, but have done. Mom, I don't agree with your views, and I never have. Earth is the center of our culture while we have nothing. I want to be a part of Earth. I don't want to be independent. What do we have on this rock?"

"You. . .why I'll tell you—"

"No Mom," I interrupted. "Save your speeches for someone else—I've heard them all. Go try and get your two-thirds vote. But you can't, can you? There are people in the Russian and Euro protectorates who feel the same as me, right? Or else you would have your precious vote, you would—"

"Shut-up! How can you talk like that in my house? I thought my own family supports me, but I can see that you've decided that you're too good for—"

"Both of you, stop it!" Dad said, rising from his seat.

I had forgotten that he was even there.

"If you two can't discuss this like adults, we just won't say anything at all. I'm surprised at the both of you. Matt, go to your room for now, we'll take this up later."

"But..."

Looking at Dad, I thought better of continuing, so I stomped to my cubical, barely waiting until I made it in before dialing the aperture shut. Grabbing my Neptune class rocket as I passed, I lay back on my bed. Holding the model above me, I lay glaring at it. Suddenly I smashed it against the wall, shattering it to pieces.

I don't believe I did that, I thought, staring stupidly at the broken pieces. I felt like a fool. I just ruined a good model because of her. I lay back down and brooded for half an hour until the bell chimed.

"Matt, it's me," Mom's voice came over the grill.

"Come in," I said, my voice low in resignation.

The aperture opened and Mom entered, shoved some clothes off the chair, and sat down. She waited a second, then cleared her throat.

"You know son, I've been doing some thinking. What you want to do will hurt me deeply, so deep that it will never be healed. It will probably ruin my chances of getting elected and hurt the chances for our cause to succeed. But it is your life. As long as you realized the pain you are going to cause, and if you still want to go, I can't stand in your way."

She looked at me expectantly.

I'd seen this act a thousand times before. Mom likes to play the martyr. She acts as if she's letting someone do something, yet she tries and uses his conscience to make him decide to go her way. But this time, it wasn't going to work.

"Thanks, Mom. I knew you'd agree."

A small look of surprise came over her face. "You mean you'd do that to your mother?"

"You said it was OK."

"I know what I said! Listen to me. You think you're so smart. Well, I'm just not going to let you go. How about that?"

"Mom, you have to let me. You know the law."

I was surprised that our voices were so calm.

"Matt, what I told you about my election just might be true. Imagine the papers, 'SON OF SECESSION MOVEMENT BOSS JOINS FOE!!' Think of what that could do to me."

"I'm sorry about that Mom, I really am. But I'm going to live my own life."

"I know how you feel, Matt, but do you have to go against your own mother? Why do you want to go, anyway?"

She spoke as if she were really puzzled, and I couldn't tell if she were acting or not.

"Mom, I want to go to space. The fleets are on Earth. What do we have here? A couple of garbage scows? In the Navy, I can be trained to handle a real spacecraft. I can go places and see things. Maybe, if I do well enough, I can even get into the Exploratory Corps. Imagine that, going somewhere where no human has ever been before. The only way I can do that, and I do mean the only way, is to become an officer in the Navy."

I felt exhilarated just from talking about it.

"So, that's it."

She picked up the Gyron model, idly turning it over in her hands.

"You know something?" Her voice suddenly became silky smooth. "I had been thinking. You know we haven't given you your graduation present yet. I had thought that a trip on one of the luxury liners around the system would be a perfect gift, sort of a last fling before career school, so to say. Only, the Academy starts early, a few days from now, doesn't it? And if you're not going to be here, it's obvious that you couldn't go."

She looked at me helplessly as if in a dilemma.

I could see that she was not going to give in. She had to win, no matter what, even if that was against her own children. I could see only one way out of this mess, so I let out a heavy sigh.

"OK, Mom, I give in. I don't want to, but I guess I don't have much of a choice, do I? But that's only if I get that trip, OK?"

She beamed victoriously at me.

"Thank you, Matt. I knew you'd understand. I knew you'd help out your mother." She replaced the model, walked over to me and kissed my forehead. "I love you, Matt. You're a good son."

She turned around and walked out of the room.

I watched her leave, closed the aperture, and looked at my chronometer.

Let's see. The flight leaves at 1100, and the ticket says be there two hours early. It's now 2100. That gives me eleven hours to get everything done.

I got my luggage out and started to pack, discarding most of my things as being too bulky. I never knew I had so many possessions. I took the Apollo capsule, even though I knew it was wasted weight, and packed it. The rest of my models I sealed in boxes to be stored. Finally, after much longer than I would have imagined it would take me, I was down to my two allotted bags, although I don't know how I fit everything in. I opened the aperture and stuck my head out. The apartment was quiet and dark.

I felt a thrill as I moved carefully around the furniture. At last I was on my way. I felt as if I were eloping and running away to the circus at the same time. I just wished I had a girlfriend that I could exchange a tearful farewell with, like they do in the shows.

Oh well, you can't have everything.

I hesitated when I got to the portal and looked back at my parents' cubicle. I'd write them and explain things to them later, once I was out of my mother's grasp. I knew I was going to miss them, though. No matter what, I loved them both. I even understood my mother's position. It was just that I had to live my own life.

I turned around and flipped the switch to open.

"One small step for man, one giant leap for me," I whispered as I stepped out. The portal hissed to a close behind me.

Jonathan P. Brazee

THE BRIDGE

This was another story for Craig Martelle, this time for The Expanding Universe 5. I wanted to go a slightly different direction from the typical grunt story, so I switched to a combat engineer team, and based this off the real-life story of Colonel John W. Ripley and his actions at the Dong Ha Bridge.

****

The sniper's round hit Lance Corporal Troy Sifuentes high on his shoulder, knocking him to his knees.

Pain engulfed him as his world exploded. He struggled to think, instinctively getting his legs under him and diving for the side of the highway. He never saw the next round that chased him as he rolled into the meager cover offered by the drainage ditch, missing him by scant centimeters.

"You OK, Tee?" Sergeant Van Meter shouted from the ditch on the other side of the road and ten meters back.

"I'm hit, Sergeant," Troy managed to croak out as he lay on his back, each breath sending waves pulsing down his body.

"How bad is it?" the sergeant yelled.

Troy gingerly lifted his left hand to his right shoulder, then raised it to his eyes. To his surprise, the hand was not covered in blood. He tilted his head to look as the waves of pain started to fade. There was a gouge in his armor shell, and the live-camo faded to utility gray from the gouge and down his right arm to mid-bicep before the camo again took over. Gingerly he rotated his right arm--wincing, but it worked.

"I think I'm OK. It didn't penetrate."

"Did you see where the shot came from?"

Troy's mind was beginning to work again, and he tried to put together what had just happened. He'd been walking down the side of Highway 42 and had just spotted the bridge when he'd been hit. He turned to tell the sergeant that he had the bridge in sight. That meant . . .

He poked his head higher to confirm when another round hit the edge of the drainage ditch, showering him with dirt and making him duck back down again.

"To our left," he shouted. "Maybe on the high ground."

"The high ground? You mean on this side of the river or the left on the other side?" the sergeant asked, switching to the team net.

"Yes, on this side."

"Are you sure?"

"Yeah. I was just turning around to tell you, and he hit me in the front."

He fingered the gouge in his armor. The cerralloy shell was indented almost a centimeter at its deepest point.

"This area's supposed to be secure. There're no Trikes here."

"Fucking grunts," Lance Corporal Liza "Rabbit" Babieux passed from where she'd taken cover. "Our own guys are shooting at us."

"Hell, that's probably it. Let me get on the hook with the CP and tell them to get that idiot off our asses. Keep your heads down," the sergeant passed before the soft click let the rest of the four-man team know he'd switched freqs.

Troy felt the anger start to fan into a flame. Life as a Marine combat engineer was dangerous enough without having friendly forces fire on them. Infantry grunts were too trigger-happy as it was, but a sniper should have been able to see that Troy was a Marine, not a Tricameral.

Another soft click told the team that the sergeant was back, and then he passed, "The CP says there's no sniper team in our pos, at least from them. They could be from Force, and they're going to go up the chain to find out."

"Meanwhile, we suck dirt," Rabbit said.

"Can't we just call out to them?" Private Dare Nichols asked.

There was a moment of silence, then the sergeant said, "Hell, our boot's got a head on his shoulders. Let me try."

A moment later, the sergeant's amplified voice rang out, "Up there on the hill. We're Federation Marines. Do not fire! I repeat, we're Federation Marines."

There was a moment of silence, then Rabbit asked, "Do you think he heard us?"

"One way to find out," the sergeant said before activating his loudspeakers again and saying, "I'm going to step out into the road now. You can see we're Marines."

"Here goes nothing. Cover me," he passed on the net before he stood up.

Troy lifted his head slightly, trying to keep out of the line of fire. He brought up his M91, wincing as he raised his right hand.

He could just see the sergeant's head as he stepped out onto the highway. The NCO looked up to the high ground and waved his hand. Nothing happened, and the sergeant turned back and passed, "Looks like that did it," when another round was fired, and the sergeant spun to the ground, grabbing his right arm.

Troy didn't see where the round came from, but he blindly emptied a magazine of 100 darts up into the hillside while Sergeant Van Meter pushed himself on his ass with his heels for cover. The boot ran out, grabbed him under the shoulders, and dragged him into the opposite drainage ditch.

"Mother fuck!" Sergeant Van Meter said over the net. "The bastard got me!"

"Guess he didn't hear you," Rabbit passed.

With the sergeant under cover, Troy ducked back down before the sniper could engage him. The adrenaline washed away most of the pain in his shoulder. He'd sure feel it tomorrow, but for the moment, he was sore but functional. He took another look, closer this time, as he fingered the damage. The round, whatever it was, had actually penetrated the shell before skimming along. Either the oblique angle of the round or the inner liquid layer—probably a combination of both—had saved his shoulder.

Marine-issued magnetorheological armor was pretty substantial, proof against most small arms. Whatever that guy up on the hill was using packed a big punch, and that meant he'd probably have top-notch optics with it . . . which meant that he'd have seen that they were Marines . . . which meant he was a Tricameral soldier. Troy mentally kicked himself. He should have realized that as soon as he was hit and kept Sergeant Van Meter from exposing himself.

"Sergeant, what's your condition?" he passed on the team net. "That guy's packing something big."

"I don't want to look. The boot's applying a pressure patch."

"It's pretty bad," Private Nichols passed. "Most of his arm's hanging on by a thread."

There was a sound of retching coming over the net, then, "Thanks for telling me that, Boot. I didn't look at it for a reason," Sergeant Van Meter managed to gasp.

Troy was the next senior in line, and if the sergeant was messed up that bad, his medkit would be flooding him with happy nanos, and those were not conducive to Marine ops. He had to see for himself.

The sergeant and Nichols were on the west side of the highway, and the slope of the hill worked to their advantage. Rabbit was on the same side as he was, which exposed her, but also gave her a better firing position up to the still hidden sniper. She also had the IAW, an automatic slug thrower, the heaviest of the team's weapons, which would be better at keeping the sniper's head down than any of the other three Marine's M91s.

"Rabbit, can you cover me?" he passed on the DM channel. "I've got to check up on the sergeant."

"Make it quick, Tee, but yeah, I've got your six."

Troy leaned back for a moment, breathing heavily. He was very, very aware that somewhere on the hill above them, a Tricameral sniper had them in their sights. If the sniper had shifted his attention back to him, he could be taken under fire the instant he showed himself.

No getting around it.

Just do it, he thought as he gathered himself, drawing his legs underneath him. He was about to spring when he remembered something his senior drill instructor had said back in boot camp. It was an offhand remark, something that had probably been drilled into every infantry grunt, but Troy was a combat engineer. All Marines were riflemen, true, but his training was to blow things up, not fight enemy snipers.

Instead of jumping up and running across the highway, Troy edged along the drainage ditch, face hugging the cerrocrete bottom until he'd gone about ten meters.

"You gonna do something, Tee, or are you just playing with yourself?" Rabbit asked.

"Yeah. I just had to displace so that bastard won't have an easy shot. I'm ready, though. On three." He took five deep breaths, then said, "One . . . two . . . THREE!"

Jonathan P. Brazee

On "three," Troy jumped to his feet and ran across the highway, feeling terribly exposed. A shot rang out just before he reached the other side, but he wasn't hit, and an instant later, he dived into the opposite drainage ditch, smacking his bad shoulder.

"Son-of-a . . ." he started before biting off his words. His earlier assumption that he was OK was forgotten and waves of pain coursed through him. He knew he could initiate his own medkit, but with the sergeant down, he had to keep a clear head.

"You OK?" Rabbit asked. "Did he get you?"

"No, he missed. Just hit hard."

Troy twisted around the other way. Five meters down the ditch, the sergeant was flat on his back. Sitting next to him, a wide-eyed Nichols was staring at him in surprise. Troy realized he'd never told the private that he was coming, a mistake that could have resulted in him eating a round from the boot.

He shifted his gaze to look up at the high ground. The trees nearest them, all nicely spaced in the terraforming style of a hundred years ago, gave them a degree of cover from farther up the hill. He wasn't about to stand up, but he was pretty sure that the sniper couldn't see them. Rabbit was still exposed, but the three were temporarily safe.

He crawled forward to the sergeant and Nichols. The pressure patch had molded around Sergeant Van Meter's right arm from just below the elbow and down to cover the hand. The patch was misshapen, indicating that there was significant damage, but at least most of it was still there, which meant the Navy docs would have more to work with.

"How're you feeling, Sergeant?" Troy asked as he crawled up alongside the NCO.

"Not bad, all things considered."

That wasn't what Troy was expecting to hear, and he tore his gaze from the sergeant's hand and shifted to his face. Sergeant Van Meter wasn't there, at least the tough, take-no-prisoners sergeant who'd been a mentor to Troy for the last two years. He was smiling, his eyes unfocussed.

This was Troy's first combat deployment, and as a combat engineer, he hadn't gotten into any direct fighting up until now. Sergeant Van Meter was the first person he'd seen who'd been shot, and more pertinent, he was the first person he'd seen who'd been filled up with happy-nanos. He didn't need to have seen it before, however, to know that the sergeant was off somewhere in a good place.

"Sergeant Van Meter, you with me?" he asked, despite knowing what his eyes told him.

"Oh, Tee? How's it going, my man?"

"I'm fine, Sergeant. How're you?"

"I got shot," the sergeant said with a laugh, holding up his arm. "Bang!"

"I'm going to call for a CASEVAC," Troy said.

"No! I'm fine," the sergeant said, sitting up, a shadow of his normal self fighting through the medically-induced haze. "We've got our mission."

Troy hesitated a moment, not sure of what he should do. Sergeant Van Meter was in charge, after all, but the man had half his arm shot off.

"I need to call the lieutenant," he said, then as the sergeant started to protest, he added, "We've got to see if they can take care of our sniper problem."

That seemed to mollify the sergeant.

Troy flicked to the platoon net and subvocalized to the AI, "Sifuentes, Troy, connect to platoon commander."

179

The comms AI ran its voice match and verified he was, in fact, Lance Corporal Troy Sifuentes, then patched him through to Second Lieutenant Horvath.

"What's your situation, Sifuentes?" the lieutenant asked before Troy could say anything. "I'm still working on finding out who might be on that hill. S2 says no way it's the Trikes, and S3 can't find out if it's Force. We need you to bypass whoever it is and get on with the mission. The CO's getting on my ass about it."

"We've hit a problem. Whoever the sniper is shot Sergeant Van Meter."

"Van Meter? Shit. Wait one while I pull up his specs." Troy gave the sergeant a smile of encouragement while he waited. It took a long minute before the lieutenant was back with, "His vitals are strong, but he's been juiced to the gills. He's not combat effective."

No shit, Lieutenant.

Troy lowered his voice to a bare whisper and said, "I think we need to CASEVAC him, ma'am."

The lieutenant hesitated, then said, "Let me check. I'm not sure we've got the resources. The grunts are heavily engaged all along the First Division's front." Again, Troy waited, this time reaching out to put a hand on his sergeant's leg.

"What's going on, Tee?" Rabbit asked over the DM.

"Hold on. I'm on with the lieutenant. I'll get back to you."

"That's a negative on the CASEVAC, Sifuentes," the lieutenant passed. "Sergeant Van Meter is stable, and the CASEVAC birds are needed elsewhere. You're in charge now, and you're to proceed with your mission."

That wasn't what Troy wanted to hear. Him in charge? This was his first time in combat, and this was his first real-time mission, something other than building defensive positions and laying mines. And what about their friend up on the hill?"

"Uh . . . Lieutenant, we can't move forward. We've got the sniper up there. Can you get us some support?"

"That's a negative on that. You're in an RFA, and the fire support coordinator will not request authorization for a strike there unless we know for sure that the sniper is a Trike."

"He shot Sergeant Van Meter, ma'am," Troy snapped. "I think he's the enemy."

He was seething. He didn't care if they were in a Restricted Fire Area. He didn't care if that was another Marine or a Tricameral soldier who somehow was already on this side of the river. Whoever it was, they'd shot the sergeant, and they had to be suppressed.

"I know how you feel, Sifuentes. But it is what it is. You're almost at the bridge. Maneuver how you can to get there, then see if you can use the bridge itself for cover. I'll keep working on the sniper issue from my side. Understand?"

"Yes, ma'am," Troy said, biting back what he really wanted to say.

"And Sifuentes, I should give you a head's up. The situation is fluid. Very fluid. The Trikes look like they are in fact trying to flank First Division, so we need that bridge down. Sergeant Yellen's already rigged the Harris Ford Bridge, so, it's only yours that's left."

"Roger that. We'll get moving."

Troy sat for a moment, gathering his thoughts. If the Tricamerals were trying to flank the Marines, then taking down the Spire Bridge was paramount. First Marine Division was engaged with the Tricameral Ninth and Fifteenth Cohorts down on the Plains of David. The cohorts outnumbered the entrenched Marines, and if they were able to move through the mountains to the north of the plains and get into the Marines' rear, that could change the course of the war. One of the grunt battalions was holding the main bridge over the Hesperia River, but up here in the hills, there weren't enough units to hold the Harris Ford and Spire bridges, the only two other crossings on this side of the Sawtooth Range. Division decided to prepare both bridges for destruction should the Tricamerals try and cross them.

Sniper or not, Troy had to rig the bridge. The question was how could he do it.

"Rabbit, do you have eyes on the hill?"

"I would if I raised my head up, but that fucker would take me out. Why? What're we doing?"

"They're not CASEVACing Sergeant Van Meter. They say he's stable, and we've got to rig the bridge anyway. They're also not going to give us any support for the sniper—"

"What the fuck? Why the hell not?"

"Because they think he's one of us."

"Who's got us pinned down!"

"I know, but that's the way it is. I'm going to take Nichols and do a little recon. I think we can get to the bridge without him getting a shot at us. I'm going to leave the sergeant here—"

"And you want me to come over there and stay with him," she said.

"No. I want you to stay there, and if the sniper spots us, give us some covering fire."

Troy loved Rabbit to death, but she always assumed she was right, and she was never shy about sharing her position.

"What about the sergeant?"

"They say he'll be fine. They're monitoring his readouts."

"Well, OK. If you think that's the way to do it. You want me to just sit here until that guy fires on you, then try and light him up?"

"That's the plan."

"Pretty sucky plan."

Don't I know it?

"Get ready, Nichols. You and I are going to do a recon. If we can, we'll rig the bridge."

"What about Sergeant Van Meter?" he asked, nodding at the NCO who was now mumbling to himself.

"The El-Tee says he's stable." Troy leaned over the sergeant and said, "Sergeant, Nichols and I are going to recon the bridge. You stay here, OK?"

"The bridge?" The word seemed to break through his happy haze. He struggled to sit up. "I'm coming."

Both Nichols and Troy pushed the sergeant back down. "No, you stay here. The El-Tee ordered it, OK? You understand?"

Sergeant Van Meter looked at him with a confused look.

"You stay here and monitor the net, Sergeant. Wait for the lieutenant."

Sergeant Van Meter furrowed his brow as he tried to concentrate, then he nodded and lay back down. Troy hoped he'd stay that way. The last thing he needed would be for the sergeant to get up and wander out into the road. He contemplated changing his mind and bringing Rabbit over, but that would leave them without a base of fire. Instead, he opened the medkit strapped to the sergeant's belt and flipped the selector to transport. The kit wouldn't do anything to endanger the sergeant, but it might up the happy-nanos. Probably knock him out.

"Got your enginkit?" he asked Nichols, who nodded and patted the engineer kit under his assault pack. "Then, let's move out."

Troy led the way, continually checking the trees to the left to make sure they had concealment. At one point, where the treeline faded back to the hill, the two Marines had to low-crawl up the ditch for 25 meters, but they made it to the edge of the bridgehead without drawing another shot. Troy hoped that meant the sniper had left, but he wasn't going to bet on that.

The Spire Bridge was a Sasumi bridge, with two main spires on either side with the bridge hanging from a series of interlocking W cables. Sasumi bridges were extremely strong and were usually formed where traffic was particularly heavy— not up in the mountains on a local highway. This was the first Sasumi bridge Troy had seen, but his en-pad had all the specs for knocking one of them down.

Troy pulled out his pad, scanned the bridge, then waited for the answer. He wasn't surprised that it wasn't the spires that would be his rigging points but rather the three nexus points. That was what Staff Sergeant Limba thought it would be during the mission brief. The spires might be the logical choice. Knock one down, and the integrity was gone. But the spires were made using the latest in braided-weld techniques and with high-strength materials. In other words, they were mighty hard to knock down, even with a combat engineer's bag of tricks.

"That's where we'll emplace the charges," he told Nichols, showing him the readout.

"What about the sniper? He's not going to let us just walk across the bridge and lay the charges."

Troy glanced up the hill. He wished he knew exactly where the sniper was, but no matter what, Nichols was right. If he could engage the sergeant and him on the road, he could engage them on the bridge. Suddenly, Troy felt a certainty that was exactly the unseen sniper's mission. He'd been inserted into Marine-held territory with the mission to protect the bridge . . . which meant the Tricamerals were going to try to envelop the Marines.

But they might still have time. It would only take them 30 minutes to emplace the charges.

"We'll wait here for a bit to see if the FSC can get permission to light up the hill," he told the private. "Let me tell Rabbit what's going on, then we'll plan this out."

The two spent the next twenty minutes planning their emplacement. One nexus would blow a chunk out of the bridge, but the rest might still stand. Two would almost assuredly take down the entire thing. His en-pad recommended four of the B53 charges per nexus. The B53s were small, but powerful high-speed explosives that cut structures. Each engineer carried three of them, and Troy wanted to kick himself. Sergeant Van Meter had already told him the bridge would require eight, and between the two of them, Nichols and he only had six. He should have taken Sergeant Van Meter's.

He was about to go back himself when he remembered the lesson in the NCO course, which he took online, that stressed delegation. They both didn't have to go back, and he felt better with him prepping the B53s than letting Nichols do it, so he sent the private back to fetch the sergeant's charges.

He sent Nichols on his way and had prepped five of the charges when the lieutenant came back on the net, "Lance Corporal Sifuentes, give me a sitrep. How far along are you?"

"I'm at the bridgehead. I've got five charges prepped, and we're waiting to see if the FSC can get permission to give us some help with the sniper."

"Damnit, Sifuentes! I didn't tell you to wait. We've got confirmation that the Trikes are on the move. You've got maybe half an hour before they're at your pos. I've given Sergeant Yellen's team the order to blow their bridge, and we need to see yours down, too."

"What about the sniper, ma'am?"

"If the sniper is still there, then work around them. Just get it done. I'm sending the platoon sergeant up to you now, but I don't think there'll be time before the Trikes get there. Just get it done, Sifuentes. I'm counting on you."

"Roger that, ma'am. I've got it."

But do I?

He looked down at the bridge, the first anchor just five meters from him. He wasn't sure how much of the bridge the sniper had covered, but he had to assume the entire length of the roadbed was.

Can I go underneath?

Nichols came up behind Troy, making him jump.

"How's Sergeant Van Meter?"

"He's out cold but looks OK. I just took his entire kit," the private said, holding it up for him to see.

"Good, we may need it. We just got the order to blow the bridge."

"Are they going to hit the sniper?"

"Nope. She told us to work around it, whatever that means."

Troy thought the lieutenant was OK for an officer, but he was feeling somewhat resentful toward her at the moment. It wasn't her ass out here on the line.

Private Nichols didn't say anything, and it took a moment for Troy to realize that the private was waiting for orders. He was waiting for the senior Marine to take charge.

Shit, that's me. Come on, Troy. Do your damned job.

"OK, this is what we're going to do. That blasted sniper's still up there, and he's not going to let us waltz on down there and emplace the 53s. So, we're going under. There're beams we can use to make our way, and the bridge itself will give us cover. Let me brief Lance Corporal Babieux."

He switched to the DM. "Rabbit, we've got the order to blow the thing. The Trikes are on the way."

"What about the sniper?"

Just let me talk, Rabbit! Stop interrupting.

"That's what I want you to take care of. Look, once he sees us, we're going to grab his attention. You start scanning the hillside for him, and if he tries to move into position to hit us, take the bastard out."

"Where should I look?"

"I don't know, Rabbit," he said, letting a little bit of his frustration show through. "Look where you'd be if you were a sniper."

"I'm not a sniper. I'm a fucking engineer," she countered.

Troy ignored her. He'd told her what to do, and now it was up to her. He loved Rabbit like a sister, but sometimes, he just wished she wasn't so ornery.

"First, we've got to get under the bridge," he told Nichols.

From where they were in the drainage ditch, they were a good 20 meters down the slope to where the highway started lifting off the ground to form the bridge. The ground continued on for another ten or fifteen meters until the edge of the cliff face. Twenty meters was a long way to scramble down and still maintain control—too quickly, and they could stumble, and it was a long 140 meters to the river below.

More pertinent to their safety was the fact that 20 meters of unsure footing would give the sniper time to engage them. Troy's only hope was that he was still scanning the highway, searching them out there.

"You ready?" he asked Nichols, and when the private nodded, he passed to Rabbit, "We're going now. Cover us."

He put his hand on Nichol's shoulder, then said, "One . . . two . . . THREE!"

He jumped up out of the ditch and ran down the rocky slope, expecting any second another round to hit him right in the back. Nichols scrambled down behind him. Troy reached the edge of the cliff and darted under the bridge when the expected shot finally sounded. Troy half-fell, half-dove for the cover of the bridge's roadbed, landing hard. He started laughing in relief as Nichols tumbled on top of him.

"I guess we're too fast for him, right, Nichols?" he asked.

The private didn't answer, and as Troy slid out from under him, he said, "I think he got me."

All levity gone, Troy turned to Nichols, who was on his side, breathing heavily. "Where're you hit?"

Nichols pointed toward his back, and Troy turned him over. The private's armor shell was shattered, and blood was spreading across the magnetorheological layer next under the shell. Troy released the catches, and the armor fell away. Nichol's back was torn up from just under the scapula down to the lower back, and Troy's breath caught in his throat. It looked bad. Carefully, he pulled away the private's utility blouse, then used it to wipe away the blood. To his surprise, there was no gaping entrance wound, just several small punctures, as if he'd been hit with a grenade.

Troy might not be a grunt, but he knew the sound of a rifle versus a grenade launcher, and the sniper was using a rifle . . . a big one.

"You guys OK?" Rabbit passed. "I didn't see anything."

"Wait one, Rabbit. Nichols was hit, and I'm checking him out now." He turned back to the private and said, "It's not so bad, Nichols. Hold still and let me look."

He poked one of the entrance wounds, eliciting a grunt of pain from the private, but he couldn't feel anything there. He tried another and felt something hard. A quick dig with his fingers, and he popped out a piece of metal, turning it over a few times before he realized what it was.

"Hell, Nichols, the round shattered when it hit your armor. You're one lucky son of a bitch."

"Lucky? I don't feel lucky. It hurts like hell."

"Yeah, lucky. You saw what it did to Sergeant Van Meter. That asshole's using something big, and if the round had held together, you'd have a giant hole in your back right now. I don't know why or how it shattered, but like I said, you're lucky."

Troy checked Nichols' medkit. He was being pumped with anti-infection nanos, but the shock meds and pain meds were at the minimum level. Troy started to dial them up, then hesitated.

"Nichols, I need you here with me. Can you handle the pain?"

There was a long pause, then, "I think I can."

Troy gave him a little pat, then said, "Good. I need you."

Troy pulled out his enginkit, then removed his three B53s and placed them on the ground in a line. He added Nichols's and two of Sergeant Van Meter's. Eight B53s—they should be enough for the job. As an afterthought, he added the sergeant's last one. Better safe than sorry. Then he added the gecko pads so he could attach them.

The next step was to arm the detonator. All Marine Corps field explosives used the MCBM-4, the "McBoom," to detonate the charges. Simple and almost Marine-proof, it had to be synched with the explosives first for it to work. Troy touched it to each of the receptor pads on the charges, making sure the indicator light turned green before moving to the next one.

"OK, you know how to use this?" he asked Nichols once the detonator was synched to all the charges.

"Yes. We used them in—"

"This is a manual detonator," Troy said, cutting the private off. He knew Nichols had been trained with them at Camp Wachika, the Marine engineer school, but the guy was a boot, and it could be his ass on the line. "This lever here is in the safe position. If anything happens to me, or if the Trikes start coming over, you're going to have to push it down, then to the right," he explained, miming the action. "That will make it hot. Then, you push the detonation switch."

"What's going to happen to you?"

"I don't know. But if anything happens, you get out from under here and detonate it."

Troy didn't want to think about the possibilities of what could happen. But with a sniper on the hill, a Tricameral unit on the way, and a 140-meter fall, well, his imagination could fill in the blanks.

He emptied his kit of everything he didn't need and placed the synched M53s back inside, making sure they were secure. He didn't need to be dropping any of them.

With a glance toward the hill, he shifted to his right and looked up into the understructure. His armor would make climbing difficult, so he shucked it. With whatever the sniper was using, the armor was barely effective at best, and a fall from this height would be deadly. He slung his enginkit again, then reached up to grab one of the cross girders under the bridge. The movement made his shoulder bark out in pain, and he momentarily considered giving himself a jolt of pain-killers, but this was going to be tricky, and he wanted to be in full control of both mind and body. Ignoring the pain, he pulled himself up into the understructure.

Most of the support for the bridge structure was from the cables, but the road itself needed to be supported from the bridge. A series of girders and beams provided that support. The main loadbearing ones were typical H-shaped girders with a horizontal bottom connected to the top by a vertical piece— from his engineering classes, he dredged up that the horizontal parts were called flanges, and the vertical were called webs. Each side of the bottom flange extended a good 18 or 20 centimeters out from the web. Between them were smaller, supporting beams. Troy was going to have to traverse the support beams to get to the nexus points.

"What's your status, Sifuentes?" the lieutenant came onto the net.

Just what I need now.

"Emplacing the charges now, ma'am."

"You're running out of time. Forward elements are less than three klicks away."

"Roger that. I'm working on it," he snapped with more emphasis than he'd intended.

The lieutenant must have heard the tone and didn't reply. Troy shook it off and stepped for the girder. The space was tight, but doable. He managed the first three easily, bad shoulder and all, until he was out over the edge of the cliff and the structure changed. The girders got smaller, and the space above the crossbeams disappeared. He couldn't walk over them.

He didn't like what he was going to have to do next, but there was no choice. He was going to have to go under the beams.

Troy leaned forward, grabbing each side of the girder, then let his legs fall free. He swung forward until his legs reached up in front of him. Desperately, he tried to lodge his heels on the edges of the girder. His right heel caught, but his left slipped off. He started to panic, but he forcibly calmed himself, reaching up with his left leg and hooking the edge of his heel above the girder's bottom.

Hanging ass-down like some sort of baby sloth gripping his mother, he wasn't really locked in, though. If his hands slipped, his heels wouldn't hold him, and he'd be in for a long fall.

Troy walked his hands forward, one after the other, about 40 centimeters. Then, gripping as tightly as he could, he pushed with his feet, extending them and advancing his body.

Only ten more of these and I'm at the first nexus. Easy peasy.

Once, twice more, he edged forward. His bad shoulder was barking at the abuse, and his forearms began to shake, but he had no choice. He had to push across.

"What's going on, Tee?" Rabbit asked on the DM.

"Not now!" he said.

He really didn't need the distraction. Slowly but surely, he made progress. Five more meters to the nexus, four, then three. He looked under his arms to see how close he was, and the slight twist of his body was enough to lose his footing. First, the right heel slipped, immediately followed by the left. His body swung down in an arc as he desperately hung on with his hands.

Somehow, he held on, his body swinging like a pendulum. He tried to swing his heels back up, but he could barely get them halfway, and each kick threatened to knock loose his grip. He was focused on the transom a little more than a meter away when a lone shot rang out, and a round hit the web, spraying his fingers with tiny bits of the environmental coating. Spurred into action, he hand-over-handed it forward, reaching the transom where a small diagonal strut braced it against the large vertical post. He swung his feet up, and with them wedged in, he was able to take the weight off his failing hands. Another round hit the edge of the beam, and exhaustion forgotten, he scrambled up on top of the transom and back into the guts of the truss system.

This was only the first nexus, and by almost falling, he'd been spotted by the sniper. Any more mistakes, he'd be dead meat. Perched like a gargoyle, he swung his kit around and pulled out the first four M53s. He slapped the four charges onto the cable connectors, the gecko pads holding them securely emplaced. It was almost too easy after the climb he made to get there.

One down, one more to go.

At least if something happened to him now, Nichols could take down one nexus point and put a gap in the bridge. But he still had one more to rig if he wanted to knock down the entire bridge.

The beam at the nexus point was larger, and Troy was able to step over the girder. But then it went back to the previous structure, and once again, Troy had to swing underneath and crawl along the support beams, all the time afraid that the sniper had moved his position and had him in his sights.

He was glad he'd ditched the armor and glad he'd already gotten rid of four of the M53s. He wasn't sure he'd have the strength lugging the extra weight. At least he could relieve his arms for a moment at each girder. Not for long, however. He had to rig the last point and get back before the Tricamerals came up the road.

His shoulder was beyond screaming when he reached the last nexus point. He had to expose his head for a second to look up and confirm he was at the right spot. He attached the final five, then brought Nichols on the team net and told him the bridge was rigged. It was up to the private to blow it.

Time to get back!

He contemplated swinging himself up and running back on top of the bridge in one mad dash, but he'd be sniper bait if he did so. Without armor, he wouldn't stand a chance if he was hit.

No, as much as he hated the idea, he had to go back the way he came. Eleven more times, he dropped under the beam and edged his way along, eleven times that his hands cramped up and his arms screamed. The only saving grace was that his abused shoulder was numb. In the end, it was his feet that failed him. As he reached the edge of solid ground, he looked up, and his right leg slipped. He managed to hang on long enough with his hands to start swinging, giving him just enough momentum to kip him over to the ground where he tottered for a second, in danger of going over, before Nicholls grabbed him and yanked him to safety.

He was paralyzed, his muscles cramping, but giddy that he'd made it. He'd hung on by pure force of will. But at least it was over. A simple detonation and the mission would be a success.

"Thanks, Nichols. You saved my ass, but how about we blow this damned thing now?"

Troy brought Rabbit and the lieutenant up to speed as he and Nichols went to the other side, away from the sniper, and low-crawled 15 meters past the edge of the bridge. It was too close for safety. As the bridge went down, the spire could take out a chunk of the supporting ground with it, and that extended to where they were. But Troy also thought it was too dangerous to try and reach the drainage ditch. The sniper would be ready, and even after donning his armor again, Troy wasn't at all confident that it could protect him.

"You want the honors?" Troy asked Nichols.

"Really, you'd let me do it?" the private said, his eyes lighting up.

"Sure. You took a sniper round in the back, and you saved me from going over. I think you earned it."

Nichols pulled the detonator out of his pack. He looked at Troy, who nodded, and with sure hands, armed it. Both Marines turned to the bridge as Nichols detonated the charges. Two huge explosions rocked the bridge . . . which stayed intact.

"What the . . ." Nichols started, astounded.

As was Troy. The bridge was supposed to go down. His engineer pad, the bible of all things engineering, had said it would go down. He'd even added an extra charge. But his eyes weren't deceiving him. The bridge was up. There was a wrinkle of sorts at the nearest nexus point, but the bridge was intact.

"What's going one?" the lieutenant broke in. "I see the detonation on my display, but it looks like the bridge is still up."

"It's still up, ma'am,"

"What the hell did you do wrong, Sifuentes?" she almost screeched.

"Nothing, Lieutenant. I did it by the book!" he protested, getting angry.

"Staff Sergeant Limba, you've got to get a move on and fix this mess," she passed on the open platoon net. "You've got . . . oh, hell. The Trikes are five minutes out. Sifuentes, you'd better come up with something right now—"

Troy tuned her out. He stared dumbly at the bridge. It should be down, but it wasn't. He knew he'd done nothing wrong. Rabbit still had three M53s, and maybe they would work on one nexus point now that it was damaged, but no way he could go back and emplace them in five minutes.

He started going through what he had in his kit while the lieutenant railed on. The B88. No. Not big enough. T-chord? Great for trees and smaller-diameter metals and ceramics. No way against the bridge. The B20s? Too slow . . .

Wait a minute!

The B20 filled with x-pyre, a nano-thermite mixture that burned much slower than a monomolecular explosive but with extreme power-to-density. This made it perfect for moving things like buildings, bunkers, dirt . . . and rock.

Troy looked back to the nearest spire. It stood some 40 meters or so tall, coming down until it split 15 meters up to straddle the road. Both sides of the split then disappeared into cerrocrete stanchions that were buried into the cliff face. The B20 wouldn't touch the spire itself and probably the stanchion as well. But what if . . .

"Rabbit, I need your B20s now. Come down the drainage ditch and meet us under the bridge," he passed, before turning to Nichols and saying, "Prep the B20s. All of them."

Troy didn't have time for a full analysis. He stepped back and examined the area. He stood on loose-packed dirt on top of solid rock, this world's answer to granite. Granite was brittle, not ductile. It had been cut for the highway and then to drop the stanchions. From the stanchions, it dropped gradually to the edge of the cliff that Troy had almost gone over, where the drop steepened for 20 or 30 meters down before the sheer cliff took over.

"Here, here, here, and here," he told Nichols, indicating spots on the ground. "Use your powerpick and get the B20s in the rock, ten centimeters deep."

Thirty centimeters would be better, but there was no time.

He bent slung his own enginkit around to get his powerpick out when the sniper fired again. Troy ducked down, but the shot wasn't targeting him. He looked up to see Rabbit pelting down the middle of the road, enginkit in hand.

"Rabbit, get in the ditch," he yelled.

She caught his eyes, a sardonic smile on her face. She gave a tiny shake of her head as her legs pumped to close the distance. The next shot caught her low in the hip, a spray of pink exploding in the air as she tumbled bonelessly face-first to the ground. She hit hard, bounced once, and fell over the edge of the road.

"Rabbit!" Troy screamed, taking a step forward to rush to her aid when her enginkit came flying over the edge of the road and sailed to him, landing just a few meters away on the edge of the highway.

"Forget about me. Take down the bridge," Rabbit's weak voice followed the kit.

Troy stopped. He knew she'd been hit, and it looked bad, but he still had his mission. Marine lives depended on taking down the bridge, and she knew that better than he did. The sniper hadn't fired at her again. No need to—she was out of the equation. He wasn't, however. Troy choked down his emotions and started digging boreholes with his powerpick. Tears threatened to cloud his vision, but he wiped his eyes and drilled, trying not to think of Rabbit bleeding out.

The lieutenant was trying to reach him, but he muted her. He didn't have time.

Eight B20s. Would they be enough? Was he emplacing them correctly? He couldn't second guess himself as he synched each one and slid them into the holes. Within a minute, six were ready. That left Rabbit's two, just at the edge of the road, where the sniper undoubtedly had them zeroed in.

"Nichols, take this," he said, handing him the McBoom. "If that asshole gets me, set the charges off, and run like hell."

He edged to where the roadbed still gave him cover. He could almost reach the kit, just a couple of meters in front of him. But he was also sure that the sniper was waiting for that.

"Here goes nothing," he muttered as he stepped out, then immediately jerked back an instant before a round cut the air centimeters past his head.

His feint had proved his point. If he tried to get the kit, he was a dead man. He thought he needed it, however.

"Lance Corporal Sifuentes!" Nichols shouted, catching his attention. The private pointed back down the bridge.

It was only then that the low hum of armor registered with Troy. The Tricamerals were almost at the bridge. There was no time left.

Troy knelt and pulled out his 2020 line. Lightweight, it had tremendous tensile strength. But the line itself wasn't going to do much. He needed a hook, but there were none in his enginkit. The best he could find was a set of nonreactive pliers. They would have to do. He pulled them from their loop and tied one handle to the line and left the other spread open.

"Give me two more bores five meters downhill from the centers. Make them as deep as you can," he yelled over his shoulder at Nichols, as he judged the distance to the kit. With the armor approaching, he wasn't going to get many chances at this.

Swinging the pliers on the end of the line, he built up some momentum and let them fly. They sailed beautifully over the kit, the line falling on top. Surprised at his success, Troy started carefully reeling the line back, slowing down as the pliers reached it. The open handle caught on the kit's straps and nudged it toward him, but his heart dropped as the pliers slipped free . . . just as the sniper fired again, his round hitting dead center on the kit and sending it skipping backward . . . and over the edge of the road.

Troy stared at the kit in shock. The idiot had shot the kit out of his line of sight, and that meant he couldn't target it anymore. Troy couldn't believe his luck. He dropped to his belly, inched up, and hooked one of the straps with his finger. He edged back down, Rabbit's kit in is possession.

As soon as he could sit up, he pulled out her two B20's, ran to Nichols to retrieve the detonator and synched them. Twenty seconds later, the two were in their holes.

"Keep low and get the hell out of here," he told Nichols, pointing to the east. The sniper may or may not have a shot at him, but it was the best he could tell the young Marine.

The bridge shook above his head. The Tricameral armor had arrived.

"This had better work," he said.

He took five steps to the east, just beyond the edge of the array he'd laid, then as Nichols limped away, he whispered a little prayer and detonated the charges.

Dirt and dust plumed out of the holes, but the bulk of the blasts were directed farther in. The entire ground around the stanchions shook as if punched by some giant as the rock structure was fractured. Troy stood there for a long moment, his hopes fading when with an audible crack, more of the rock split, sending the ground under Troy downhill half a meter.

"Run!" he yelled at Nichols, only ten meters beyond him as he turned to follow suit.

He managed one step when the brittle granite—that huge beautiful slab of granite—gave way. The ground swept him off his feet as the cliff face started sliding down. Joy turned to panic as he tried to crawl to safety, and he was spun around, just in time to see the stanchion start to slide, the massive bulk no longer held up on one side by solid rock. Despite the danger, as he slid farther down the cliff face, he stared in awe as the south spire gallantly tried to hold firm, but just as Troy was no longer in control, neither was the spire. Almost in slow motion, it fell, twisting to the west as the roadbed itself acted as an anchor. Fifty meters of spire slammed into the hillside on the west, clearing trees like a scythe through winter wheat before it bounced twice and disappeared over the side.

Troy kept scrambling on the moving pile of rock as it slid downhill, but his eyes were on the bridge. With the spire gone, half of the bridge immediately went with it. Cables snapped like guitar strings, and the rest followed, along with the first two Tricameral APCs as they started their short journey to the river below.

Troy wanted to cheer, but even on the edge of the broken cliff face, he was quickly approaching the long drop as well to join the two APCs. With a last mad scramble, he somehow managed to grab the branch of a tree that leaned out over the sliding hillside, half of its root system caught in the rockfall, half still in solid ground.

The rocks and dirt grabbed at him like a riptide determined to take him out. The branch cracked and bent, and the tree leaned farther and farther over as it fought to remain in place. Troy hung on for dear life, dredging up prayers that he'd long forgotten, making promises to a god he hadn't considered in years. Whether it was the prayers, whether it was the promises to lead a better life, or whether it was just the way things worked out, the flow stopped.

Afraid to let go, Troy twisted around to look. At the base of the bridge where the cliff had been, there was now a gaping hole, some five or six meters deep, a gouge running to the now lower cliff face. The stanchion was gone, torn from its previous home and now somewhere far below. The southern spire was gone. He turned to look across the gap. The northern spire was still standing, as was a good ten meters or so of bridge. An APC was on that remaining section, the crew cautiously climbing out. Soldiers on foot were swarming forward, and Troy realized that he was in a pretty precarious position. He was an easy target, fewer than 120 meters away.

He tried to pull himself up, but that caused the tree to jerk and lean forward even more. Troy froze, afraid to do more when a hand reached out. Private Nichols was leaning out, one hand grabbing the next tree over, the other stretched to him.

With a final lunge, Troy grabbed the hand, and with Nichol's help, scrambled to safety.

Shouts from across the gap caught their attention. They turned to see several soldiers pointing at them. Without a word, both of them jumped back into the concealment of the trees.

"Again, you saved my ass, Nichols," Troy said as he pulled the private to a stop once they had some concealment.

"That was pretty fucking amazing, Lance Corporal Sifuentes. You were scrambling on top of the rock like it was solid ground."

That wasn't how he remembered it.

"It's Tee. They call me Tee. And what was your nickname in bootcamp? Did you have one?" Troy asked.

"Uh . . . my friends call me Digger."

"OK, Digger, let's go see what happened to Rabbit."

They slowly made their way through the trees, keeping out of sight of both the sniper and the troops on the other side. They didn't have to go south far, but they kept low on their bellies as they approached the road. As the adrenaline dissipated, Troy felt new cuts and scrapes he'd manage to accumulate in the blast.

They reached the edge of the trees, and Troy cautiously called out, "Rabbit, you still there?" afraid he'd hear nothing.

"Where the fuck do you think I'd be? Get your ass over here and make sure this damned medkit is working. I don't think it's giving me the right painkillers."

"Sshhh! You'll give away your position to the sniper. Just hold on, and we'll figure out how to get to you."

"Sniper? I guess you didn't see. Look up on the hillside, where the spire cleared it."

Troy didn't know what she was talking about, so he raised his head to look at the mess of torn-up trees, bushes, and mostly furrowed dirt.

"Right there," Digger said, pointing.

Troy squinted his eyes. There was something there, a bundle that he couldn't make out. He pulled his binos out of his enginkit and focused in. The sniper, or what was left of him, was in a twisted pile in the dirt. His back was twisted in a way in which a human body was not designed to be. It didn't look like the kind of place that would have served as a sniper hide, but maybe the guy had been making his way down so he could fire upon them under the bridge. If that had been his plan, he'd waited too long.

"Damn, the spire smashed his ass," Troy said in awe.

Without the sniper, Troy felt better about making a dash to Rabbit. The soldiers on the other side of the bridge hadn't taken them under fire yet.

On "three," the two bolted for the drainage ditch, diving in beside a Rabbit who looked about ready to bite someone's head off. She'd managed to get a pressure patch on her hip. There was a lot of blood showing from the edges of the pack, but as long as it was on, Troy couldn't see how much damage there was.

"Hey, these are happy nanos," Troy said as he checked her medkit. It was pumping her full. "You're not happy."

"Eat me," she said. "I don't think it's working."

"Sure is. You're just a natural-born asshole," Troy said, a smile on his face. He'd been afraid of what he'd find, but this was the Rabbit he knew and loved.

"What's wrong with you, Boot?" she asked Digger, directing some of her ire at him. "You're standing there gawking like a little old lady."

"Digger took a round in the back, but he's OK," Troy said.

Rabbit raised an eyebrow at his use of a nickname, but if Troy said the boot was no longer a boot, then that was that.

"And so, what do we do now, oh fearless leader?" she asked him.

Troy raised his head to look across the highway. Sergeant Van Meter was in the ditch on the other side. The sniper might be gone, but there was a passel of Tricameral soldiers on the other side of the bridge, pissed off soldiers. With the sergeant cocooned up, there wasn't much any of the three could do for him now, and they certainly couldn't take on the enemy troops.

He pulled up the platoon net and connected with the lieutenant.

"The bridge is down, Lieutenant, along with two APCs. The Trikes are on the other side, pissed, but stopped in their tracks. We've done our job. How about sending up our damned infantry now to clean up the rest of this mess and get us out of here?"

Jonathan P. Brazee

THE PUMPKIN ACE

Gracie Medicine Crow has proven to be one of my readers' favorite characters, but I think Floribeth Salinas O'Shea Dalisay has her beat. Readers seem to love the diminutive Navy fighter pilot. There are four, soon to be five books on her, and one of them, Fire Ant, was the 2018 Nebula Award Finalist for best novella.

This story was originally published in Bob's Bar 2 in a slightly different form, and the action is again described in the novel, Ace. In this version, Beth has been transported to a bar in the multiverse where she is telling a sea story to characters from some of my friends' novels.

****

Beth, looked at the expectant eyes, waiting for her "sea story," as the robotic bartender had called them. While she still hadn't figured out what Artur was, the others around the table were pretty high on the food chain, and she was a petty officer, an enlisted sailor. The tall blonde was an admiral. The general rode some kind of magic plane. Heck, there was a queen and a princess among them. High society for a girl from New Cebu.

But hell, none of them is a Navy fighter pilot, and fighter pilots kick ass and take names. See what they'd do facing a flight of FALs in their crystal fighters. If they want a story, I'll give them one!

I can tell them about . . . no, the statute of limitations isn't up on that one.

Beth still couldn't grasp exactly who the other people were. She didn't think they were from her universe, if that was even possible, and that should send up all sorts of flares, but it didn't really bother her. Even if they were from a different universe or dimension, she wasn't going to take the chance that one of the officers might be able to reach back into her universe and report her up the chain.

So, what to tell . . .

"I'm Petty Officer Second Class Floribeth Salinas O'Shea Dalisay, Navy of Humankind, and I'm a fighter pilot. My callsign is Fire Ant, and my ride is the *Tala II*."

"Feck me, that's a mouthful," Artur remarked.

"You might not want to know that one of my LTs has been dubbed Anteater," Ridge said. "There might be comments if you flew in the same squadron together."

"You sure you're big enough to reach your fighter's pedals?" BA said with a laugh.

Kelsey, who was only slightly taller than Floribeth, glared at BA. "We folks on the smaller side can start at the ankles and wear you down just fine."

Rika laughed and winked at the two women. "I'm about your height—when my legs are pulled off."

"I bet you're pretty popular with the guys when they are," Floribeth said.

"Well, anyway, my brother was getting hitched, to my best friend and wingman Mercy. Mercy Hamlin. Callsign Red Devil. With the war footing and all, leave was canceled for the duration, or at least until we could stand up a fourth Mike squadron."

"What's a Mike squadron?" Cain asked.

"The premier Navy one-seater is the Wasp, but the FALs were making mincemeat out of them," she said soberly. "We were losing lots of good pilots. Most were flying the FX6 Indias and Kilos, which are good birds, but outclassed by the crystals. I was flying the Mikes, though, the best Wasp ever made. We didn't have very many yet, only enough for three squadrons, and it was our mission to hold back the tide until all the new fighters and capital ships were online and we could really take it to the FALs."

"Wait a minute, you're losing me. Is it universal that fleet speaks in code?" Cain wondered. Brutus rolled to his back and gazed at Floribeth.

Beth stopped, then with a slight roll of her eyes, answered in the tone of a mother explaining gravity to a four-year-old. "The crystals are the alien race that's pushing out through the spiral arm. We didn't know much about them. Hell, we still don't know much about them, but they want our planets, and they take them by force."

"And the 'FALs?'"

"'Fucking aliens.' That's what we call them in the Navy"

"Hah," Amanda laughed.

"Once again, so glad we have no aliens," Rika added.

Kelsey gave the woman two thumbs up.

Bethany Anne raised her drink. "I have to agree to the shorthand."

"So, if you're all caught up, can I go on?" she asked, looking at the others. They nodded, so she continued.

"So, anyway, like I was saying, we were stuck on the *Victory*, no leave authorized for the duration. But Mercy got her ass shot up, and she was in rehab back on Innamincka Station until her nerves knitted, so she put in a special request for three days to get married. She and Rocky, my kid brother had met a year before, and well, you know how it is in war . . ."

"Fight today so you can live to see tomorrow. Fight like hell today or tomorrow may never come." Cain looked at his drink with a solemn expression on his face.

"That's why I married Talbot. Take what joy you can today, because tomorrow might never come. Or worse, it might come and take you both forever."

"Yep, that's the way it is. Any day could be your last."

She shook her head, as if to clear memories of those no longer with her.

"Mercy was one of those rich kids, you know, with everything given to her. But she wanted to do something in her life on her own merits, so she joined the Navy, wrecking whatever plans her parents had for her. With the war and us sort of being heroes," she said, looking embarrassed for using the term, "they began to accept her. That's until she said she was going to marry Rocky."

Rika's brow furrowed. "Wait, it sounded like marriage was a good thing with your people. How does that make her unaccepted?" "Why? or words to that effect.

"You've got to understand, my family, well, the only way to make a decent living is to become an Off Planet Worker, taking factory jobs and working as maids for the rich folks, folks like Mercy's family. My dad did it for more than twenty years, spending time away just so we could go to school, so we could have a roof over our heads. And it killed him. He died, lightyears from home in a construction accident. So, for Mercy to marry a penniless . . . *servant* was not acceptable," she said, anger bubbling up through her voice. "So, the assholes disowned her. Just like that!" she said, snapping her fingers. "You can't just disown family. I mean, that's *family*! But they sure did."

"I wish I had family," Blackhawk said, the first comment he'd made other that when telling his story.

Floribeth nodded at him, a slight frown on her face before she continued. "She said screw them and decided to get married on New Cebu. My family, who was going to be her family now, was going to make sure she had a proper wedding. The whole kit and caboodle. And me being her best friend and Rocky's sister, she asked me to be her maid of honor."

Rika looked bored and asked, "So, your story is about being a maid of honor?"

"Seriously?" Kelsey asked. "Let her tell her story and be bored on your own time."

"Yes. I mean, no. That just sets the stage. I wasn't going to let my wingman and brother get married without me there. So, I asked the commander if I can get just one day on New Cebu, not even a full day, to be there. Commander Tuominen—he was the Stinger's CO—took it all the way up to Admiral Nzama, the task force commander, but she said no, she couldn't make any exception, not even for me."

"That's a long way to run it up the chain," Rika commented. "Bad ju ju to catch the Old Woman's eye."

Beth looked embarrassed, then in a quieter voice, said, "I was kind of a big thing, then. I was the first human to make contact with the FALs, back when I was a civilian scout, and then when I got pulled into the Navy, I sort of did OK."

Rika, gave her a long, pointed stare, eyebrows raised in question.

"I was tied with Capgun—that's Lieutenant Jim Caplan—for the most confirmed kills at four. One short of an ace, and there was, how did the Public Affairs Officer put it? 'Significant public interest in the 'Race to Ace.' There hadn't been a Navy ace in almost 200 years. That and my Platinum Star made carried some weight . . . but not enough for her to cut me a break. She turned my request down."

"Let me guess. You went UA," Cain said.

"Yeah. I mean no, not technically. I just sort of bent the rules a bit. It was Josh who thought of it. AT3 Joshua Frye, my plane captain. You see, I was pretty pissed. I mean, one frigging day? After over a year in the middle of the fight, I can't get a day? Give me a break.

"But while I'm bitching, he says there's something wrong with my synch comb. The readings aren't matching. Now, I know there's no way he's telling the truth. I mean, he loves the *Tala II* more than I do, and it's like he only *allows* me to borrow it and take it out into the black. He may be a strange duck, but he's the best plane captain in the squadron, maybe the entire Navy. He'd never let the *Tala* degrade that much. I started to protest, but he put his hand over my mouth to stop me.

"'I'm going to reset it. You're going to need to take it out for a couple of gate jumps to make sure it starts synching.'

"And I know what he's doing. He's giving me the excuse to go off on my own for a day . . . and it's only two gate jumps from Washburne IV to New Cebu. I can get in and get out before anyone knows it. Oh, they'd know later, but what are they going to do? Ground me when we need all the experienced pilots we can find? Or suspend me, letting Capgun become the first ace? That would piss off a lot of the indentured class who wanted one of their own to be the first.

"'So, when would you reset it?' I asked Josh."

"'Give me a day to try and find a workaround. If I can't, then the day after that,' he told me. 'Let me know what you want me to do.'

"Which was the day of the wedding. I already knew exactly what I wanted him to do, but I had to play the game. I got him to show me the numbers and pretended to study them. But I'm a pilot, not a tech, so I didn't know what the heck they meant. I just nodded and told him to try and fix the *Tala*, and if he couldn't, just reset the synch comb.

"I spent the rest of the day doing admin work before going to White Duck right after chow. White Duck had the concession for Station 3, the only non-military store there. Run by retired Lieutenant Commander Tracy Ruiz and her son, it was the sailors at the station's lone touch of civilian life—and it was the only place for receiving commercial orders. I downloaded the file Mercy had sent, entered my measurements, and printed out a bright orange, calf-length gown—my bridemaid's dress. I tried it on in the dressing room, and, as much as I love Mercy, her fashion sense sucked. The orange was bad enough, but from the strapless top down to about the knees, it puffed out in a bubble. I looked like a damned pumpkin. There wasn't much I could do about it, though, so I just paid for it and went back to my quarters where I stuffed it under my mattress.

Bethany Anne mused. "Bad fashion is the expectation for bridesmaids. I'm never sure if it is because the bride's fashion sense sucks, or the bride doesn't want to be upstaged."

"Knowing Mercy, even as much as I love her, I'd say you nailed it with the second reason," Floribeth said.

"Anyway, late the next day, I went into the Flight Ops to schedule my check flight. Of course, I went late enough that I couldn't go out that day—the Navy was hell bent on maintaining strict flight hours for routine flights. A check flight having to deal with transiting gates needed a minimum of three jumps. I only listed my first destination, the Pyrus System, one of the junction complexes with no fewer than forty-two other gates— one being to New Cebu. When he asked me for my next gate, I told him I'd see what the traffic was on the other side before I made that decision.

"That was a little out-of-the-ordinary, but not enough so to make him question it. He reminded me that I was dead-lined until the check flight, barring a FAL attack somewhere.

"That night, I lay awake, dreading an alert. Normally, I'm a little excited to go into action—scared, but excited. I wanted the FALs to pay for Lieutenant Hadley, for Hurl, and Trout. This time, I prayed that the bastards would take the night off. For once, the capricious gods of war had mercy on me, and I woke up bright and early for my check ride. I had my bridesmaid dress stuffed in my survival kit, and Josh had stashed the shoes inside the nose compartment. It was already 1200 local at Malapascua, my home village on New Cebu, and that meant I had about six hours to make it there. That would be cutting it tight, but it should be doable. The *Victory* was in orbit around Washburne IV, taking on supplies, and the station's gate was only a few light-seconds away. On the other side, transferring between gates at Pyrus would be quick. The longest delay would be after arriving through the New Cebu Gate. It would take me over an hour to land at the small shuttle port at Bogo, then catch a ride to Malapascua for the wedding.

"Josh was waiting for me, and he went over the entire pre-flight check-list, to include the synching procedures. I just wanted to get going, but even if he was helping me commit a potential court martial offense, the *Tala* was still his baby, and there were no cutting corners. I had to sit there and keep the grimace from my face until we completed the checklist.

"Finally, we were done, the yellow shirts ferried the *Tala* to the launch rails, and once given the release from the Flight Officer, we took off, slotting in our gate entry. The interesting thing about the Washburne IV gate is that it is multi-faceted. That means—"

"I hate to be the one who keeps asking, but when are you going to get to the good parts?" Rika asked.

Beth blushed, then said, "Sorry. I can get a little long-winded, I know. OK, to cut to the chase, I get to the Pyrus system, then track to the gate to New Cebu. I clear it with Gate Control, but I didn't report back to my command until ten seconds before entry.

"Well played," Rika chuckled. "Just on this side of asking for permission rather than forgiveness."

Floribeth gave a wry grin, but didn't deny the intent.

"I pop out in the New Cebu system, but the time is getting short. I didn't think I could land at the nearest shuttleport and catch a ride in time, but a Wasp can land anywhere, so I called up Mercy and told her to hang on, I was coming and would land just outside of town. Mercy, being Mercy, had a few choice words for me, but I think that was more nerves than anything else.

"Time was still getting tight, so I decided to cut some time while approaching the planet. I squirmed out of my flight suit—"

"In a fighter? A single-seat fighter? No fighter I know has that much room in it," Blackhawk said, his second comment since the others starting telling their tales.

"In case you didn't notice, I'm 4'6" in my bare feet and weigh 72 pounds. That's 33 kg and 137 cm. There was room," she said, sweeping a hand across her body. "It was tight, though.

Rika lifted her right arm, which still bore the body of her GNR-41C. "You realize you weigh less than this, right?"

"Maybe, Rika, but I'm a hell of a lot better looking than that thing.

"So, I start changing, and as soon as I'm in my birthday suit—"

"Ye mean naked?" Artur perked up.

Kelsey rolled her eyes.

"Yes, naked, if you must," Floribeth said, turning red. "As I was saying, as soon as I was *naked*, I get a call from my CO, over the visuals. I don't know what to do, so I just held up my flight suit in front of me and took the call.

"'Dalisay, where the hell are you?' I can see he's royally pissed, so I tell him, 'I'm at Quebec-Romeo-Papa-Four-Niner-Niner,' which is the G-Number for New Cebu, hoping he won't realize that.

"Kind of stupid on my part. Not much ever got past him.

"'And why are you at New Cebu?'"

"I'm doing my synch check, sir."

"'Any particular reason you picked New Cebu, other than your brother and Petty Officer 1 Hamlin are getting married there today?'"

"With all due respect, sir, I have authorization to use any gate that does not lead to a restricted area for my check flight."

"'And, of course, you're going to land on the planet?'"

"'If I wish to conduct an external check of the ship, I am authorized to land on any non-restricted planet or Navy ship to conduct said check,' I said, holding my breath. The CO was pretty cool, but he was a stickler for the regs."

"'You know just as well as I do that you planned this. I've already sent for AT3 Frye. If either of you have falsified records . . . suffice it to say, it won't be pretty. The instant you return from your check flight, I want you standing tall in front of me in my office.'"

Rika giggled and said, "Can you do that? I mean stand *tall*? Sorry, sorry, I couldn't resist."

Beth just rolled her eyes, then continued. "I was scamming the system, sure. And maybe Josh made up the problem with the synch comb, but even if it was a miliscosh out of alignment, he had ever right to reset it, and that required the check flight. And I had every right to choose New Cebu. But if they could prove that there was nothing wrong, then we'd probably get brig time before being discharged. I knew the CO liked me, but he'd do his duty, whatever he thought that was."

"He cut the connection, and I lowered my flight suit. He had to have seen that I was naked, at least from the waist up, but he'd never mentioned it.

"I wasn't going to be naked for long. I pulled out the orange dress with matching bra and panties, then started the contortions to get them on. It took five minutes, but at last, except for being barefoot, I was dressed as well as I could make it for the wedding."

"So, you're in a fighter in a civilian wedding dress?" Bethany Anne asked.

"Why not? People fly in space in civilian clothes all the time. The flight suit is to help with the Gs and protect us in case our cockpit is breached. I was just gliding in for a nice, easy landing, no high-speed maneuvering. I was already in the glidepath for entry and the *Tala* had taken over. I was hand's off, trying to apply a little makeup when the call came through.

"'Navy Foxtrot-six-mike-zero one-niner, this is New Cebu Control.'

"I tell you, my heart sunk. I figured the commander had contacted them to deny me landing rights. That didn't sound like him, but you can never tell with officers if they think you've dissed their authority.

"'This is Navy fighter Six- six-mike-zero one-niner on a check flight. What do you have for me?' I asked the system control, trying sound innocent."

"'Maybe nothing, Navy. We've just had some strange readings for the last hour, and we can't make heads nor tails of it. Then you popped in, and the director thought that since you're Navy, maybe you've seen this before or have better scanners.'"

"My heart skipped a beat, and a sense of foreboding swept over me. The person on the other side of the comms hadn't given me much, but still . . .

"Give me the coordinates, New Cebu. I'll check it out.

"'*Tala*, full sensor array,' I ordered, then sat there biting my lip as the systems came online. I'd only had nav, gate synch, and comms online. I wasn't on a combat mission, after all.

"It took about thirty seconds for the *Tala* to be completely operational. I inputted the coordinates and went right to the TSM-4, the main scanner array. I saw what was bothering them on the Kilting band. Nothing concrete, but a definite flux in the wave, something that shouldn't be there . . . and something heading straight to New Cebu, like a bow-wave of a torpedo closing in on a wet-water ship. The torpedo might not be visible, the bow-wave sure was.

"This was exactly what we'd seen at Niue, and before we'd figured it out, we'd lost four fighters. That was a quarter of the galaxy away, deep into the center, but I knew the two anomalies were FALs and their crystal ships.

"New Cebu Control, go to General Emergency Condition Alpha!" I shouted as I adjusted my course to bypass the planet and intercept the approaching ships. "And contact the Navy Command Center, give them my ship designator, my current heading, and tell them two Crystal ships have appeared in system."

"'Crystals? That's impossible. They're on the other side of the galaxy,'" the comms operator said."

"'Impossible or not,' I told him, 'They're on their freaking way to you right now. Just do what I told you!'"

"To be honest, I didn't know if the FALs were on an attack run or not. They could be on a recce; hell, they could be FAL tourists, if that even existed. But I had to stop them. Without any defenses, New Cebu could be devastated by even two of their fighters—and my family was down there.

"I armed the *Tala*, and turned on the new clone projector. We didn't even know if the thing worked yet. It wouldn't be the first new system that R&D developed that was rushed into service and ended up being useless. The clone projector didn't try to hide my Wasp. We hadn't had much luck with stealth tech against the FALs so far. What it did was clone twenty more Talas, each slightly different than the other. It was designed to hopefully make the FALs break contact and run at best, to target the cloned images at worst. The thing is, we didn't know if it worked yet.

"I had to report in, no matter what happened. I couldn't trust the civilian Traffic Control to do it without going through all the steps up their reporting chain, and that could be too late.

"'Commander Tuominen, this is Petty Officer Dalisay--'"

'I know who you are, Dalisay,' he snapped at me. 'What do you want?'"

"'I've got two FALs, sir, heading in to the planet. I told Traffic Control to report the contact to the Navy, but you know civilians. It might take awhile.'"

'Is this some sort of BS game, Dalisay, to cover up the fact that you are on an unauthorized flight just to get to your brother's wedding? If it is, so help me God, I'll have your hide, no matter how much you think you're the public's hero. This is just too far.'"

"'Pull up my telemetries,' I told him as I started running fire-control solutions for my three weapon systems. 'Check my TSM-4.'

"I had a choice, at this point. I didn't even consider my L-20 laser, which had so far proven to be about worthless against the crystal ships. I had my G-21 railgun, and I'd gotten two of my four kills with it, but that was an anomaly. The railgun was only for close-in fighting, atmospheric air-to-air, or ground support. The rounds, even at hypervelocity speeds were just too slow. Fire too early, and even a mining barge could dodge out of the way.

"That left two choices, my M-57 torpedoes or my P-13 Hadron Coil Particle Beam. Of the two, the P-13 was a light-speed weapon, but it took awhile to knock out a crystal ship, and the longer it was fired, radiation and heat buildup in the Wasp became problematic. The torpedoes locked onto and chased the crystal ships, and if they hit, they could knock any ship out, FAL or human. Getting them to hit, however, was the problem."

Rika reached back and tapped the barrel of her GNR. "Sounds like my gun-arm and your ship have a lot in common. Granted, I'm hardened against the rads."

"The commander came back and said, 'Try to divert the FALs. If not, engage, Dalisay. Keep them off the planet. We'll have three flights there in three hours, and I've already set the alert with HQ. If they have anything closer, I'll let you know.'

"'Aye-aye, sir. Understand.' And I did. At interstellar distances, a battle might barely advance over three hours, but this was in-system. Three hours was a long time, and whatever was going to happen would have happened by then. All I could hope for was to beat the two crystals, or if they were going to splash me, divert them away from the planet long enough for the cavalry to arrive.

"You still in your pumpkin dress?" Bethany Anne asked. "That had to be comfortable."

"Yep. I thought about trying to change back, but the flight suit is far easier to take off than get back on. Normally, we needed someone to help with the final connections, although it could be donned in an emergency—but probably not sitting in a cockpit. I decided not to risk getting tangled up trying to get it on. Besides, I could beat them around the planet and intercept them at the speeds the compensators could handle. I thought.

"I was still one-point-eight million klicks from the planet when the FALs upped the ante. If I thought they might be a recce flight, they dispelled that notion when they fired one of their round torpedoes, not at me, but at the planet. The torp was immediately visible as it exited whatever hid the crystal ships, and it was a big one, bigger than any I'd seen before. The mass and speed alone could make this an extinction event, like with the dinosaurs on Earth. But those were my family down there, not dinosaurs. I was not going to let that thing reach the planet.

"Without thinking, I hit G-shot and increased my speed. I was below the orbital plane, while the FALs were above it. I had to close the distance if I want my torps to have a shot at diverting the thing. I could eventually disable it with my hadron projector, but the hulking thing would still continue on its trajectory, and even a dead lump of crystal would cause a tremendous amount of damage.

"What's G-shot?" Cain asked, wincing.

Beth looked confused for a moment, then said, "G-shot. You know, so a person could survive heavy G. Without it, my body would be smushed into red jelly at the Gs we were already pulling.

"It would be better if I was in my flight suit, but it was what it was. And if you don't know what a G-shot is, you wouldn't know that it hurts! It's like fire was injected into your veins. We only do it as a final option.

"The *Tala* jumped forward like a racehorse, and we closed the distance. My comms lit up from the panicked Traffic Control. They'd have seen the torpedo as well, but with the G-shot taking over, I didn't have time nor inclination to calm them down. I had to focus.

"'Keep running the firing solutions,' I told *Tala*. I would never get a 100% probability of a kill, so I had to take my best shot. The graph kept changing as more data poured in, but it looked like my best would be seventy-two percent. Good, but when I'm dealing with five hundred million on the planet, that wasn't good enough. I started to target all three of my torps, but what if the FALs had another one? I had to keep back one of the torps for that.

"My first alarm went off. I was under fire from their beam projector. The eggheads were still not sure just how they worked, but they were deadly. Somehow, they found the molecular resonance of a Wasp's shields, then the outer skin and set up a resonating frequency that vibrated the molecules, building up heat until the fighter came apart. Cooked. The *Tala* had a latticed polycarbon web surrounding the hull in hopes that it would slow down the resonance. It hadn't helped Mercy on her last mission, though.

"Or maybe it did. She lost her fighter, but she survived," Beth said, a little quieter. She shook it off and continued. "But I didn't know if I would last long. Only one of the crystals was firing at me, best I could tell, but my shields were ablating. In only ten seconds, I was down to eighty-eight percent.

"I had to fire. The torps did not have the same shielding as the *Tala* had, and they could not survive long. I'd already programmed a divergent approach, coming in on the FAL torp from different directions. The probability of a kill hit sixty-four percent, but started dropping as the combat AI considered the enemy projector.

"'Fire one and two!' I shouted before turning in and up to the two FALs. With the combined closing rate of the three torpedoes, two of mine and one of theirs, I'd know in thirty-three seconds if I'd taken it out.

"Immediately, the FAL projector shifted from me to one of the torps. I had to keep their attention on me. I still had one torp and my hadron cannon. I targeted the torp on where I thought the second crystal was and opened fire with my cannon on where I thought the one firing at my torp was. I had to make it take evasive action.

"With our dogfights so far, the winner was generally the one whose shields could outlast the others'. We could maneuver to break contact for a moment, but the effects were cumulative. I couldn't break contact. I had to bear in, to make *them* break contact. A big game of chicken, to see who'd blink.

"The enemy fighter didn't blink. My cannon beam disrupted its scan shielding enough that it failed, and suddenly two crystal ships popped on on my display. The one firing looked like a normal crystal fighter. The second one, the one that had fired the torpedo, was twice the size. I didn't know what that indicated, nor did I have time to contemplate that. I had to disrupt the smaller one, and with them visible, now I could focus my beam tighter, to put more energy on the target in hopes of burning though. There was no maneuvering now, just three ships closing in on each other."

Bethany Anne tapped a finger to her lips. "Sounds like knights jousting."

"Yeah, maybe it was at that," Beth said as if considering the imagery for the first time. "If knights jousted two-against-one. And had long-range weapons.

"And it was the smaller FAL fighter's weapon that drew first blood. At nineteen seconds to impact, my first torp was knocked out. I had one left to take out the FAL torp, and I regretted only firing two. I was already past the perpendicular to the enemy torpedo, and while I could spin on my axis and fire the third one, instead of closing, it would be chasing, and with the two FALs much closer to it.

"I had to stop the crystal that was firing. If that FAL torpedo got through to the planet, I didn't want to imagine how many lives would be lost. I switched the target of my third M-57 torpedo to the smaller crystal and fired. The *Tala* was already at point-seven-two-C, and my torp had a good lock. As it shot ahead, it would reach the FAL crystal in ten seconds—but would it be soon enough? I came close to redlining my cannon as I pour power into it, and my radiation levels were climbing dangerously.

"My mind was getting fuzzy around the edges from the G-shot and acceleration, but I was latched to the first torp's telemetry. Its little shield started to fail just as my third torp hit the FAL ship. The pilot had played chicken and lost.

"I shifted my course to cut off the bigger ship when my first torpedo hit the planet killer, exploding it into its component atoms. Part of me, the still sane part, wanted to cheer, but it took all my effort to focus on the second ship. My brain felt like it was in a bag full of cotton, and I wanted to sink into its embrace of oblivion."

"'No, Floribeth! Not yet!' I had to scream. I told *Tala* to target the ship with the beamer, then to max the acceleration to close the distance. I didn't know how long I could stand it. I had taken the G-shot, but I was in the pumpkin dress, not my flight suit. Normally, maybe three minutes. Now . . . ?

"But I was closing. I thought about ramming it, but the numbers were wrong. If it remained on its course, I could get within forty-two-thousand klicks, a stone's throw by interstellar standards, but not near close enough to ram. I had to keep pouring hadron beam into it and hope for the best.

"The *Tala* shuddered, and alarms blared. I couldn't concentrate, and it took me a moment to realize my P-13 cannon had been knocked out. The *Tala* started bleeding acceleration, alarms blaring for my attention. My hand automatically reached up to check my helmet seal before I remembered I was not in my flight suit, and that struck me funny. I started laughing until a blip appeared in front of the FAL ship and started to accelerate. Death on the way. That shocked me sober, the cotton mind gone.

"The second enemy torp was almost a million klicks away and separating. The *Tala* was at point-seven-three-C. All I had was my G-21 railgun, which fired depleted uranium rounds at five-thousand meters per second. Add on the Tala's speed and that was three-hundred-thousand meters times point-seven-three and an oblique of . . . hell, even with a clear mind, I didn't have the math for that, and I couldn't mumble out the commands clear enough for the targeting computer to do the calculations.

"The railgun was fixed in place, and was aimed by spinning the entire fighter around. The ship would keep traveling on its previous course, but the prow—and railgun—would now be aiming at the target. With shaky hands, I switched the targeting system to manual, spun the *Tala* around, and using the crosshairs and more then a bit of Kentucky windage, fired off three long belts of ammo, sending six-hundred quarter-kilogram inert rounds at the enemy torpedo as it started to accelerate to New Cebu, which was hanging large in the black of space.

"The gods of war are a capricious lot, and they loved nothing better than to screw up the strategic experts who have a plan for every contingency. Sometimes, they also love to reward the stupid and unprepared. I must have been their quota for that second category. Somehow, against all odds, one of those 600 rounds hit the enemy torp as it sped off. Even a quarter-kilo travelling at those speeds is deadly. The torpedo came apart into a million pieces. They'd still reach the planet, but most would burn up in entry, giving the people a nice show.

"But there was still the last FAL ship. I didn't know how many torpedoes it had. The *Tala's* alarms went off again, this time from the FAL projector. My shields were down to thirty-four-point-one and dropping. I really didn't care about that. All I could think about was the enemy ship. We'd be at our closest point in about ten seconds. I could have told *Tala* to target the enemy ship, but like I said, my mind was pretty much shot by now. All I could think of was to kill it. I spun the *Tala* around, zooming in the railgun's targeting scope, and targeted it. At forty-thousand-whatever kilometers, even on manual with the targeting assist, I couldn't miss. I started firing, emptying the last twelve-hundred rounds. The FAL ship seemed to realize what was going on, but too late. It started to move to the side when the first rounds slammed into it and that's all she wrote."

"Wait a minute, you hit a torpedo, and then an enemy fighter, with a manual slug-thrower, at a million klicks?" Rika asked. "I'm not gonna go so far as to call bullshit . . . but that's hard to swallow."

"I believe her!" Kelsey declared.

"I'm here. New Cebu is still here. Either I hit the sucker or it spontaneously blew up on its own," Beth said, shrugging her shoulders before reaching out to take her drink, relishing a long swallow.

"Or," Bethany Anne smirked, "This is a story of a practice run you cooked up, and New Cebu was never in danger?"

Kelsey threw Bethany Anne a look before turning back to Beth. "So, what happened after that? Did you get to the wedding?"

"Sort of," Beth said with a wry grin. "I mean, I got there. The *Tala* was damaged, and I had to get it on the ground. Before I passed out, I told *Tala* to land at the coordinates I previous gave her. It took a couple of hours to come back around, but I landed outside of Malapascua about forty minutes before the cavalry arrive in-system. I was out the entire time. G-shot charged a heavy price, and I was going to need two weeks to recover. I woke up when my canopy opened and Mercy and Rocky looked in.

"'Satan's balls, girl, where the hell have you been?' Mercy asked me. I managed to croak out something about two crystal ships and G-shot, and she got the rest to pull me out of the *Tala* and sat me on the ground. My mother gave me a glass of melon, which felt wonderful going down my parched throat.

"'Sorry I missed your wedding,' I said.

"'You haven't missed anything. We delayed it because we didn't know where you were. You were on your way, but then you weren't, and I couldn't raise you. We were worried sick. But never mind about that. We need to get you to the hospital. Is anyone coming for you?'"

"'I expect the Stingers will get here in an hour, maybe less. They'll know where I landed.'"

"Mercy, wedding dress and all, leaned into the cockpit, ass and legs hanging out, and I could hear her reporting in. I just relaxed, happy to have someone else taking over. She popped back out and told me the CO himself had led three flights into the system, and a flight would be on the ground in a little over an hour. She sat down and wrapped her arms around me.

"'I'd never have forgiven myself if you got yourself killed on my wedding day, Beth,' she said."

"'You know me. I'm tougher than that. Besides, it's not your wedding day yet.'"

"'Don't worry about that. Now, we've got to get you taken care of.'"

"'We've got an hour.'"

"'What do you mean?' she asked me."

"'Jeeze you can be dense sometimes, Mercy. And I'm the one who's brain is muddled from the G-shot. Rocky, are the guests still gathered at the church?'"

"'Most of them. Some are in the square drinking. Some are here,' my brother said, waving a hand at the ten or so people standing around.

"'Well, I'd think it is obvious. I don't think I'm up to a walk to the church, so if you want me to be your maid of honor, you'd better get everyone here, and within the next hour. If you don't mind not using the church, that is.'"

"There was dead silence for a moment before my mom went into overdrive, running around like a chicken with its head cut off to get everyone moving. Her son was getting married, and her oldest daughter only had an hour. Nothing was going to get in her way. I drifted in and out, but fifteen minutes later, everyone was gathered around the Tala for the ceremony. We finished, with Mercy and Rocky married, just as four Wasps, led by the CO, landed."

"What happened with the brass. You did break a bunch of rules, and you said he was pissed," Cain asked.

"Not much the brass could do. I'd saved a world, after all." She pointed to the top ribbon on her chest, and said, "Gave me the Order of Honor, only the third living recipient. And I was the Navy's first ace in 200 years. Someone went back and approved my leave to make it all above ground. They digitally fixed the images released to the media so I wasn't wearing a bridesmaid gown. Can't have a *hero* wearing that while she goes to war, don't you know," she said with only a moderate tone of sarcasm when she said "hero."

"I'm not sure what half the things were that you were talking about," Ridge said, "but I know what it's like to get awards and recognition that you don't feel you deserve. I also know a thing or two about dresses now. I agree with your media that it's hard to be heroic in them."

"So, how was the wedding, if you don't count being loopy," BA asked.

"I don't rightly remember. I was pretty out of it. At the time, most of the wedding party just thought I was drunk. I don't remember lots of that next week, and if it weren't for the holo, I'd had thought I'd dreamed it all in a G-shot-induced fantasy."

Rika leant forward. "Holo? Can we see it?"

"I don't carry it around."

"OK, now I'm calling bullshit." Rika shook her head, fixing Beth with a level stare. "You were at a wedding for your brother and best friend. You have it."

She looked around the table, hesitant. Finally, she nodded, and said, "You have to remember, I was out-of-it, and I was wearing that gown. I don't look good."

She reached into her thigh pocket and pulled out a tablet, unrolled it, opened the images file, and whispered a password. She looked at it, grimaced, and turned the tablet so the others could see.

There were several intakes of breath as the group took it in. The *Tala* stood prominent in the photo with the wedding party arrayed in front of it. The bride and groom, looking lovely, were in the middle. The best man and the groomsmen, some male, some female, were lined up beside the groom. Beth was standing beside the bride, with a line of bridesmaids, all in the orange gowns, stretching out. Everyone in the holo had smiles, except for Beth. She looked like death-warmed over, a zombie, in a dress that was . . . the best that could be said was that it was merely hideous.

"Ok," Bethany Anne smiled, "Nobody would be caught dead in that dress for a practical joke. Totally believe you."

"Ooh, I see what you mean about the dress, you look like a pumpkin with legs," Amanda commented.

"Yeah, that's me. The Pumpkin Ace."

You can find Fire Ant, the first book of Beth's Navy of Humankind series on Amazon or other outlets.

Jonathan P. Brazee

VENUS

This is just a fun little story I first imagined when looking at Venus of Willendorf at the Naturhistorisches Museum in Vienna. I don't think it might be that far from the truth.

****

Nik stared across the glen, his thoughts drifting despite his father's earlier admonition to keep alert. The Tujat had been encroaching on Nadal land lately, and the disappearance two days ago of Lokit could have been the result of a Tujat raiding party. Tujat women seemed to have a hard time surviving, so the Tujat men were constantly looking to steal mates.

But the sun was warm on his face, and the Tujat seemed a long way away. He leaned is bony body back against the large boulder behind him, feeling the boulder's radiant heat seep through his back, and contemplated his young life. Things were good for the Nadal, and for him in particular. His father had been chief for over three years now, so Nik carried a small degree of reflected status. Food was plentiful, and the band's health was generally good. In a few more years he would join the men in the hunts, but for now, he hunted small animals like mice and frogs with the other boys or stood on watch as he was doing today.

He heard a grunt and looked over to Jun, his watch partner. Jun was behind a fallen tree, supposedly looking over the same glen as Nik. But Jun seemed preoccupied, his back towards Nik and facing away from the glen. Nik was puzzled. It didn't look like Jun was taking a piss, and who would piss right in his hide spot anyway?

Was he...? Nik stood up to get a better look. He was! He was yanking!

Sex was not particularly hidden in the band. At such close quarters, it would be difficult to do so. But boys were not privileged to spill milk. They had to wait until they were raised to men, to become full members of the band.

Oh, of course all the boys did yank when they became old enough that their bodies cried for it, but always off in private, out-of-sight of the others. And they never yanked while on watch.

With one more glance across the glen first, Nik started to creep forward. If he could make it over to the tree, lean over it, and pull on Jun's shoulders, Jun would shit right then and there! That would teach him!

It only took a few moments for Nik to make it the short distance to the tree. Not that Jun would have noticed a cave bear if it had come up to him, Nik thought. He started to reach over the tree trunk to grab Jun's shoulders when he saw that while one hand was occupied yanking, Jun's other hand was holding something. He couldn't quite make it out.

"What is that?" he asked, curiosity overcoming him.

Jun's reaction was gratifying. He jumped up in the air and spun around, one hand still on his horn. His face flushed red as he stumbled back a step. There was a look of horror on his face for a moment, but it faded to a sheepish grin as he shrugged his shoulders and held out his other hand, palm open.

Jun held out a piece of limestone, a little smaller than his palm. But the limestone was a figure of a woman. Her huge breasts and belly were prominent, as was her oversized honeycomb. Nik reached out to pick it up.

"How...where did you get this?" he asked wondering, turning the small figure over in his hands.

Jun bent down to pick up an antler tine which he brandished at Nik. "I made it. With this."

Nik imagined he could feel the heat of a real woman emanate from the stone. The detail on it was remarkable. The breasts hung ponderously to rest on a huge belly. The honeycomb unnaturally protruded, and he thought he could almost see inside. Huge haunches made up the figure's butt. A large hooked nose made up most of the face. There was an anklet carved above each foot, and only one woman in the band was allowed those.

"This is Teerak!" he shouted, almost dropping the figurine.

"So, I'm a good artist, then?" laughed Jun.

Teerak was the band's shaman. An immense woman, she was more powerful than anyone else, even Nik's father. Nik hurriedly handed the carving back to Jun as if it would burn his hand.

"Why her? Aren't you afraid? She could cast a spell and make your horn fall off."

Jun laughed. "Why not her? She's a woman, right?"

"But she is our shaman!"

"Yea, and she always wears the girdle, right? Haven't you ever wondered about her honeycomb?"

The women in the band wore clothes only for warmth and protection, and nudity was not part of the band's taboos. Only Teerak hid her genitalia with her shaman's crow-feather girdle. And as much as Nik feared her, he had to admit that he did wonder if there was something different about her honeycomb.

"Yea, but, well, she's so fat! I thought you liked Kud, and it would take three Kuds to make one Teerak!"

"Kud's pretty sexy, yeah, and I'm going to take her when I'm raised. But I am an artist," he said, with mock sincerity, "and this piece of limestone just called out to release the Teerak in it."

Nik took the figurine back. "Well, it does look pretty good. And you did this all yourself?"

"Just me and my bone!" He held the antler tine down to his crotch, aiming it up.

Nik laughed and turned the figurine around, touching the antler tip Jun was holding erect to its prominent honeycomb. "How is that?"

"Oh, Teerak, I love your huge ass, your huge tits! Let me do you hard!" he replied with a theatrical tone of ecstasy.

Nik never felt the blow against the side of his head which knocked him to his knees. He tried to get his thoughts together. Had the Tujat come? Were they attacking?

He felt more than saw Jun on the ground beside him. He managed to look up, and he almost wished the Tujat had come. His father stood over him, face red in anger. He reached down and grabbed Nik's bone and nuts, then lifted him up to his feet. Nik cried out in agony.

"So, this is how you stand watch? This is how you protect The People? By playing vile little games with each other?" He twisted Nik's bone. "I should rip this worthless worm off, because you are never going to be a man, you are never going to use it on a woman!"

Nik was still holding the figurine, and his father took it from his hand. As he took in the features, his face went from red to white.

"Are you two crazy, or just stupid? Teerak? What spirit possessed you? I won't need to rip your little worms off. Teerak will make them shrivel up and turn black!" Spittle flew from his mouth as he ranted.

"This is a perversion! " He turned and cocked his arm back before heaving the figurine out over the glen. Nik watched the small stone turn over and over before it fell into the grass and was lost from sight.

24,000 Years Later . . .

"So, this is her. She's, she's beautiful." Dr. Sarah Planchett bent down to examine the small figure in the secure viewing case. It was held in the standing position by a few unobtrusive wires. It stood on a mirror so the bottom view could be seen, was well-lit by small spotlights, and had three large magnifying glasses strategically placed so viewers could see the figurine's details.

"I told you, she is simply remarkable," Dr. Ernst Gruber replied. "This is one of the finest figurines ever found. You can tell she was made by an expert, a Paleolithic Michelangelo."

"The jpegs you sent me didn't do her justice. This just takes my breath away."

"Well, enjoy her now. We expect a huge crowd in after opening. The Venus has received tremendous press, as you know."

"And I appreciate you giving me access early, Ernst."

"Professional courtesy, Sarah, professional courtesy."

"It is more than that, Ernst, and you know it."

"Well, Sarah, I admire you greatly, you know, and I have been a fan since your seminar at Lyon. So it seems right that you get a special peek at our girl, especially given your field of expertise."

Dr. Sarah Planchett smiled back at Dr. Ernst Gruber for an awkward moment before he hurriedly continued.

"Ah, well, as you can see, as we wrote in the journal, the extreme exaggeration in the vulva, to the extent that is it almost prolapsed, while similar to the Magdalenian Venus and its incised vaginal opening, is very unique among other figures discovered so far."

"Yes, the opening is very visible. And your team believes that this signifies fertility?"

"Well, beyond the obvious manifestations of what Paleolithic man thought of as beauty, the immense breasts and the very exaggerated vulva lead us to believe that this figure represents fertility, most likely a goddess. Even if heavy, even obese women are considered attractive at the time, no real human woman could have attained such size given the diet of people in the region. So she must be a goddess. See the anklets?"

She nodded.

"Dr. Martens has postulated that those represent fertility of the soil as indicated by worms."

"Worms? That wasn't in the journal article." She took a closer look. "But now that you mention it, yes, they do look segmented, like an earthworm."

Truth be told, she wasn't sure about the veracity of the worm analysis. But they could be worms, she admitted to herself. The fact that she even had feet made her unique from most other figurines.

"The most telling argument that this represents a goddess is where she was found. There were no other artifacts with her. No sign of any human habitation. Most figurines can be found with middens, other artifacts, et cetera. This one was alone in deep loam. She had to have been buried there with all reverence due a goddess, although one of our Ph.D. students has postulated that maybe she was a sacrifice who was then buried alone."

"You've never found anything else in the vicinity?"

"Nothing. It's a miracle that the good Herr Spitz, the excavator operator, even saw her while he was digging. We didn't have anyone on site due to the location of the construction, but he saw her as his bucket pulled up a load, and he jumped down and dug through the dirt with his hands until he found her again."

She shuddered to think of this priceless artifact being trucked away with the rest of the leavings, never to be seen again.

"And you think she is 50,000 years old? That's at the limits of the Upper Paleolithic. That is pretty early for religious sacrifice. And that is pretty early for Pleistocene Overkill."

"Well, without the middens or other artifacts, we can't carbon date it. But given the depth of the soil and other tests done at similar levels, I would bet my position here at the university that we are within 5,000 years either way." He paused for a second, wiping his brow. "Pleistocene Overkill is overrated, anyway. I agree with those who hold that simply eating a meat and fat diet from naturally grazing animals just can't produce the obesity we see here. "

They fell into a companionable silence for a few moments. Dr. Planchett stared at the Venus de Langerich. The small representation of a goddess must have been held in such high esteem by her makers, by her worshipers. And now she had come back to life, to welcome the adoration of a new age of men.

Jonathan P. Brazee

The Accidental War

This story was originally published in a different format in Bob's Bar: Tales from the Multiverse. The idea was for a handful of writers taking their characters, then having them meet in a multiverse bar and tell sea stories. I was the editor for the project, and it was the proverbial herding cats, but I think the end result was worth the effort.

My character is Ryck Lysander, the main character in my main United Federation Marine Corps series. The story is a compilation of two events in Vietnam, one by a US Marine Captain, the other by an Australian Air Force pilot.

****

"So, we're going out with the fuckdicks again?" Sams asked, hitching up his battle harness.

"That's Federal Civil Development Corps troopers," Lance Corporal Samuelson," Second Lieutenant Patrick Surrey said, in the voice of someone who knew he was trying to beat back the tide.

The platoon commander wasn't a bad guy. He arrived in the battalion full of righteousness and morality, something that three months with the platoon was slowly eating away. Sams, in particular, seemed to enjoy "knocking a sense of reality into the butterbar's head."

"And yes, you're going out with them one more time. We need to support our fellow troopers. We're all on the same side, after all."

Lance Corporal Ryck Lysander, United Federation Marine Corps, fought not to roll his eyes. Sams had it right. The sooner the lieutenant climbed down from Federation Fantasyland and understood the reality on the ground, the better.

Ryck had not joined the Marines out of a sense of patriotic fervor. He'd needed an escape from his home-planet of Prophesy, nothing more. He'd changed over his tour, though, learning to appreciate the brotherhood and sense of purpose the Marines offered him. Even as a relatively newbie, however, he understood this mission was less-than-noble.

Second Battalion, Ninth Marines, had been deployed to Saint Hollis, not to fight back invaders, not to root out a Soldiers of God incursion. They were here to maintain the status quo.

Saint Hollis was a Class-1 world only certified for about ten years. The Sea of Kansas Corporation did the terraforming, and they're were out the big credits for it. Only some of the settlers didn't think they need to pay Sea of Kansas back. They formed up, called themselves the League of Justice, and they essentially told Sea of Kansas to go pound sand.

Ryck didn't know who was in the right. As a dirt grubber on Prophesy, he'd seen how the corporations could squeeze settlers in a python's grip, strangling their ability to survive. He could sympathize with the League of Justice, but he really didn't have a dog in this fight.

Not so the Council. It was taken as a fact of life that the corporations had the government in their power. So, when Sea of Kansas complained to the council, the council said, "Send in the Marines."

No Marines, at least the enlisted grunts, wanted to be a hammer for the corporations. The Marines famously served the people. But orders were orders. Refusing to obey would mean brig time and a Dishonorable Discharge. It wasn't as if these types of missions were commonplace. This was Ryck's first. The Marines shouldered their packs with a hearty "Fuck them all" and hoped the next mission would be more in line with their stated mission.

Even with just the battalion on the planet, the Marines could march into the so-called capital of the league in a couple of hours and show the LOJ leadership the error of their ways. The "revolutionaries," as Sea of Kansas called them, had only had a thousand or so militia under arms. Hell, even a fuckdick company could have crushed them. But there was too much media attention on the situation. The Federation might be there at the behest of the corporation, but it didn't want to come across as the bullying bad guys. So, the operation was not under First Ministry command. Second Ministry was in charge, and they had instituted some seriously tight ROEs. The Marines could fire only if fired upon first, and the league wasn't stupid. They were not about to initiate hostilities that they could not win.

The Marines were not even the main force on the planet. The fuckdicks, who fell under the Second Ministry were. The Marines were officially there to support the fuckdicks—as if an infantry battalion was a support unit. In reality, they were there as a visible sword hanging over the LOJ's heads. The diplomats wanted the Marines there as a threat, but preferred them to be a toothless tiger, sitting on their collective asses, bored out of their gourds.

The battalion CO, though, wasn't just going to let the Marines be a target. The LOJ might not be much, but all it took was one suicide bomber to unload a world of hurt on the battalion. So, he initiated continual patrols, diplomats be damned.

Ryck didn't know why Sams was complaining. They weren't really going out with the fuckdicks. Rather, the fuckdicks were flying the fire team in one of their Mayflys, and the little flyers were a fun ride.

The Marines didn't have any of the three-fan carriers in their T/E. They were small, carrying only four pax and the pilot, and were unarmed. They might be fine for fuckdick police work, but were hardly useful to the offensively-oriented Marines. With the ROE, however, the CO was willing to use them to get bored Marines out from behind the wire and to be seen by the LOJ, to remind them that the Marines were there.

The lieutenant finished with his operations order, which despite all the in-the-weeds detail, was essentially, "ride in the Mayfly and look around." Corporal Sparta, the team leader, assured the lieutenant that the fire team was up for the mission, that he could count on them.

Twenty minutes later, Ryck, Sams, T-Rex, and Corporal Sparta arrived at the airfield, which was a grandiose term for the cleared patch of grass where a Mayfly was waiting for them.

"Hosef," the war pilot said, hand out as they walked up to him. "You my jarheads?"

"Sure are," Corporal Sparta answered.

Hosef was a warrant officer, technically senior to the Marines, but he was younger than Corporal Sparta, and in fuckdick fashion, he insisted they call him by his first name. Marines didn't use warrant officers for pilots, but the FCDC did, and a little Mayfly only rated the most junior of them.

They climbed aboard. This was Ryck's second Mayfly ride. The little planes did not look substantial enough to carry the pilot, much less the fire team, but it jumped up into the air as if eager to leave the confines of the ground. Within moments, Hosef had the Mayfly dancing over the treeline as they headed to their patrol route.

T-Rex nudged Ryck, then pointed at Sams, who looked green. Ryck laughed at his friend. With no sides on the Mayfly, if Sams lost it, he could just lean out and fertilize the ground below.

Corporal Sparta motioned for the others to lock and load. This was against ROE, but they'd be flying the border in plain sight. The LOJ militia were not SOG soldiers, but someone could decide to take a potshot at them.

Sixty klicks from the base camp, Hosef banked the Mayfly and took it up to 300 meters, then started following the trace of the border. Ryck watched the heavily forested ground below, wondering how he was supposed to spot anyone down there. It was easy to get drawn in by the green, to lose focus as the klicks passed beneath them.

"Hey, there's a Venus!" Sams yelled, snapping Ryck back to the mission at hand.

"Where?" T-Rex asked, crowding Sams.

"Over there!" he said, pointing toward the border.

We all crowded over, and the little Mayfly tilted before Hosef could straighten it out. Sure enough, along the border below them, the flag rose above the trees, fluttering in the light wind. It was beautiful.

The Marines had taken to calling the League of Justice flag a "Venus." Their militia might have been a joke, but they had some great artists. The blue flag was bordered in gold, and in the middle was an image of a Greek-goddess-looking woman, left hand holding a set of scales, right hand a sword, and the left breast exposed—and to the Marines' gutter minds she was smoking hot. Ryck, with this love of history, had looked up "Lady Justice" on the net, and her real Greek name was "Themis," but with the Marines, "'Venus'" stuck, and she became an object of collective lust. If the Marines ever did get ordered to invade, every grunt knew the laws about trophy-taking are going to be roundly ignored.

Hosef banked the Mayfly around and angled it over for a better look. Five sets of covetous eyes watched the flag flutter in the light breeze.

"Is that in government territory?" Corporal Sparta asked hopefully.

"'Wait one,'" Hosef said as he checked his nav screens, then, "'No, it's five fucking meters on their side.'"

There really weren't any formal borders of government and LOJ-controlled territory, but the Second Ministry had designated a No Fire Line that the Marines and fuckdicks couldn't cross. The League knew exactly where that line was. They were flying that flag just to taunt the Marines.

"I could reach that flag if you got us closer," Sams said.

"Five meters is five meters," Sparta said, but he didn't sound very convinced to Ryck.

And then Hosef, to Ryck's surprise, asked, "What say we go try and snag that thing?"

"You said it was five meters on their side," Corporal Sparta said.

"Shit, you jarheads are so by-the-fucking-book," Hosef said. "We Dog Soldiers take the initiative when we see the need."

Ryck frowned. Marines sometimes used the historic nickname for themselves, but when Hosef said "jarhead," he made it sound like an insult—sort of like when Marines called them fuckdicks or doggies.

He reached under his control box and flipped something, then said, "OK. We're now twenty meters farther into our side of the line."

Ryck turned to look at the corporal to see his reaction. A smile broke over his face, and he said, "Oh, hell yeah. If you're sure about that, let's do it."

"I'm sure," Hosef said as he swooped lower and closer, slowing to a stop about twenty meters away before crabbing the Mayfly closer.

The downdraft from the fans whipped the flag about, the gold catching the light of the late afternoon sun. She was beautiful. The distance closed and Sams leaned out, one hand holding the edge of his seat, the other reaching to grab the prize. He touched it, but the flapping kept it out of his grasp.

"Come on, Sams, grab the damned thing," T-Rex shouted.

As Sams reached, the flag started to lower. Sams shouted and lunged . . . and disappeared over the side as T-Rex tried and failed to grab him.

"Land this thing!" Corporal Sparta yelled at Hosef.

"I can't, not here in the trees!"

"We're going down," Sparta said, pulling a mono out of his cargo pocket.

He gave it a twist around the Mayfly's side strut, then dropped the line, shouting "Gloves!" before he grabbed it and descended. T-Rex was next, right on his ass.

"What am I supposed to do?" Hosef asked as Ryck whipped on his gloves and grabbed the line.

"Just stay on our side of the line. We'll let you know," he shouted as he went over.

Mono lines were great pieces of gear, but they were not good for fast-roping. They were too thin, so despite his gloves, his hands were screaming as he dropped through the trees to catch up to T-Rex. He tried to slow down, but he can't get a good enough grip, and he hit T-Rex's helmet with his feet, knocking him off the line. T-Rex fell the last three meters, hitting Corporal Sparta who'd just reached the ground. Ryck reached the ground right after, the only one of the team on his feet.

To his right, Sams was groaning and trying to stand. Under him was a very still militiaman. Then Ryck spotted a second militiaman standing just to his left, his TK-15 at the half-ready, his mouth open in shock. Ryck took three steps and swung his M-99 in a vicious butt-stroke, smashing the militiaman's TK-15 out of his hands and connecting with his shoulder. The man staggered back, hands in the air as Ryck's finger starts to squeeze the trigger to send a dozen hypervelocity darts into the man's chest.

"I surrender," he shouted, and somehow that registered with Ryck, and he held back.

"Get down on your face and let me see your hands," Ryck shouted before asking over his shoulder, "You OK, Sams?"

"I think so. This guy broke my fall. The bastard was trying to lower the flag," he said, nudging the unmoving militiaman.

T-Rex is on his feet by this time, and he said, "Nice move, Ryck. Lucky you didn't kill me," before he stepped over to Sams and the militiaman. "Hell, Sams, I think you killed this guy."

When he heard that, Ryck kept the other guy covered but stepped over to where he can see the body. The militiaman's neck was at an angle necks aren't designed to make. Under him, the edge of the flag peeked out. He'd tried to save Venus, but it had cost him his life.

Ryck looked at the other three Marines, wondering what they were supposed to do. They were in deep, deep shit. They were on the ground in League territory. They'd just killed a league militiaman. They were going to the brig for a long time, that was for certain. Ryck looked at Corporal Sparta hoping he had an answer. He was on the comms with someone, but Ryck couldn't tell if that was with the lieutenant back at camp or with Hosef.

"Hosef can't land here, and he can't hang around, or battalion'll know something's up, so I told him to continue his track, then come back for us," Sparta said.

Ryck looked at him in surprise.

Does he really think we can somehow get out of this with our asses intact?

"Uh . . . Corporal Sparta, we're in League territory, and Sams just killed one of their militia," he started to say.

"Not my fault," Sams protested. "He was just under me when I fell."

"Just listen to me. Hosef's got an idea, and it might work. When he comes back, he's going to say that he's taking fire. *We're* taking fire, since as far as anyone knows, we're still in the Mayfly with him. He's going to say he's hit, and he's got to land at an open area about five hundred meters from here to check the damage. We've got twenty minutes to get to there."

Ryck listened for a moment, mouth open and ready to argue, ready to tell him they'd just had to come clean with the lieutenant, but nothing came out. He didn't want to get court-martialed, and that plan, as stupid as it sounded, could work.

"Grubbing hell, let's do it," Ryck said. "I mean, we're already in deep shit, right? So, how much worse can this make it?" He pressed on. "If this cockamamie plan Hosef's gonna work, we're going to need to take one of their weapons. To put a hole in the Mayfly, you know. To make his story look like what really happened."

T-Rex bent over and picked up the dead militiaman's TK-15. He gave it a glance, then said, "Won't work. It's bio-locked."

All four of Marines swiveled toward their prisoner. He was still prone on the ground, but he'd shifted his position to stare at his dead compatriot.

"What's your name?" Ryck asked, stepping over to him.

"Giddeon. Giddeon McManus, sir," he answered, his voice quavering.

He didn't give his rank, just his name. It was obvious that he wasn't aware of the Harbin Accords. He was nervous as all get-out, and Ryck could see him trembling.

Ryck looked at Corporal Sparta and tilted his head toward the militiaman, his eyebrows raised in a question. Sparta hesitated, then nodded.

"Well, Gideon, do you want to live?" Ryck asked him.

"Yes, sir," he squeaked out.

"OK, it's like this. You come with us. When we reach the LZ, you fire your fifteen where we tell you. If you do that, we'll let you go. Understand?" Ryck asked.

"Yes, sir, I'll do that. No problem," he said eagerly.

Ryck look at him in surprise. He thought the militiaman would offer some resistance, and he'd have to threaten the guy, maybe rough him up. But he just capitulated like that without even trying to negotiate or ask for assurances? Ryck didn't really want to beat on him, hoping mere threats would work, but the militiaman gave in too easily.

"Just like that?" Ryck asked. "What about your buddy there?"

He shrugged his shoulders and said, "He was an asshole. I just want to go home, and if you'll let me do that, I'll do whatever you want."

He's OK with us killing his buddy because the guy was an asshole? Either he's playing us, or the guy has no loyalty to his cause.

Ryck leaned to the former, but the fact was that there were four Marines and one him, so there wasn't much he could do. Ryck looked at the other three, and as one, they shrugged their assent. Ryck pick up Giddeon's TK-15, slung it over his shoulder, and told him to get up. T-Rex stepped forward to search him for other weapons, then gave the other three a thumbs-up.

"You're going to walk in front of me. If you even twitch sideways, you're a dead man," Ryck told him.

"Don't worry, I'll do what you want," he said, tentatively standing up, his eyes locked on the muzzle of Ryck's M99.

"What about him?" Sams asked, pointing at the dead man.

"We have to take him. We can't leave anything to focus attention here. T-Rex, you've got him," Sparta said.

T-Rex was a heavy-worlder, so the dead man's weight was nothing to him. He hoisted the body onto his shoulder as Sams took the point, and they headed out. They had five hundred meters to cover, and not that much time. Luckily, they weren't in enemy-held territory, so they could move quickly through the trees back to their side of the border.

Ryck watched their prisoner closely, but as he followed Corporal Sparta, the militiaman didn't have the look of someone who was going to try something. His head was down, and his shoulders slumped as if he accepted his situation.

Which is a look that someone who's going to attempt something would try to portray.

"Hosef's on his way in, so pick it up," Corporal Sparta told the others when they were still three hundred meters out.

Ryck took a quick look behind him at T-Rex, and the broad-shouldered Marine gave him a thumbs-up. They had to do something with the dead militiaman, and Ryck didn't know what Sparta planned for that."

"Fuck!" Sparta shouted. "Hosef reported getting shot at, and battalion wants to know from where. They want a call for fire."

They all stopped dead. None of them thought the CO would want a fire mission. Since there haven't been any real rounds fired, Navy surveillance wouldn't have picked anything up, which wouldn't be that odd. But now it looked as if battalion was itching to get involved."

The ROE was that the Marines could only fire if they were fired upon first. No one in the League had really fired a weapon, but by trying to cover their asses, the four Marines had just given the battalion CO the excuse he needed to unleash some firepower.

Corporal Sparta pulled up his display, then pushed a position onto theirs. The fire team had been moving diagonally away from the NFL, which was now about a hundred and twenty meters to their left. Just over the NFL was a slight rise, and that's where the corporal highlighted.

"T-Rex, Ryck, haul ass. Drop our dead friend there and then boogie back to the LZ. Give me that fifteen," Sparta said.

"Wait," Gideon said, the first time he'd opened his mouth since they started. "Take this," he added, taking off his helmet. "The visor is ceroline, so it'll stand up to whatever you use to hit the place. And you can take the TK too."

"Can't take the fifteen," Ryck told him as he grabbed the militiaman's helmet. "We need it to shoot the Mayfly."

"No, you don't," he said, holding his hands out for them to see. "I'm not trying anything, so don't forging shoot me now."

He slowly reached down to his boot, then used his thumb and forefinger to pull out a wicked-looking handgun. Ryck dropped his M99 on him as the militiaman laid the handgun on the ground.

T-Rex, who'd searched the man earlier, gaped open his mouth in surprise.

"It uses the same round. I can still shoot your ride, and you can leave my TK at the site. I want it to look like I was there when you hit it."

"You want to disappear," Ryck said as it hit him. "You don't want anyone to know you're alive."

He shrugged, then said, "It seems like a good idea. I've been thinking about the recruiters for Rio Tinto 2, but I'm still under contract."

Officially, the Federation didn't permit indentured workers, but in reality, if someone was recruited by a company, they were stuck for the length of the contract. Penalties were just too high for anyone to buy out their contracts. So, if Gideon was "dead," then he'd be free. And hiring a dead man wouldn't give any competent recruiter pause.

Corporal Sparta considered what Gideon had said, then told Ryck, "Take the fifteen. Leave it on the hill. And you," he said, turning to Gideon, "Pick up your handgun and follow me."

Ryck was surprised that Sparta told Gideon to take the weapon, but he didn't have time to worry about it. He and T-Rex bolted through the trees, racing to the high ground that Sparta had selected. T-Rex was strong as hell, but he didn't have Ryck's stamina, and the taller Marines shot ahead as he crossed back over the NFL and climbed the low hill. He dropped Gideon's helmet and the TK-15, then headed back down to meet T-Rex, who was huffing as he climbed.

"Back down," Ryck told him, taking the dead militiaman's body and running to the bottom of the hill. He ran another thirty meters and put the body face down, his head against the bole of a tree.

"You don't want him up there?" T-Rex asked as he stumbled up to him.

Ryck understood T-Rex's unspoken question. If they left the body up there, it would be destroyed under the barrage that would soon hit the hill. The man's weapon and helmet would give more credence to the fact that he'd been firing at them. But the guy hadn't fire. He'd just tried to protect his flag before Sams landed on him. Ryck didn't know how good the resurrection process was on this planet, but with just a broken neck the man should be a reasonable candidate. If he had any chance of coming back, Ryck couldn't take that away from him. He didn't execute the enemy, and that's what it will be if he left him up on the hill.

"This is good enough," he said, not wanting to get into an argument.

"Your call," T-Rex said.

"Now, let's haul ass," Ryck told him.

Ryck passed to Sparta that they were clear as they ran through the forest toward the others. He kept expecting to hear incoming, but there was nothing as the two Marines burst into the LZ. The Mayfly is already there. Gideon raised his handgun and fired two shots into the rear assembly, then tried to hand his weapon to Sparta, who waved him off.

There was a crack of ionizing air behind us, and Ryck spun around to see the distortion in the air that tracks the path of an orbital energy beam as it reached down from a Navy ship and hit the hill.

"Oh, wow, get some!" T-Rex said with awe in his voice.

Ryck and T-Rex joined the other four at the Mayfly, then climbed on top among the fans to get a better view as beam after beam hit. Hosef pulled up a cooler, and they all popped some beers and cheered at each strike.

"We've got more incoming," Sparta said. "Battalion told us to keep our heads down."

That brought a round of laughter, and they toasted their battle. A minute later, a missile streaked right over their heads to crash into the hilltop. The meson beams packed more energy, but there was something about explosives that made Marines hard. They jumped up, hooting and hollering as smoke billowed into the air.

"That's it," Corporal Sparta said after a few minutes. "Battalion is ordering all of the patrols back."

"Well, I officially declare the damage to the *Hothead* is minimal," Hosef said, poking his finger into one of the bullet holes in the Mayfly.

"Shit," Sams said. "All that for nothing. We didn't even get the Venus."

"Yes, we did," Ryck said, opening his utility blouse to show a flash of blue.

"You picked it up?" Corporal Sparta asked, reaching over to touch the flag.

"I sure the grubbing hell wasn't going to leave it there," Ryck said, pulling it out for everyone to see it in its glory. "But it's going to have to stay hidden. I don't want to have to explain anything to anyone."

Battle trophies were illegal, but each of them wanted to hold it. The Venus was beautiful.

"We have to get back," Hosef finally said, pointing at his Mayfly. "They're asking if the Mayfly is damaged."

"What about him?" T-Rex asked, pointing at a suddenly wary Gideon.

Corporal Sparta didn't hesitate. "Can you hump out of here OK?"

"Yes, sir. No problem. Nice and quiet. I've got an uncle in Baggerstown who can get me off-planet."

"Then I suggest you get going. I don't know what's going to happen now, but the shit might hit the fan."

The young militiaman shook each of their hands, then after a salty salute, disappeared into the brush.

"I kinda like that guy," T-Rex said as the boarded the Mayfly for the flight back to battalion.

No one said a word as they flew. They could still be in deep kimchi. The Marines had wasted a missile worth more than the combined salary of a Marine rifle company. More than that, they might have just shit-canned all the diplomacy done to date.

They needn't have worried. The battalion was a beehive of activity as they landed, and other than the lieutenant telling them he'd debrief them later, they were quickly forgotten in the chaos. The battalion was ready to move out, cross the NFL, and put an end to this conflict. The four Marines gratefully rejoined their squad and got ready for a fight.

But it never came to that. It was one thing to stand up to a Marine battalion that was behind wires and out in the sticks. It was another to contemplate that same battalion marching on their declared capital. Already unnerved by the bombardment on the hill, they folded only minutes after the lead company crossed the Line of Departure. The conflict was over without firing a shot—a shot fired at an actual person, that is.

Within a week, the battalion was embarking aboard ship for transport back to Camp Alexander. The Venus was stuffed in a DSK-99 case, hopefully to be recovered once they got back.

Ryck lay in his bunk, not for the first time marveling at how they managed to get away with what they'd done. It went beyond improbable to impossible. Even just a week later, it seemed like the remnants of a fevered dream.

He had to see it again. Ryck pulled out his PA and followed three encrypted paths to the target folder. He held the PA to his eye for a retinal scan, and the folder opened, revealing the file. Ryck looked around the berthing space to make sure no one else could see, then opened the file. It was a clear image. Six men stood in front of a Mayfly in a small LZ: Four Marines, an FCDC trooper, and an ex-militiaman. All six had huge smiles, and they held a gold-trimmed blue flag with the image of Lady Justice in the center.

Grubbing hell, it really did happen.

Ryck's story starts with the first book in the United Federation Marine Corps series, Recruit.

Jonathan P. Brazee

Thank you for reading *Where the Battle Rages*. I hope you enjoyed it. If you liked it, please feel free to leave a review of the book from wherever you bought it.

If you would like updates on new books releases, news, or special offers, please consider signing up for my mailing list. Your email will not be sold, rented, or in any other way disseminated. If you are interested, please sign up at the link below:

http://eepurl.com/bnFSHH

Other Books by Jonathan Brazee

<u>Gemini Twins</u>
Gemini Twins
Gemini Rising (2026 Nebula Award Finalist)

<u>Werewolf of Marines</u>
Werewolf of Marines: Semper Lycanus
Werewolf of Marines: Patria Lycanus
Werewolf of Marines: Pax Lycanus

<u>The United Federation Marine Corps</u>
Recruit
Sergeant
Lieutenant
Captain
Major
Lieutenant Colonel
Colonel
Commandant
Legacy Marines
Esther's Story: Recon Marine
Noah's Story: Marine Tanker

Esther's Story: Special Duty
Blood United

Coda

Rebel (Set in the UFMC universe.)

Behind Enemy Lines (A UFMC Prequel)

The Accidental War (A Ryck Lysander Short Story
Published in BOB's Bar: Tales from the Multiverse

Ghost Marines
Integration
Unification
Devotion
Fusion

The Navy of Humankind: Wasp Squadron
Fire Ant (2019 Nebula Award Finalist)
Crystals
Ace

The United Federation Marine Corps'
Grub Wars
Alliance
The Price of Honor
Division of Power

Women of the United Federation

Marine Corps
Gladiator
Sniper
Corpsman

High Value Target (A Gracie Medicine Crow Short Story)
BOLO Mission (A Gracie Medicine Crow Short Story)
None Left Behind (A Gracie Medicine Crow Short Story)

Weaponized Math (A Gracie Medicine Crow Novelette,
Published in The Expanding Universe 3. 2018 Nebula
Award Finalist)

The Return of the Marines Trilogy
The Few
The Proud
The Marines

The Al Anbar Chronicles: First Marine Expeditionary Force--Iraq
Prisoner of Fallujah
Combat Corpsman
Sniper

Call to Arms Capernica
Conscientious Objector
POG
Veteran

Soldier

Animal Soldier: Hannibal

To the Shores of Tripoli

Wererat

Darwin's Quest: The Search for the Ultimate Survivor

Starship in a Bottle

The Goblin General

Short Stories

Venus: A Paleolithic Short Story

Secession

Duty

Semper Fidelis

Checkmate (Published in The Expanding Universe 4)

Recon Pilot

The Bridge

Silent Hero

Sentenced to War (with JN Chaney)
Seeds of War
Children of Angels
Song of Redemption
An Uneasy Alliance
A Broken Alliance
An Alliance Reforged
When Worlds Fail
What Lies Behind
Gods of War

United We Kill
Marines Never Die
Nexus of Chaos
Exiled to Perdition
Into The Void
Brave New Dawn

Undead Marine (With JN Chaney)

Undead Marine
Proof of Concept
Mission Creep
Marine Corpse
A Meeting of Minds
Dead to Rights

Seeds of War (With Lawrence Schoen)

Invasion
Scorched Earth
Bitter Harvest

Non-Fiction

Exercise for a Longer Life

The Effects of Environmental Activism on the Yellowfin
Tuna Industry

Author Website

http://www.jonathanbrazee.com

Twitter

https://twitter.com/jonathanbrazee

Jonathan P. Brazee

The Effects of Environmental Activism on the Yellowfin Tuna
Industry

Author Website
http://www.jonathanbrazee.com

www.ingramcontent.com/pod-product-compliance
Lightning Source LLC
Chambersburg PA
CBHW071133170626
46809CB00002B/597